REASONS TO HATE ME

SUSAN METALLO

REASONS TO HATE ME

SUSAN METALLO

CANDLEWICK PRESS

This is a work of fiction. Names, characters, places, and incidents are either products of the author's imagination or, if real, are used fictitiously.

Copyright © 2025 by Susan Metallo

Excerpts (pp. 33–34) from *The Poems of Emily Dickinson*, edited by Thomas H. Johnson, Cambridge, Mass.: The Belknap Press of Harvard University Press, Copyright © 1951, 1955 by the President and Fellows of Harvard College. Copyright © renewed 1979, 1983 by the President and Fellows of Harvard College. Copyright © 1914, 1918, 1919, 1924, 1929, 1930, 1932, 1935, 1937, 1942, by Martha Dickinson Bianchi. Copyright © 1952, 1957, 1958, 1963, 1965, by Mary L. Hampson. Used by permission. All rights reserved.

Excerpt (p. 91) from *Into the Woods* by James Lapine and Stephen Sondheim. Text copyright © 1987 by James Lapine, Inc. Lyrics copyright © 1987 by Rilting Music, Inc. Published by Theatre Communications Group. Used by permission of Theatre Communication Group.

Excerpt (pp. 281–282) from *The Crucible* by Arthur Miller, copyright 1952, 1953, 1954, renewed © 1980, 1981, 1982 by Arthur Miller. Used by permission of Viking Books, an imprint of Penguin Publishing Group, a division of Penguin Random House LLC. All rights reserved.

Lyrics (p. 299) from "Your Fault" from *Into the Woods*. Words and Music by Stephen Sondheim. © 1988 Rilting Music, Inc. All Rights Administered by WC Music Corp. All Rights Reserved. Used by Permission. Reprinted by Permission of Hal Leonard LLC.

All rights reserved. No part of this book may be reproduced, transmitted, or stored in an information retrieval system in any form or by any means, graphic, electronic, or mechanical, including photocopying, taping, and recording, without prior written permission from the publisher. Additionally, no part of this book may be used or reproduced in any manner for the purpose of training artificial intelligence technologies or systems, nor for text and data mining.

First edition 2025

Library of Congress Control Number: pending
ISBN 978-1-5362-4035-1

25 26 27 28 29 30 SHD 10 9 8 7 6 5 4 3 2 1

Printed in Chelsea, MI, USA

This book was typeset in Baskerville.

Candlewick Press
99 Dover Street
Somerville, Massachusetts 02144

www.candlewick.com

EU Authorized Representative: HackettFlynn Ltd, 36 Cloch Choirneal, Balrothery, Co. Dublin, K32 C942, Ireland. EU@walkerpublishinggroup.com

For my family

MIGHTY-PEN-JESS
Aug 17

An Open Letter to the Cyberbullies of Stone Bridge High

Dear Hannah, Brooklyn, and Alexis:

Can I tell you how flattered I am that you've chosen me as the main character for your story?

Very.

Exceedingly.

Inordinately flattered.

To be honest, flattery wasn't my first emotion when I saw your blog. At first, it felt more like someone had subjected me to a bizarre temperature-change experiment—a wash of ice, then heat, then the uncomfortable warmth of perpetual humiliation. It took five Milky Ways and two cans of orange soda to restore my body to its normal state of being.

But once I was jangling with excessive sugar and caffeine, the flattery set in. It's not every day that three esteemed high school socialites take notice of an autistic nerdling. I guess I should be grateful for Noah's SMS confessional, although I'm kind of hurt that you didn't notice me before then. After all, I *was* the leftmost Capulet sword fighter in act 3, scene 1 of *Romeo and Juliet* last fall (thank you, please hold your applause till the end). Someday, when I'm a Tony Award–winning playwright, you'll regret that you didn't pay more attention to me in high school. Or maybe I'll wind up unemployed and living in a cardboard box in Central Park, which unfortunately seems more likely.

But I'm not here to talk about me.

Let's talk about *you*—specifically, your repetitive, lackluster blog posts.

In your latest post, you used the word "slob" seven times. I mean, you're not wrong—I'm currently lying in the alcove under my stairs on a blanket that hasn't been washed in two or three years, coated in a fine layer of Cheetos dust, with my hair snarled up into some sort of mud-colored postapocalyptic halo—but you could at least use a thesaurus.

And while I don't deny that I am ugly or nerdy or badly dressed or even a "boyfriend-stealing slutbag," isn't that content getting a little stale? Despite having collected 100 percent of your information from Noah, you seem to have your facts straight about the events of last Memorial Day. But you've been writing that story for *months*. Could it be that you've run out of creative insults?

Well, starting tomorrow, I will be the senior editor of your (yes, *your*) SBHS literary magazine, so it is now my sworn duty to help you with your writing. In the interest of supplying you with more engaging material, I have launched this blog. Here you will find a trove of my many embarrassing and/or hate-worthy mistakes and flaws to improve your web content. I will continue posting until you feel completely overwhelmed by my dazzling terribleness.

Because, sluttiness aside, there are plenty of reasons to hate me, girls. You just need to get to know me.

Yours insincerely,

Jess "That Whore" Lanza

MIGHTY-PEN-JESS
Aug 18

REASON #1:
Because of me, you will never date the hottest guy in school.

I let Cam drive me to school today. Mom didn't have a shift, so she wanted to go to an old-lady Bible study at church before dropping me off. I definitely did *not* want to go to an old-lady Bible study at church, but neither did I look forward to a twenty-minute ride crammed into a yellow tin can with two dozen other teenagers who might have seen your charming hate blog. Thankfully, Cam has wheels.

The wheels in question are attached to a 2011 Chrysler minivan that was, in its youth, white but is now a sickly milk-at-the-bottom-of-the-Lucky-Charms-bowl gray. Cam was already in the van, fingers drumming against the wheel, when I trudged out of my apartment. His mom watched through their cracked-open door, I guess to make sure that I didn't get abducted by aliens during the ninety-second walk down the stairs to the parking lot? (It's nice that she cares, but I'm not sure what Mrs. Lewis in her fluffy pink bathrobe could do to protect me that her gargantuan sportsball-star son couldn't do better.)

I waved at Mrs. Lewis, and she waved her cup of coffee back at me as Cam leaned across to unlock my door. I clambered in, my jeans squeaking across the duct tape on the seat.

"Wow." He gave me a skeptical once-over. "So, your new look is, what, Juliet after she takes the poison? Macbeth the morning after the murders?"

"Don't name the Scottish Play or your car will explode." I pulled down the sun visor and examined myself in the mirror.

"I'm pretty sure that's not a thing."

"Devi Sharma named the play backstage during *The Wizard of Oz*, and the lighting board blew out within the hour." I prodded the grayish bags under my eyes. I should have filched some of my sister's excessive quantities of makeup before she left for college.

"First, that was actually in a theater, which I think is a key component of the curse," Cam said. He shifted into drive with a squeal and series of thunks that did not bode well for our making it to school in one piece. "And second, it was a coincidence."

"It can't be both a curse and a coincidence."

"I'm just saying that either way, my car is not going to explode if I say 'Macbeth.'" He rolled through the stop sign at the entrance to the apartment complex, and the brakes wailed. I said a silent prayer to Jesus and/or Lin-Manuel Miranda that we would at least get to 7-Eleven before the car died. I was not going to make it through the day without sugar.

About the only thing in Cam's car that always works is the radio. Unfortunately. He grumbled when I shut it off. "Can't you make an exception to your stupid rule today?"

"No exceptions," I said.

"I'll pay for your Slurpee."

"I do not respond to bribes."

"You used to be fun," he whined, but he was smiling.

Do you know Cam? If not, you wish you did. He is easily the hottest guy in our grade. It could be his height, or his muscles, or the careless tangle of blond hair flopping over his tanned forehead. But mostly, it's his shoulders.

I get a perverse sense of pride when girls like you see me with Cam. Jealousy radiates from your lustful eyes and drool-moistened lips. But I'm not friends with Cam because of his hotness or his sportsball prowess—though proximity to his shoulders is certainly a perk. We're friends because when I show up for school looking like an extra in *Night of the Living Dead*, he makes a Shakespeare joke and lets me turn off the radio.

My Slurpee was more sugar syrup than slush—just how I like it. It's not breakfast unless it turns your teeth blue. I chewed the straw and let the ice freeze my prefrontal cortex as we turned into the dogwood-lined entrance to Stone Bridge High. I wondered who planted those trees. Was it some fresh-faced assistant principal, straight out of grad school? ("But if it doesn't *look* like a soul-sucking hellhole rife with the fumes of Axe body spray and unfinished math homework, then surely...")

Cam's minivan crawled down the drive and through the traffic circle, where parental SUVs abandoned underclassmen at the crosswalk, then looped up the hill toward the student lots.

"We're not juniors anymore," I reminded him when he passed the entrance to the coveted Senior Lot. "Why are you parking so far out?"

"Because no one else does. I don't want anyone denting my sweet ride."

His sweet ride already had its fair share of dents. But when I looked back at the cheerful bustle of the Senior Lot, I was relieved to be moving farther from it.

He pulled into an isolated spot in the overflow lot and shifted into park with an emphatic clunk. Back down the hill, you three had emerged from your vehicles and converged on Chloe's Volt. My ex-best-friend's high bun of raven-colored twists bobbed up from the open door. Your squeals of greeting carried across the lots between us. Chloe was squealing, too. She'd have her "friendly allistic girl" smile pasted on, I knew, and she'd be looking at your eyes, or just so slightly above them that you wouldn't be able to tell the difference.

Her mask has always been better than mine.

"You gonna be okay?" Cam asked.

"Of course." I forced my fingers to stop drumming

against my cup and sucked down another memory-freezing gulp of slush. "I'm a hundred percent focused on the Senior Year Plan."

Cam grinned and counted on his fingers. "One, have fun. Two, get into college, and three . . ."

"Get the hell out of here," we chorused.

His smile faded. "But you're sure you'll be okay? Has Chloe texted you back yet?"

"No, but she will. She just needs space—you know us autistics and our unwieldy emotions. Soon she'll realize she misses me and accept my apologies."

Cam quirked an eyebrow, looking about as convinced as I felt. "Okay . . . But until that happens, you'll let me know if you need me to beat the bullies up for you?"

A laugh burst out my nose. I don't know which was more ridiculous: his mock sincerity or the idea of gentle, laid-back Cam in a fight. I let the scene play out in my head.

SETTING: The upstairs Senior Hallway of Stone Bridge High. Aggressively purple lockers flank the classroom doors, a stark contrast to the dirty beige tile floor.

AT RISE: CAMERON has cornered three girls in field hockey uniforms: Sporty-Elsa, Sporty-Tiana, and Sporty-

> Belle. Though he has several inches on the tallest of them, none of the girls looks particularly intimidated. CAMERON squares his magnificent shoulders.

                CAMERON

Hey, so you really hurt Jess's feelings, and, uh, please stop, you know, being mean. And, uh, stuff.

              SPORTY-BELLE

And you'll stop us how?

SPORTY-BELLE steps forward. CAMERON stumbles back.

                CAMERON

What do you mean? I said "please."

              SPORTY-BELLE

She-demons, attack!

Bewildered, CAMERON stands stock still as they surround him in a flurry of Puma Purple skorts and lip gloss.

CAMERON
Uh . . . Please . . . Ouch! . . . If it wouldn't be too much trouble . . .

"Why are you smirking? What do you know that I don't?"

"Nothing," I said. "I'll be fine. I should never have showed you that blog."

"No, you should have showed me it sooner."

"You've made your opinion on that known."

He had, last night when I finally showed him your homage to my sluttiness. There wasn't much hope of keeping it from him when we all got back to school anyway. You will be disappointed to know that it didn't alter his opinion of me.

"Everybody makes mistakes," he'd said. "That's no excuse for torture."

And so I smiled into the sun-visor mirror—a deliciously blue-toothed smile. Because despite your many advantages over me (popularity, athleticism, inexplicably clear skin, etc.), Cameron Lewis—and his shoulders—will always be far more mine than yours.

MIGHTY-PEN-JESS
Aug 19

REASON #2:
I assault innocent people with baked goods, and I am reluctant to apologize for it.

You want to know how I ended up friends with someone as awesome as Chloe.

To understand that, you first have to understand that I live in an apartment. My mom will tell you we live in a town house, but she is in denial. It *is* two levels like a town house, but town houses don't have people living above and below them. Plus, the sign definitely says ACADIA APARTMENTS. But if my mom called it an apartment, she'd be admitting how far we'd come down in the world since Dad got laid off. (We've come down even further since Mom drove Dad away, but this particular story takes place five years ago, and back then, we were still playing Big Happy Family in the *Yes-Jessica-It-IS-a-Town-House*.)

We had moved in right after sixth-grade graduation, and by November, I was mostly okay with it. It wasn't terrible—I was particularly fond of the space under the stairs that I filled with pillows and blankets as a comfy homework cave—but it felt small compared to the house we used to rent. I could cross my bedroom in three paces, and the kitchen was so narrow that two people couldn't pass each other. Since my mom believes all foods need to be boiled and prodded with wooden spoons for at least three hours before being soggy enough to eat, I'd taken to squirreling away snacks in my bedroom, thereby avoiding the whole frazzled-mom/bubbling-cabbage-pot situation.

One such snack was a pink buttercream-slathered birthday cake. I'd baked it for my sister Julia's Sweet Sixteen, but since Julia stopped eating cake at like age twelve when she discovered makeup and boys (God forbid an ounce of fat would mar the otherwise perfect line of her black satin sex-dress!), it was really for me. Unfortunately, the cake was a disappointment. Not only did it lean precariously, but the icing tasted like oily candy powder, and the cake itself was salty. (It is possible I misread the abbreviation "tsp" as "tbsp.") As a result, I hadn't managed to choke down much before it began to mold.

The molding cake must have grated on my mom's nerves when she went into my room to vacuum, but she had promised not to throw away any of my leftovers after the Unfinished Brownie Debacle, so it just kind of sat there on my dresser, rotting away. A month after the ill-fated cake's birth, I decided to put it out of its misery. Crumbs trailed along the scuzzy carpets as I proceeded ceremoniously down the stairs with the cake plate, a mournful dirge droning in my head. The kitchen trash can awaited, the cake's final resting place.

But I never made it that far. I stopped at the kitchen entrance, my gaze fixed on the large living room windows. Movement outside had caught my eye—a bare branch unsettled by a leaping squirrel. Still clutching the plate of ex-cake, I crossed the living room, past the armchair where Julia was sitting, eyes suctioned to her phone as usual. She ignored me, also as usual.

On the balcony, I peered down to the gully floor some twenty feet below. We're only the second apartment up, but the hill is so steep that the back half of the building needs stilts just to keep up with the front. Even the bottom-floor apartment has a balcony. The squirrel jumped from one tree to another, careless of the certain death that awaited him if he should slip and fall to the ground below. I shivered, my hole-riddled socks and threadbare *Hamilton* T-shirt poor protection against the November wind. I wondered how that squirrel could possibly store up enough food for the winter when it was already so cold.

And then, in a millisecond, my brain made an enthusiastically definitive decision.

In retrospect, I don't know if squirrels should really be eating birthday cake. Apparently it makes dogs sick. It didn't occur to me at the time. Things frequently don't occur to me until it's too late.

I tipped the cake plate over the balcony. I expected to

hear a crunch as the cake met the leaves at the bottom of the gully, but instead I heard a splat, too soon and too close. I leaned over the railing.

The cake had landed on the balcony below.

I don't know how. Maybe the wind caught it. Maybe I tipped it at the wrong angle (physics has never been my strongest subject). But now, hot-pink buttercream spattered the railing and white wicker patio furniture on our neighbor's balcony.

It wouldn't have been so bad if it were still those two community college students living there—Dan and Matt, or Dan and Mark (Dave and Mark?)—because they always left the balcony trashed with empty beer cans and soggy potato chips and occasionally vomit. Moldy cake would be an improvement. But Dan/Dave and Matt/Mark had moved out in September, and someone new had just moved in. He was oldish (maybe my mom's age), bald, and Black, with hipster glasses and long-sleeve button-down shirts that he wore even while lugging furniture into the apartment. He drove a Subaru and left for work so early in the morning that I figured he must be a teacher or a barista. I had observed no significant other.

(I realize that last paragraph makes me sound like a stalker. That is not inaccurate.)

But one thing I could be certain of: New Neighbor was not the type to leave beer cans or potato chips or vomit on his balcony. And he was sure to notice the moldy cake.

I lingered, staring down at the pathetic remains until the wind numbed my cheeks and fingers, and then I wandered back inside. I felt a bit dazed, standing in the middle of the living room, clinging to the empty plate like it was my last link to reality. My tongue scrubbed frantically against my gums like the motion could fling me back in time.

Julia didn't look up from her phone. "What did you do?"

"I dropped the cake on the downstairs neighbor's balcony."

She looked up, frowning like she wasn't sure why I would make such a weird joke. Then she saw my face. "Oh, Jesus. You're serious."

I nodded. She threw back her head and let out an exasperated roar. Then she tossed her phone on the couch and stomped onto the balcony. I followed.

Side by side, Julia and I are a strange pair. You'd never guess we were sisters. She has curves where I just bulge. Her hair shines while mine frizzes. She got our father's smooth olive skin while I am pasty with an irregular smattering of freckles. She is a gazelle: svelte and graceful and perfectly put together. I am an aardvark: short and stubby and awkward.

I used to wonder if I would outgrow my awkward the way she did. (Because she was definitely your average braces-wearing, model-UN, know-it-all nerd in elementary school.) I'd kind of figured when I hit puberty, I would also suddenly develop an interest in my appearance and dating people and remembering to wear deodorant. (Still waiting on all counts.)

Julia peered over the railing, scowling. "How did you even do that?" Then she started to laugh. I laughed, too. It was more hysteria for me, panic at the consequences of my terrible life choices, but it was laughter.

"Oh my God, you are such a ridiculous person. Get a broom."

That was the most bonding I'd had—or have had—with my sister since she entered high school: lying on our stomachs, swinging a broom over the edge of our balcony, trying to brush the cake off our new neighbor's patio furniture. I gave up when I dropped the broom. I imagined what New Neighbor would think. Did a witch fly up there, smear cake on his possessions, and then jump to her death in the ravine below? Also, would my mom notice the broom was missing?

"You're going to have to go down there," Julia said.

"Can you do it?"

She snorted. "Um, no. You threw the cake, weirdo. Apologize, and don't forget to ask for the broom back."

"You're really going to force your autistic sister into a confrontation with a stranger?"

"You left out the part where my autistic sister chose to throw moldy cake at the stranger. So, yes."

I sighed. I had always known it would come to this.

My black orthopedic shoes (as comfortable as they are unstylish) resounded against the stairs with hollow clangs, every step bringing me closer to the lower apartment. There are many perks of having a brain like mine, but chatting with unfamiliar humans is not an area in which I excel. I paused at the door with my hand raised to knock, but my muscles wouldn't obey.

I'd seen the Subaru in the parking lot. New Neighbor was definitely home. But what would I say? *I'm sorry I dropped a cake on your balcony?* I wasn't sure I'd be able to get the words out without cracking up again. Even just thinking about it, a few stray giggles escaped.

I fled back upstairs.

"He wasn't home," I told Julia.

"Bullshit," she said. "His car is there. You're just chicken."

"Can't we wait until Mom gets home? She can bring him some apology cabbage."

Julia skewered me with her no-nonsense, future-lawyer stare.

I moaned and went back outside.

I could run away. I could take blankets from my bed and camp out in the gully. I could see if Mrs. Teplitsky in B10 would let me stay with her in exchange for walking her little yippy rat-dog.

Or I could just knock on this door and apologize.

I sucked in my cheeks, biting them to control my hysteria-giggles, and knocked.

It was a long minute before the door opened. It wasn't New Neighbor, though, in his button-down shirt and hipster glasses. It was a girl about my age with twists of raven-black hair down her back and a constellation of freckles like my own across her warm brown cheeks, and when I forced myself to quick-glance at her eyes, they weren't searching for mine.

And that's why I told you this five-year-old story. Not just to illustrate my impulsiveness, or my instinctive cowardice, but because, in a way, the Cake-Dropping Incident is the root cause of your hatred of me. Because if I hadn't dropped that cake, I may never have met Chloe. And then she wouldn't have met Noah. And none of this would have happened.

MIGHTY-PEN-JESS
Aug 20

REASON #3:
I am so awkward that freshmen feel sorry for me.

There's a rumor out there that autistic people can't lie. I am proof that this is untrue.

In fact, I spend my entire life, or at least my entire school day, lying. I'm constantly forcing myself to nod and smile, to pretend I get what people are saying, when in reality my brain is like a full sixty seconds behind on processing their words. Have you ever noticed how *loud* it is in this building? It's a chaos of sounds—conversations and laughter and slamming lockers—creeping under my skin like hundreds of spiders, drawing my focus until I feel motion-sick and can't even keep my eyes open.

Sorry not sorry if that weirds you out. You're not the ones who have to live it.

Chloe understands sensory hang-ups. The first time we hung out back in seventh grade, her dad dropped us off at that Mexican place on Maple, and I noticed right away that one red tile on the front of the bar was out of place. I started feeling dizzy and nauseated, and I was mortified. I mean, what would the cool new neighbor kid think of me if I randomly puked into the basket of complimentary tortilla chips? But then Chloe said, "I think we have to go. There's this red tile—" and I was like, *"YES!"* and we threw a five on the table for the chips and ran out together, both laughing in our relief to finally have met someone who *gets it*.

That was the moment for both of us, I think: the moment we knew what kind of a friendship we'd lucked into. You three will never understand her the way I do.

I was feeling pretty dizzy and nauseated yesterday, weaving through the hordes of chatting, shrieking, chewing teenagers who clog the hallways and breezeway between classes, and I practically ran the last few yards into the Creative Writing room. It was a relief, the quiet empty classroom with the familiar workshop tables, scent of pencil shavings, and classic movie posters on the wall.

Then one of our Drama Freshmen showed up.

Technically, Emily Fernandez is a sophomore now, but I still think of her as a freshman. She did stage crew for *R&J* and *Into the Woods*, and she was always quietly on top of it, not like many of the giggly, overenthusiastic, still-haven't-figured-out-they're-not-king-of-the-school-anymore freshmen. Sometimes she joined Dee, Carly, Noah, and me for vending-machine dinner during break, though she didn't say much.

All of Emily's clothes are black, but her thick mane of hair is an ever-changing explosion of neon. When she first walked into the *R&J* crew meeting last year, it was lime green. This week, it's cobalt. I studied her Chucks, silently willing her to take a seat on the other side of the room.

"Hi?" she said quietly, like she'd just intruded on a private, romantic moment between me and the desk.

"Hi." I couldn't bring myself to force eye contact. This week had already been too much.

"Can I, uh . . . ?" She eased her messenger bag over the back of the chair next to mine.

My inner asocial curmudgeon gave a resigned groan. "Oh . . . yeah, sure."

"Thanks."

"Yup."

The warning bell put the barely existent conversation out of its misery. As other students trickled in, Emily pulled her notebook out of her bag and made a show of painstaking concentration as she wrote the date, period, and class title at the top of a page. Her ears had turned copper, the blush creeping its way onto her cheeks like she was having a sudden, violent allergic reaction to my presence.

And that's when I realized.

Emily knows Noah. And based on her five-alarm embarrassment, she probably saw Noah's text. Did he send it to *everyone* in his phone?

> I know a text message isn't the best way to share this, but I can't keep this secret

> any longer. I can't keep accepting your
> friendship when you don't know what kind
> of person I really am—what I've done.

It was my turn to blush, the warmth of shame not stopping at my skin but seeping deeper, constricting my lungs. I'd assumed only the people in Chloe's circle (and whatever readers have bravely suffered the tedious prose of your blog) knew what I did, but in reality, even the freaking freshmen knew.

> When she kissed me, I was like wtf bc she's
> Chloe's friend, but I also didn't want to
> hurt her feelings. Maybe that's why I gave in.

My legs started jiggling. I was definitely going to have to amend my school survival strategy. Arriving at class early was obviously a failure. Perhaps lurking in the bathroom until the warning bell?

> I still can't believe my gf's best friend
> would want to—

"Jess! Our illustrious editor in chief!" Mr. Barton strode into the room, clutching one of those rock-hard natural granola bars they sell in the vending machines. He was beaming. He was always beaming, at least when I was around. He had on one of his signature blue-stripe button-down shirts, and he'd gotten new hipster glasses over the summer. They were black like his old ones but slightly thicker so that the bottoms of the frames extended almost to the tip of his nose. "I can't believe I didn't see you all summer. I was so bummed when Chloe told me you couldn't come with us to the Outer Banks this year. Did you and your sister have fun in New York?"

"Oh. Yeah," I lied. Julia and I definitely did *not* have fun in New York, mostly because Julia and I definitely did not *go* to New York. But who am I to tell a man that his daughter's been lying to his face?

"I'm glad someone had fun. When you couldn't come, we ended up having to invite *Noah*." He gave an exaggerated fake-grimace, running a hand over the shadow of hair on his mahogany scalp. "Can you imagine being a third wheel to your own daughter?"

I hoped that he interpreted my wince as sympathy and not a response to the pulverizing, soul-thrashing wallop of pain the thought of Noah provoked.

"What about you? Write anything good this summer?"

"Not much." That wasn't a lie. Instead of being full of story ideas and character sketches, my current notebook was a mess of scribbles and eraser smudges. Of course the summer I needed to write college essays, I couldn't string three words together.

"Are you still planning to apply to the Goldberg program?" he asked.

"Yeah."

"Have you started your portfolio?"

"Not really."

"You need to get working on it. Fall will fly by."

"Right." In some ways, I wish that were true. Obviously, I need as much time for my application as I can get, but if fall is anything like this summer, each day will feel like a thousand years and none of them will be productive.

The second bell rang, and Mr. Barton began his standard icebreaker explanation (two truths and a lie). Emily leaned toward me. I braced myself for the inevitable *I-know-what-you-did-how-dare-you?*

"What's the Goldberg program?" she whispered.

"Oh. Um, a dramatic writing program at Tisch. You know, the NYU arts school?"

"Whoa. Do you have to audition? I don't think I'd ever be brave enough to audition for Tisch."

"You don't have to audition for the Goldberg program, but you do have to submit a portfolio, and it's just as competitive as the performance tracks," I whispered. "I think I have about as much chance of being accepted as I have of being struck by lightning. Twice. While wrapped in a rubber tire."

Emily held in a laugh that partially escaped as a snort. I smiled innocently when Mr. Barton glanced our way and waited for him to look elsewhere before I whispered, "No, seriously. I have major writer's block. I don't think I'll get the application done in time."

"Mr. Barton will help. He's the best."

I glanced up at Chloe's dad, who was beaming (of course), and ignored the dull stab in the vicinity of my heart. "Yeah," I said truthfully. "He definitely is."

Mr. Barton called on me to give my two truths and a lie.

I have never stolen anything.

I have never been to the Outer Banks.

I have never dated anyone.

No one guessed right.

MIGHTY-PEN-JESS
Aug 22

REASON #4:
I am the Aaron Burr of Chloe's love life.

It should be illegal for people to fight before noon. Not federal law illegal, but laws of physics illegal. Morning fights should be prevented by our circadian rhythms, like how some plants only sprout when there have been a certain number of warm days after a frost. We should only start arguments with other humans a certain number of hours after our particular patch of Earth has been facing the sun. Because if someone does get in a fight, say with their boyfriend, first thing in the morning, then someone else, say their ex-best friend who was the catalyst of the relationship drama, will have a whole day to feel shitty about it.

When I came out of the stairwell into the Senior Hallway, Noah was shouting, "Yeah, you keep *saying* that. But it's what you *do*, Chloe. I know you blame me, and I can't take it anymore." He hitched up his backpack and slammed out the door.

"Walking away won't fix this," Chloe called after him. As tight as she held her voice, it still wobbled. I stepped toward her, but you already had her surrounded, sweeping her toward the refuge of the girls' bathroom. A gaggle of anxious underclassmen scurried out when you opened the door to usher Chloe inside. Hannah, you paused long enough to look over your shoulder at me, tossing your perfect brunette curls in a way that was intended to either menace or land you a gig selling shampoo in low-budget infomercials.

You needn't have worried. I had no intention of following you. It wasn't difficult to imagine how *that* would have gone.

```
AT RISE:      JESS slips awkwardly into the
              bathroom. The battered wood door
              closes behind her with a miser-
              able creak. HANNAH, BROOKLYN,
              ALEXIS, and CHLOE turn slowly
              from their sink-side huddle.


                     HANNAH
Oh. My. God.


                     CHLOE
                   (shrieking)
How dare you come in here! Don't you know
this is all your fault?!
```

I do, actually, know it is all my fault. In fact, I have a habit of ruining Chloe's relationships; though, in fairness to myself, I must point out that my actions last May were not premeditated. I liked Chloe and Noah together. I wanted it to work.

I cannot say as much for several of the earlier boyfriend casualties.

She was dating Mason when we met. He had an annoying laugh like Ernie from *Sesame Street*, and if that wasn't bad enough, he was also a jerk. Not just to me—to pretty much everyone who wasn't Chloe. His mom. His little sister. The security guy at the skate park. (Oh yeah, he was a skater, so there was also that.) I started commenting on every instance of his jerkishness, and they added up. She broke up with him the day after Valentine's.

She started dating Raheem in time for freshman-year Homecoming. I liked him at first, but after a while, I realized that he was a taker. He needed all her time, all her energy, all her attention. He got offended if I joined them for anything—even supremely non-romantic things like helping Dr. Barton hand out voter registration paperwork. It was weird. And once I pointed it out to Chloe, she agreed. Eventually.

You all know what happened with Leo at the Summer Picnic before sophomore year, and I'm sure you agree that even if I hadn't accidentally broken his precious Nintendo D-whatever, anyone who can curse that loudly for that long over something that inconsequential has some deeper anger management issues to work out before he can be in a healthy relationship.

I knew from the moment I saw Noah onstage at his audition for *The Importance of Being Earnest* that he was the right guy to help Chloe get over Leo. Sure, he was a freshman and we were sophomores, but he exuded more confidence than most of the college guys Julia brought home. Julia's boys were always aesthetically pleasing, but if they had personalities, they kept them pretty well hidden. (They spent most of their visits locked away in her bedroom, and I have this working theory that Julia views men as sex toys who can tell her *of course that dress looks good on you.*)

Noah, on the other hand, had *charisma*. He was handsome, in that classic Coca-Cola ad way, with a wave in his sable hair, smooth, golden-tanned skin, and dreamy dark eyes. He was funny—witty funny—and most important, polite. I've never developed much of an interest in dating, but Chloe thrives on those dedicated, emotionally close relationships. Noah was just the sort of nice guy who could make Chloe stop moping about Leo.

(And yes, I was sort of hoping I'd get to hang out with her more if she were dating a theatre guy. Selfish, but that is the theme of this blog, so.)

After auditions, I found Noah in the cafeteria fighting with the vending machine over a package of Oreos.

"Great audition," I said.

"Thanks. I'm Noah."

"Yes, I know. I saw your audition sheet." Then, since that sounded super stalkerish, I added, "I'm the stage manager."

"Oh, right, right. Jenn?"

"Jess."

"Jess. Cool. Well, hopefully we'll be seeing more of each other. If I make the play."

"Oh, you'll make it. But on the off chance you don't, we always need techies!"

"Great." He was holding his slightly damaged Oreos and clearly looking for a way to escape the conversation, though he was too nice to just walk away. (Another bonus point.) I glanced up at the clock. I couldn't tell him *please just wait five more minutes so you can meet my friend who I want to set you up with*. (In retrospect, maybe I could have. Noah would probably have been intrigued rather than weirded out.) Finally, he held out his hand.

"Very pleased to make your acquaintance, Jessica," he drawled in his best Lady Bracknell falsetto.

I took his hand and bowed over it. "Adieu." I watched him swagger away.

"Who was that?" Chloe asked. I hadn't heard her come up behind me.

"Your future husband," I said. She tilted her head skeptically but knew me better than to comment.

I invited them both to join me for a viewing of the 2002 Oliver Parker film adaptation of *Earnest* that Saturday morning. Noah might not have been able to tell how much Chloe liked him, but I could. She was watching him out of the corner of her eye, and her fingers kept happy-fluttering while Noah monologued about his favorite musicals, most of which lined up with Chloe's (and mine). And that made my heart happy-flutter, too. Because maybe I hadn't just set Chloe up with a convenient theatre-centric rebound. Maybe I'd found Her Person. Maybe they'd be Together Forever!

Or maybe I'd accidentally pulverize their chance at romantic bliss, surprising us all with my unpremeditated sluttiness.

> *I didn't want to hurt her feelings. Maybe that's why I gave in.*
> *I still can't believe my gf's best friend would want to have sex with me.*

I waited until the warning bell rang and still none of you had come out of the bathroom. I was tempted to go in and check on Chloe, but that might have made things worse. So I tore a sheet from my notebook and filled it with the only two words I seem to be able to write these days: *I'm sorry.*

I didn't sign it. We know each other's handwriting like our own.

As I crossed the hall, I folded the note, doing my best to flatten the creases between my chewed-off fingernails. I had the note poised at the edge of one of the vent slits of Chloe's locker when the bathroom door squawked.

It was you, Alexis, cherry blush blended into the brown of your cheeks, Puma Purple gloss glistening on your lips, frown lines cutting deep between your eyebrows. The gold baubles dangling from your earlobes clinked as you looked over your shoulder into the bathroom, then back to me. I waited for you to yell at me or to call for your reinforcements. You didn't. You pressed your lips tight and watched me ease the paper through the vent.

Maybe you thought it wouldn't matter, that my words on the page wouldn't take. But I happen to believe in the power of words. The only thing I believe in more fiercely is Chloe and me. Couples fight, and relationships die, but one mistake can't kill a friendship.

Not one like ours.

Not forever.

MIGHTY-PEN-JESS
Aug 24

REASON #5:
My relationship with my mom is as messed up as Emily Dickinson's sex life.

Long Years apart—can make no
Breach a second cannot fill—
The absence of the Witch does not
Invalidate the spell—
The embers of a Thousand Years
Uncovered by the Hand
That fondled them when they were Fire
Will stir and understand—

Cam finished reading aloud from my poetry textbook with a flourish and a bow, which was slightly difficult to achieve while hunched in the homework cave under the stairs. "I'm assuming she doesn't mean a literal witch."

I slumped lower in the corner, tapping my notebook with a pen like it was a magic wand that could make my Creative

Writing assignment complete itself. "Emily Dickinson never means anything literally."

"I dunno. She talks about death a lot. That's literal, right? Or is it one of those poetic euphemisms for an orgasm?"

I flinched, then cleared my throat. "I hope not. Otherwise 'I heard a Fly buzz—when I died—' would take on some very weird connotations."

Cam drew a dramatic breath. "The Stillness in the Room / Was like the Stillness in the Air— / Between the Heaves of Storm."

"Oh my God, stop."

"The Eyes around—had wrung them dry— / And Breaths were gathering . . . *firm*!"

"Stop!" I tried to laugh it off, though the noise that straggled from my throat sounded more like the dying breath of a nearly drowned oboe. "Why do you even have that memorized?"

"At my old school, we had to learn one in ninth grade, and that's the one I picked." He turned back to my textbook, totally casual, as though having a random school assignment from three years ago memorized were normal. "Oh, okay. Apparently the witch is a metaphor for friendship when two people are together, and the spell is the bond of friendship that lingers when they're apart."

"You really should have taken AP Lit."

"Nah, because then I would have to write a paper about it."

I gave him my best not-impressed stare. He might deny

it, but Cam is a word nerd. He outed himself the moment I met him two summers ago. Because of course—*of course*—within five seconds of meeting the tall, hot boy moving in next door, I told him about my name.

Did you know that the name Jessica was invented by William Shakespeare for his play *The Merchant of Venice* because he thought it sounded super Jewish? Do you care?

You answered no to both questions. It's why we're not friends. (Well, one of the reasons.)

But when the hot boy next door popped over for introductions, and I told him my name was *Jessica, you know, like from* The Merchant of Venice, he responded, "Shylock's daughter. Nice. Not nice how she steals all his shit and leaves him to die, but nice name."

And that is how I know he could write an AP Lit paper if he weren't too lazy to try.

Cam reached one of his oversize arms across the homework cave and plucked the mostly blank notebook out of my lap. "Is this your portfolio for Tisch?"

"No." I lunged for the notebook, but he dodged back in what must be some sort of advanced sportsball evasive maneuver, leaving me grasping at carpet fuzz.

"His smile, however lopsided, always made her feel warm and safe," he read. "Aww, Jess! Are you writing a story about me?" He twisted his lips into an exaggeratedly lopsided smile.

"I wasn't." I lunged again, this time snatching the notebook. Clicking my pen, I added another sentence. *"It was such* a shame that he had the mental faculties and charisma of a three-week-old stalk of limp celery."

Cam chortled. I did not, partly because chortling is a ridiculous-sounding form of laughter that should be avoided whenever possible, but mostly because that last, utterly unusable sentence was the best thing I'd written in that notebook all day. In months, actually. Since Chloe stopped speaking to me.

"You look depressed," Cam said. "Are you depressed?"

"No."

He ignored me. "I know what will cheer you up! Shakespeare movie night. Ian McKellen *Richard III*, nonnegotiable."

My lips twitched. "You *would* choose the Shakespeare movie with the biggest guns. But unfortunately, I can't tonight. If I don't clean the kitchen, my mom will boil me with tomorrow's cabbage."

As though my mention of cabbage were a summoning spell, the deadbolt on the front door clunked open. Cam scrambled out from under the stairs as the-killjoy-otherwise-known-as-my-mother entered the apartment.

If you've been thinking I'm too hard on my mom, you probably haven't met her. Or you *have* met her but were taken in by her demure *I'm-just-an-innocent-NICU-nurse-who-loves-Jesus* schtick. (I mean, she *is* a NICU nurse who loves Jesus, but definitely not an innocent one. I found her college yearbook in the attic a couple of years ago, and I came very close to scrubbing my eyes with a Brillo pad after.) For most of my childhood, she split her nonworking hours pretty evenly between church stuff and hanging around the house, nagging my dad. But eventually my dad left, and Julia went to college, so now my mom focuses all her nagging on me.

She sighed in the doorway of the kitchen, no doubt taking in the open microwave drenched in exploded mac and cheese and the Jenga tower of empty soda cans on the counter. But when she made it to the living room, she forced a smile.

"Hello, Cameron. How is the football season going?"

I rolled my eyes.

"Great. Thanks, Ms. Lanza. We've got our first game on Friday night."

"Good luck! What a shame I have to work, but I'm sure Jessie will tell me all about it after."

Cam and I exchanged a look. We both knew I would go to a sportsball game the day Stephen King wrote a rom-com.

"Jessie, did you try on the jeans I left on your bed?"

"Not yet."

"The thrift store only has forty-eight-hour returns, so I really need—"

"I'll do it tonight," I snapped. It was bad enough that my oh-so-stylish mom jeans came from the hospital thrift store, but worse when she mentioned it in front of my friends. Friend.

She wavered on her feet in the living room, the weight of decision-making threatening to topple her. Then she said,

"It's always nice to see you, Cameron, but it's time to go home. Jessie has work to do."

"Of course." Cam scooped up his backpack and textbooks with the urgency of Richard III on the run from Henry Tudor's panzer tanks.

"You don't have to go, Cam. Mom, he doesn't have to go."

"It's cool," Cam said. "I'll see you tomorrow morning. Bye, Ms. Lanza."

I waited until the door thunked shut before I lost it. "You didn't have to kick him out."

"Jessica," my mom said on a sigh. She hadn't known Shakespeare invented my name, either. She'd been unimpressed when I'd told her.

Sometimes I wonder if we're really related or if I'm just some baby she stole from the NICU. Like somewhere out there, I have a real mom who wouldn't be flabbergasted when I inform her that science is the most tediously awful subject area I am forced to learn about. A real mom who would be delighted to watch Branagh's *Hamlet* at the first ever Lanza Girls' Family Movie Night, instead of looking panicked and saying "Isn't that really long?" and siding with Julia in forcing me to watch *She's the Man*. (That was also the *last* ever Lanza Girls' Family Movie Night.)

"Jessie, we agreed that on my workdays, you'd clean the kitchen."

"I'm going to. *God!*" I stomped to the kitchen.

"Don't swear."

"I didn't swear. That's not a swear." I swept the soda cans toward the recycling with such force that one of them skittered across the counter and clanked to the ground, spilling the last drops of soda on the linoleum. Because of course it did. I grabbed a paper towel.

Mom hovered in the doorway. "When you're done, you can try on—"

"The jeans. *Yes*. Though I don't know why it matters. I can always safety-pin them. I couldn't make them any less fashionable than they already are." I pounded up the stairs.

"Jessie—"

"It's *Jess*," I shouted. "I'm not five anymore."

They weren't mom jeans. Inexplicably, my mother had actually selected two pairs of J.Crew ankle jeans—one dark wash, one black. I stared at them for a full ten minutes before I tried them on. If there were any justice, they would have been too tight, but they were a perfect fit.

MIGHTY-PEN-JESS
Aug 25

REASON #6:
I am actively plotting against you.

Cam's not wrong. I kind of am depressed.

And no, it's not because you three haven't commented on my blog. Or acknowledged its existence. Or stopped blogging about me. In fact, it doesn't really have anything to do with you.

And I think "depression" might be the wrong word, because I'm not sad. I'm just . . . blah. Go to school, come home, stare at a blank page in my Creative Writing notebook for a few hours, go to bed, repeat. No tears, no angst, just solemn resignation. It's not presence of sadness so much as absence of fun. A complete failure of the first tenet of the Senior Year Plan.

Cam, Chloe, and I came up with the Plan during that heat wave last May when they canceled school because the teachers union pointed out that when the temperature in the classrooms was creeping up over eighty degrees (and the trailers were the approximate temperature of the sun), it wasn't exactly a safe working and learning environment.

This was pre–Memorial Day, so it was a period of relative bliss, except for the fact that the AC in our apartment building was on strike. Also, my mother works twelve-hour shifts, which means she's home four whole days a week, which is intolerable (there are only so many times a seventeen-year-old can endure lectures on How Your Chemistry Grades Do Not Reflect Your Best Effort before she spontaneously combusts). Also, Julia was done with college for the year, and every time I came downstairs, she was *there*, being an infuriating, sanctimonious know-it-all with assorted unwelcome advice about my wardrobe and personal hygiene. So, I guess "bliss" is only an accurate characterization when compared to the new circle of hell in which we now exist.

To avoid this hot, sweaty armpit of judgment, one day I harassed Cam until he drove us over to Chloe's mom's house.

We were lying on the floor of Dr. Barton's kitchen, letting the tile cool our half-melted bodies, when we got to talking about senior year and everything we wanted to do before we graduated.

"Graduation is obviously a good thing," Chloe said. "It's the next step toward you making the world better through your plays—"

"And you saving the world through robots and then subsequently destroying the world, also through robots," I added.

"Robotic prosthetics, and they will not destroy the world, and *it is too hot to explain this to you again.*" She finished off her admonishment singing, a riff that would have made Renée Elise Goldsberry proud.

Cam laughed, so I halfheartedly fwapped him on the shoulder. "Fine, non-world-destroying robotic prosthetics that emphasize functionality and disability justice and blah blah blah, but what about the fact that graduation means *you are moving to California.*" I attempted to sing like she had done, and I immediately regretted it. This time, Cam's laughter earned him a wholehearted shoulder fwap.

"We need to make a list." Chloe sat up, giving her glasses three quick wipes on the front of her tank top. She had her twists wrapped up in a high bun to keep them off the back of her neck, but sweat had still beaded on the bridge of her nose. "Do you have our notebook, Jess?"

"Always." I scrubbed my own sweat from my forehead with the bottom of my tee before heading to the couch where I'd dumped my stuff. I pulled our current spiral-bound notebook from the bottom of my backpack, shaking off the bits of crushed Cheez-Its and miscellaneous lint that always accumulate in the bottom of my bag. When I returned, Chloe had assembled a rainbow of pens, and Cam was raking a hand through his hair as though he found this whole process baffling.

"We can color-code by category," she said. "Do you have a preference for what color we use for day trips?"

We did not have a preference because neither Cam nor I is Chloe.

I ceded the notebook, and Chloe began listing the many adventures, activities, and achievements we needed to squeeze into our last year of togetherness. Chloe is an expert at lists. It's probably why she's so much better at keeping her life together than I am.

After a while, Cam wandered off to root through the fridge (or possibly just to use it as a source of personal bonus AC) because, really, this list was turning out to be about Chloe and me. Cam had moved into our school district sophomore year, and though he hung out with us sometimes, more often he was with the other sportsball-guys doing whatever sportsball-guys do. Chloe and I had been friends since the Cake-Dropping Incident in seventh grade, and that was *forever*. Was there life before Chloe-and-Jess? There must have been, but it's hard to remember—some hazy, distant past, the protozoan stage of my organism's evolution.

But making this list of last things, suddenly *forever* seemed fleeting. One more year. That was all the time that Chloe-and-Jess had left. In one year, I'd hopefully be packing up to move to New York, and Chloe would definitely be going to Caltech. (She says it's a "reach school," but it's not. They'll be begging her to come.) We'd be a country apart.

My fingers were flapping against the tiles, my tongue scrubbing over my teeth like it wanted to erase them, when

Chloe put down her pen. "I'm sorry," she said. "I thought it would be fun, but . . ."

"Yeah."

We sat cross-legged on the tiles, facing each other but not looking at each other. We never looked each other in the eye, but we were usually really good at *seeing* each other, understanding each other. In that moment, though, I couldn't see past the cloud of sadness that had settled between us. I tugged on the frayed threads trailing from the bottom of my jeans and willed my intestines to unknot themselves.

"You're making it too complicated," Cam said, returning from his refrigerated adventure with a soda. "Just keep it simple, and leave room for flexibility. Like, here's mine." He tore a page from the notebook, ignoring my squawk of indignation and Chloe's appalled hiss.

He wrote:

1. Have fun.

2. Get into college.

3. Get the hell out of Stone Bridge High School.

We stared at the paper. It wasn't color coded. It wasn't detailed. But looking at it didn't make me want to puke.

"I think that encompasses everything," Chloe said, her thumb working furiously over the woven bracelet she always wears on her left wrist.

"Yeah, okay," I said.

Cameron scrawled *Senior Year Plan* at the top and magneted it to Chloe's fridge. But Chloe pointed out her mom's inevitable objection to the use of the word "hell," so rather than being censored, the Plan found its way into the bottom of my backpack with the cracker crumbs and tissue fuzz. And there it stayed.

Until this morning, when Cam and I were getting Slurpees, and he was harassing me about my college applications, so I had to throw my backpack at his head (obviously), but he ducked, and it turned upside down, and absolutely everything fell out, including the crumpled, crumb-dusted Plan. And when I got to first period, I flattened it and squeezed a new goal at the top of the page–the goal I need to achieve before anything else on the list becomes possible.

Because the thing I want most in the world is to get Chloe back.

MIGHTY-PEN-JESS
Aug 27

REASON #7:
I spy on people in bathrooms.

This afternoon, after slipping yet another *please talk to me* note into Chloe's locker, I retreated to the Language Arts Hall bathroom. I figured it was an unlikely place to run into any of you three. Or Noah. Or anyone who'd gotten Noah's text.

It turns out this was yet another miscalculation on my part.

I was sitting on the toilet seat (with my pants on, which I'm just now realizing might be grosser than if I had pulled them down?), waiting for the warning bell to ring, when someone hurled the door open, probably kicked it, so it cracked against the wall.

Someone said, "—because *Mean Girls* is hella cliché. And does Regina George really resemble any of the characters in *Pygmalion?*"

"The point isn't to have a monologue that matches a specific character, just to give them a taste of what you can do."

"Still, you gotta be relevant."

I recognized the voices, of course, but until I could see them, I still held out hope that it was just some randos who happened to sound like my theatre friends.

Former theatre friends.

I took a deep breath of stanky bathroom air and leaned to the side until my view through the door gap lined up with the kids at the sinks: a short, curvy figure in a tunic and animal-print leggings with a matching wrap headband around her locs, and a tall, willowy figure in orange skinny jeans and a chartreuse-sequined top, their short wavy hair sideswept and dyed blond.

My hope wilted. It was definitely Carly and Dee.

"Okay, then," Dee said, their chain-loop fidget clacking between their fingers. "What are *you* going to audition with?"

"Puck's last soliloquy from *Midsummer*."

I shook my head. *Way too overdone.*

"Ew, way too overdone," said Dee. "And too old."

I pressed my palms into my eyes, tracing my gums with my tongue, as Carly and Dee bounced (terrible) monologue ideas back and forth. Last year we'd done this together—Carly, Dee, me, and Noah—sitting on the stage in the Drama Room. Dee had spitballed wild ideas faster than I could keep up (their neurodivergent brain is bouncier than mine) while Carly took notes. I wondered whether they were coming from Advanced Drama now. I don't even know what period it is this year, since I dropped the class before the schedule posted.

"*Rosencrantz and Guildenstern Are Dead?*" Carly suggested, rattling around in her makeup bag.

"Will you get off the Shakespeare already?"

"It's not Shakespeare. It's Stoppard."

"Semantics, babe. It should be something like *The Importance of Being Earnest.*"

"How is that *not* overdone?"

Obviously, I wouldn't be auditioning this year. Noah was without question going to land the lead as Henry Higgins, and the thought of being onstage—or backstage—with him made my mouth go dry, even though I knew it shouldn't. (It's not like I could mess things up more than I already had.)

But if I *were* going to audition for a late Victorian comedy, I would want to pick a monologue from another Victorian comedy. Wilde maybe, but not *Earnest*. Something over the top. Something . . .

"'Tommy has proposed to me again,' from *An Ideal Husband*," I decided. "That'd be perfect."

Outside my stall, there was silence. Sudden, deafening silence.

Did you know that silence is its own sound? It's not an absence of sound; that's a mistake a lot of people make. Silence sounds like blood rushing in your own ears. Like someone releasing an abrupt breath too slowly. A heeled boot shifting a millimeter on glazed tile when someone tries to stop their leg from twitching. The faint snick of lips and tongues as two people hold an unvoiced conversation.

The soft clap of my palm against my forehead when I realize I spoke out loud.

"Helloo?" Dee addressed me, their boots clicking as they turned toward the stall. "Toilet person? Want to come out and join the conversation?"

I pushed my breath out, fast, from between tight lips. *Nope. No, I do not.*

"We know you're in there," they continued. "You in the . . . frayed jeans and clunky black sneakers with Velcro—wait. Jess?"

My trembling hands snatched my backpack off the hook and clawed at the latch until the stall opened. I barely registered the shocked flush in Dee's cheeks or Carly's newly painted wine-red lips, open in an almost cartoonish O. I barreled through the door and into the hallway just as the warning bell blared. Passing students tried to ignore me as I stood there, gasping air that burned like poison.

I knew they were still talking about me in that bathroom. There were about a dozen different ways the conversation could've been going.

DEE
Wow. She's even sluttier than I remember.

> CARLY

Yeah. You think you know a person . . .

Or...

> DEE

Was that Jess? I mean, she's always been awkward, but not washing her hands after using a public restroom? Geez.

> CARLY

Can you believe we used to hang out with her?

Or...

> CARLY

Well, that was awkward. Oh hey, did you watch that YouTube link I sent you?

> DEE

Umm, yes! In what universe would I *not* watch a baby monkey video?

Or...

CARLY

You know, Jess might just be a genius.

DEE

Googling *An Ideal Husband* now!

    I stepped back toward the door, pressing my ear against the splintered wood.

    I caught one word: *Noah*.

    And then I fled.

MIGHTY-PEN-JESS
Aug 29

REASON #8:
I steal jewelry from elderly men.

To be accurate, one particular piece of jewelry from one particular elderly man.

It happened in ninth-grade English during Mr. Pasquinelli's Shakespeare unit, around the time I discovered my deep and abiding love for both Shakespeare and Mr. Pasquinelli. (Yes, I know he's so old and wrinkly he looks like he crawled out of a display case at the natural history museum, but I've always had a soft spot for a man who can read Lady Macbeth with that amount of conviction. And spittle expulsion.)

The ruby necklace he wore every time he read Lady Macbeth's part bridged the gap between my beloveds, the ancient words of a dead poet and the ancient English teacher invoking them. It symbolized the power of the text to transform an awkward, elderly man into a young, vicious murderess. Through words alone, Shakespeare had created a new reality.

I've always been obsessed with plays. It's something Chloe and I have in common. We can both list every Tony-winning musical by year. When it comes to my favorites, I can tell you the dates of the run, the dates of any revivals, the name of every actor in each production, and their birthdays. (I mean, so can the internet. That's probably why I have been told on four separate occasions by four different people that I *am* a computer, which on the scale of Things You Probably Shouldn't Say to an Autistic Person is at least a few degrees better than "You are a robot.")

But in Pasquinelli's Shakespeare unit, I learned that I didn't just love *watching* plays. I wanted to *write* them. I wanted to be William Shakespeare, Oscar Wilde, Margaret Edson. As we picked the play apart, my fingers never stopped drumming inside my desk, my tongue tracing my gumline, my mind burbling with the possibilities of creation. When Pasquinelli read Lady M's last line and pulled the necklace over his head, depositing it in his desk drawer, I felt a sudden surge of loss. Our Shakespeare unit had ended.

Only one thing would fill the void.

That Saturday, Chloe and I hung out at her mom's house. We were up in her room, under her loft bed, which, if you haven't seen it, is lined with purple beaded curtains to create a snug space not unlike my cave under the stairs.

"No," Chloe said. "Stealing is wrong." She gave her glasses three quick wipes on the front of her shirt before replacing them on the bridge of her nose, looking every bit the Mature and Responsible One. Like with most of my schemes, this would take some convincing.

"It probably cost him like a dollar at Goodwill," I tried.

"The price doesn't affect the morality."

"But wouldn't it be fun to do a heist? We've never done a heist! Ooh! And when we're done, we could sing 'Who Am I?' because we'd be thieves like Jean Valjean!"

The excitement had begun to tingle through me, and Chloe was feeling it, too. Her eyes widened and the muscles around her mouth gave a few little twitches. But then she shook her head. "We wouldn't be like Jean Valjean. He stole to feed his family during a political regime where the laws were morally unjust. One could argue that we are the opposite of Jean Valjean because 'Who Am I?' is about choosing to accept responsibility for one's crimes, even when the line of morality is blurred."

I clunked my head back against the wall, my fingers fluttering furiously against my knees. "Okay, then we could still do *Les Mis*, but be the Thénardiers instead. Or Fagin and the Artful Dodger from *Oliver!* Or Miss Hannigan and Rooster from *Annie*."

"To clarify, you are trying to support your argument that stealing would be morally acceptable by listing villains."

Sometimes people misinterpret Chloe when she speaks in that flat, straightforward way of hers. They assume she's deadpanning a sarcastic critique. They don't understand, like I do, that she is genuinely wondering whether they are making their clearly illogical arguments deliberately.

I backtracked. "Okay, what about antiheroes? Bialystock and Bloom from *The Producers*. No, Ida and Eunice from *70, Girls, 70!*"

She closed her eyes. The lamplight bounced through the curtain beads, sending lilac polka dots shimmering over her skin and hair. She looked like a goddess preparing to speak wisdom—or to sentence a mortal to eternal torture.

After a moment, she said, "I'd be Ida."

Joy fluttered through my fingertips. "Obviously." (If we were seventy-year-old women robbing ritzy department stores, she *would* be the calm mastermind. And I would definitely be the hot mess who accidentally leaves incriminating evidence behind.)

Chloe nodded. She opened her eyes wide. "Monday, then. We will do this heist."

On Monday, when I stepped into the too-crowded SBHS lobby, my brain sizzled with excitement—and some other emotion I couldn't quite identify. Maybe it was guilt. Or doubt (is doubt an emotion?) about whether this heist was a good idea. I'd had a whole weekend for the potential consequences of stealing jewelry from under a teacher's nose to occur to me. Unfortunately, those flimsy whispers about detention and expulsion and twelve-months-imprisonment-without-the-possibility-of-parole were immediately crushed by the stampede of autistic thought barreling through Heist Gorge. Trying to change the direction of my ideas is like trying to rope a mustang with dental floss.

"This is my heist," I whispered as I slid into the desk beside Chloe's in the back of Pasquinelli's class. My jiggling knees bumped against the metal legs of the desk, the heels of my orthopedic shoes stuttering against the floor. "If we get caught, pretend you didn't know anything about it."

"It's *our* heist, and the best option would be for us not to get caught," she said, not whispering, which prompted suspicious looks from a few classmates.

I barely paid attention to Pasquinelli's quavering lecture on Emily Dickinson. I was pulling every self-regulation strategy out of my old therapist's metaphorical toolbox—legs jiggling, fingers drumming, tongue sliding furiously over my incisors—but my body still sizzled with so much nervous energy that I felt motion-sick.

When the bell rang, the rest of the class bolted. Chloe took her time—way too much time, in my opinion—flipping through her notes and questions written in many colors of pen: the things she missed when her brain was preoccupied with processing other stuff, the figures of speech she didn't quite get. *Finally*, she took the notebook and approached Mr. Pasquinelli at the board.

From that time on, we were singing from the same song sheet.

JEWELRY HEIST: THE MUSICAL

AT RISE: PASQUINELLI is wrestling an interactive whiteboard back into the corner of the room. As CHLOE approaches him, JESS sidles toward the cluttered teacher desk in the opposite corner.

                    CHLOE
Mr. Pasquinelli. I have several questions about slant rhyme.

CHLOE and PASQUINELLI converse quietly.

Meanwhile . . .

With her back to the desk, JESS eases open the drawer. As her fingers close on pens, binder clips, and rubber bands—but no necklace—she begins to panic.

                    JESS
                (singing)
A stapler, a marker, a pen cap or ten.
Will I ever see Lady M's jewelry again?

                    CHLOE

The very definition of rhyme is that the word endings are identical.

                    PASQUINELLI
                (speaking in rhythm)
I know what you mean, but . . .

                      JESS
                    (singing)
Would it kill him to clean up?

                    PASQUINELLI
                (speaking in rhythm)
. . . think about it like this . . .

                      JESS
                    (singing)
I don't know what this is!

Face contorted, JESS pulls a shriveled apple core from the drawer, then drops it in horror.

                    PASQUINELLI
The ends of the words are identical if you only look at the final consonant.

                    CHLOE
"Doe" and "reply" don't end in consonants.

                    JESS
                  (singing)
I must be brave; I'll try once more,
With fingers in the fetid drawer.

Her grasping hand once again dips into the desk.

                    CHLOE
And they don't end in the same vowels or vowel sounds.

                    JESS
                  (singing)
My heart how it pounds,
My hands how they shake,
My palms dripping sweat,
My knees knocking—wait!

CHLOE and PASQUINELLI freeze in a tableau as JESS's face brightens in hopeful ecstasy.

                    JESS
                (singing)
    Is this . . . could it be?
    Rough and plasticky,
    Beads grouped in threes . . .

JESS raises her fist high, clutching a costume necklace.

                    JESS
            (singing, triumphant)
    Yes! The rubies!

The warning bell blared, and Chloe and I both flinched. I crammed the necklace into the pocket of my jeans and edged toward the back of the room.

"I have to go now," Chloe told Pasquinelli before marching to her desk.

As we stuffed notebooks and pencils into our backpacks, it suddenly felt less like a musical comedy and more like the moment in every mafia movie right before someone gets hit with a barrage of revenge bullets. The air conditioner seemed to have dropped at least ten degrees, and the necklace in my pocket bulged increasingly larger. I didn't even zip my bag all the way before scurrying from the room. First rule of heists: don't stick around at the scene of the crime.

The hallway teemed with students, any one of whom

might notice the jagged lump in my pocket. I tugged my T-shirt lower. At the corner where the Language Arts Hall meets the Science Hall, I glanced over my shoulder to be sure Chloe was following.

She wasn't.

She still stood outside Pasquinelli's room. I scuttled back toward her. My whole body shuddered with nervous energy, every locker slam and sneaker squeak on the tile was an ice pick in my ears. "What are you doing?"

"He left for the teachers' lounge," Chloe said. "So you can put it back now."

"What?" The shudders intensified.

"Pasquinelli isn't in the room now. It's safe."

I frowned so hard my whole brain scrunched up, like this would help me make sense of what she was saying. The hallway noise wasn't helping. "I already got the necklace," I said slowly.

"I know," she said, just as slowly. "And now you can put it back."

"But . . . why?"

Chloe's forehead formed its own brain-scrunching frown. "Because if you don't, it would be stealing."

"The *point* was to steal it," I whispered. The hallway was clearing out. The bell would ring soon. If Pasquinelli came back and we were lurking here, he'd be beyond suspicious. "We need to go."

"Stealing is wrong," Chloe said.

"We had this conversation on Saturday. You said you'd do the heist."

"We did the heist. Now you can put it back."

The ripples of nervous energy had become full-blown tidal waves pounding my synapses. "We did the heist because I wanted the necklace."

Students trickled into the classrooms around us, though Pasquinelli's was still empty. He must've had a planning period. Chloe wasn't budging, staring at me, unblinking. I felt dizzy and maybe like I might puke as the first streams of guilt churned into my ocean of anxiety.

"I really need it, Chloe," I whimpered.

When Pasquinelli returned from his planning period, the necklace was back among the overturned boxes of paper clips and half a dozen orphaned pen caps in his desk drawer.

And in case you're thinking, *But, Jess–then you didn't really steal it! You just borrowed it for five minutes. You're a good person after all!* please know that I absolutely would have kept it—wouldn't even have thought twice—if it weren't for Chloe.

I guess she's always had a way of getting in my head.

MIGHTY-PEN-JESS
Aug 31

REASON #9:
You are helping me pull up my math grade.

It's probably no surprise that a theatre nerd like me is not great at math, but my D on Friday's quiz was absolutely, 100 percent Cameron's fault.

It was his idea, me taking AP Calc. It was the only way we'd have a class together. I would have flat-out failed AP Physics, and Computer Science would have given me a permanent migraine. The best option would have been for Cam to take AP Lit with me, but as we have previously discussed, he *just can't* with the papers.

And so I'd agreed to Calculus.

"The end is nigh," I wailed.

Cam laughed. "You'll get it."

"No. No, I will not get it. I will fail it, and never get into college, and then my mother will cut out your intestines and boil them in her cabbage stew."

"You're disgusting. And your mother loves me."

"She wouldn't if she could see us now."

We were lounging next to each other in my cave under the stairs. We had draped a blanket over our legs since my mother insisted on keeping the apartment at approximately the same temperature as an industrial freezer. We were fully clothed, and we weren't even touching, but that wouldn't matter to my mother. She began lecturing me and Julia about the Dangers of Boys and Giving Them the Wrong Idea as soon as Julia sprouted breasts. Based on the fact that Julia had a different boyfriend every couple of months in high school, I'd say she didn't pay too much attention.

To be fair, based on the events of Memorial Day, I guess I didn't pay enough attention, either.

Cam tossed his protractor at the slats above us and caught it on its way down. "Your mom trusts me."

"She shouldn't."

His usually pale skin flushed an alarming shade of vermilion, and I immediately felt bad. It was a low blow, and not at all fair.

Since you already think I'm a slutbag, I might as well admit that Cam and I made out once last March, and it was at least as much my fault as his. Cam plays a different sport every time the weather changes, and he had come back from some kind of sportsball postgame celebration a little tipsy, and as I may have mentioned previously, he is hot.

And I was curious.

I'd never kissed anyone before, and I've only kissed one someone since, but from that limited experience, I'm not sure what the fuss is about. I have no complaints about the snuggling portion of the activity. There is something decidedly appealing about crushing yourself up against a huge rock of a guy (and have I mentioned his shoulders?), but the actual lip/tongue action is baffling. A bit slimy. Not really sure what the point is, to be honest.

"Sorry," I said. "Bad joke. You know I don't blame you for that, right?"

Cam's face was still the color of a Broadway curtain, but he put a hand to his chest in mock astonishment. "Did Jess Lanza just apologize for something? To lowly me? Where is my phone? I must record this date!"

I swung my Calc book at his head.

He rolled away. "If you kill me, I can't help you bring your grade up."

"You haven't been much help so far."

My phone dinged. It was your text, Hannah. (FYI, autocorrect changed "cheating" to "creating" and replaced a crucial "f" with a "d," but I got the message.)

"Who is it?" Cam asked, though the abrupt sobering of his voice told me he already knew.

"Do you want a soda?" I rose so quickly I bashed my head on the step above us. I literally saw stars, or at least neon explosions of color, and I was too disoriented to stop Cam from pulling the phone from my hand.

When I sank back onto the blanket, he was staring at the text.

"This isn't okay."

I massaged my battered skull. "They're just standing up for Chloe."

"No. You know you made a mistake—you admitted it—and they're still harassing you months later? If Chloe's friends with these people, why isn't she putting a stop to it?"

"Honestly, I doubt she even knows it's happening. You know how much she hates social media." I pulled my knees up to my chest, hoping the pressure might calm my churning stomach. "Anyway, she has a right to be angry. She's still getting over what I did."

"What you *and* her boyfriend did, and she seems to have forgiven him pretty quick. Are they sending *him* hate texts?"

"I doubt it. Does it matter?"

"I think it does. It takes two to cheat."

"Well, he's a guy."

"What does that mean?"

"Well, you know . . ." My face was on the verge of spontaneous combustion. "Guys get all . . . carried away and stuff."

"Do you think we can't control ourselves?" he asked, raking a hand through his tousled hair. "Is it because of what I—what happened with us in March, because I really regret my actions—"

"Oh my God stop."

"—and I value your friendship, and—"

"Our friendship is contingent on us never talking about that ever, ever, ever again."

"I'm just saying, why are they singling you out as a whore, or . . . those other things they called you, when whatever you did, he did it, too? All people get, um, horny, and—"

"Ew. Gah! Give me my phone back. I'd rather talk to the bullies."

He rolled his eyes, but he returned my phone. "Just tell me you know you're not a whore."

I dug my fingernails into the back of my phone case to stop my hands from shaking. "I know I'm not a whore. Happy?"

"Very." He dumped the Calc book back onto my lap. "Now. Derivatives."

We actually finished the problem set before my mom got home. That's the first time we've gotten through a whole homework assignment together. You see, normally, we just keep on getting distracted and goofing off. But this afternoon, we had to focus on the problem set or risk thinking about other unpleasant things.

So, thanks for the text, Hannah.

And as Cam and I agreed, you are mistaken; I am not a whore.

If I were, at least I'd have gotten paid.

MIGHTY-PEN-JESS
Sept 3

REASON #10:
I nerdified a sportsball-guy.

I've been writing this blog for a solid two and a half weeks now, and up to today, I was pretty sure no one at Stone Bridge was reading it.

I haven't mentioned my suspicions on the off chance that you were among my handful of readers; I didn't want you to think my hopes for hate-blog dominance had been thwarted. You will recall that my primary motivation was to write a blog that is better than yours, and I think we can all agree that I've succeeded overwhelmingly. And besides that, it's been surprisingly therapeutic. I may be failing at writing fiction (you know, the stuff I actually need to write for my Creative Writing class and college application), but it's nice to have some form of prose flowing from my fingertips, even if the only people who see it are internet randos who click a post by accident.

I found out my blog has a wider reach than I'd thought

this morning, in the 7-Eleven parking lot. I was halfway out of the minivan before I realized Cam was still buckled, frowning at his phone.

"What's up?"

"Since when do you have a blog?"

Gurgles of panic supplanted the Slurpee cravings in my stomach. "You found my blog?"

"Jeff Watkins found it, and he says I'm in it? Or at least . . . my *shoulders*? Jess, what—?"

"Don't read it!" I dove across the console for his phone, which was a doomed move because he is (a) seventy-five feet taller than me and (b) a sportsball-guy.

Phone held high, he continued scrolling. *"Easily the hottest guy in our grade—"*

"It was a joke!"

"—proximity to his shoulders is certainly a perk?" Cam groaned piteously. "Jessica, why?"

"I'm sorry!"

"And Jeff texted it to the whole team? I am never going to live this down."

"Please don't read any more."

"Don't worry. I won't. But . . ." He scrubbed a palm over his forehead like I'd given him a migraine. In fairness, maybe I had. "Are you sure about this? I mean, the cyberbullies . . ."

"Hey, I can't let them have all the fun. Anyway, my blog is better."

"But what if they retaliate?"

"By blogging about me more? That seems kind of impossible."

"What if they start doing more than blogging?"

My heart flash-froze for a second, because that definitely hadn't occurred to me. Then again, based on your inability to craft an engaging blog post, I assumed your creative powers were limited. "In that unlikely event, I will have to take you up on your offer to use your magnificent musculature to beat them up."

Cam's groan was positively funereal.

I think the most annoying thing about you decorating my locker before fourth period is that you may have proved Cam right. It was vengeance for my blog, wasn't it? Obviously one of the two people who clicked the last post was Jeff Watkins, but now I'm picturing you three crowded around Hannah's iPhone, squinting at the tiny text of my latest literary masterpiece. Out of curiosity, I popped onto *your* blog during my morning bathroom-lurking and noted that the hit counter hasn't changed much over there, either. Could it be that the chronicle of a boring love triangle among three nerds who no one really cared about in the first place is losing its luster?

I guess maybe that's why you're experimenting with a new medium for your hate text. Some advice for the next time you employ lipstick vigilantism: use a different color. Scarlet doesn't particularly complement the Puma Purple of my locker.

I was scrubbing at the "s" with the edge of my sleeve when Emily came over. Her September hair color is purple (not Puma Purple, more of an Elsa's-dress-in-*Frozen-II* purple), and everything she was wearing, from her torn sweater to her Chucks, was black. She didn't say anything, just pulled a pack of makeup removal wipes from her messenger bag and started in on the "l-u-t."

"Thanks," I said.

She ducked her head and flushed like she was embarrassed by her own niceness. "'Course."

When the offending word had been reduced to smears, she shoved the soiled wipe into her pocket. "Creative Writing?"

Somewhere there was a bathroom that needed a lurker, but Emily had been so nice about helping me with my locker, I said, "Sure."

We'd already reached the classroom when it occurred to me: "What were you even doing in the Senior Hallway?"

"Oh. Just . . . heard some dicks bragging about being dickish," she mumbled. "Thought you might need help."

She looked embarrassed again. I think that must be one of those allistic emotional responses that will never make sense to me. If *I* did something that nice, I would be beyond proud. I would probably put it on my college applications. *Achievements: Realized a Friend Needed Help with a Thing Before She Asked and Knew What Concrete Actions Could Support Her.*

I had plenty of time to reflect on my inadequacies during the first half of Creative Writing. It was Unreliable Narrator

Day, Mr. Barton's favorite unit, and his melodramatic reading of "The Tell-Tale Heart" took all the way until the lunch bell. While everyone else filed out, Mr. Barton held me back.

"Would you be willing to lead a small group for our discussion after lunch?" he asked, unwrapping one of his tasteless granola rocks.

"Um . . . okay?"

"Great!" He lowered his voice a little. "I'm putting Drew and Emily in your group because I'm hoping you can bring them out of their shells."

"Oh." I fiddled with the hem of my T-shirt. "Are you sure I'm your best option?"

"Jess, your classmates elected you senior editor of our lit mag team for a reason. You're a born leader! You'll do great."

"If you say so." I have often wondered why last year's seniors elected me as the new head of the lit mag, but I'm pretty sure if I asked them, their answer would not have included the words "born leader."

"How is that Goldberg portfolio coming?" Mr. Barton asked, beaming. I tried not to stare at the oat flake wedged between two of his top teeth.

"Umm, okay. I . . . actually . . . For your class, could I just revise my unreliable narrator story from last year instead of writing a new one? You know, so I can focus on the portfolio instead." My words scrambled over one another in their eagerness to escape my awkward mouth. "It's just that the realistic fiction assignment took me a really long time, and

I'm not as far as I'd like to be on the portfolio, and I just don't think I can—"

"Whoa! Slow down!" Mr. Barton put his hands up like he was trying to calm a spooked horse. "Yes, I think it would be fine to give this assignment a miss. I understand what you mean about the realistic fiction project taking time. It's certainly taking me long enough to grade them all."

"Thanks." I hurried down to the cafeteria, pondering whether telling Mr. Barton that my portfolio was going "okay" was more of a misdemeanor-level lie or a full-on triple homicide. Maybe I'm something of an unreliable narrator myself.

I managed to skirt around your table without much trouble. You were pretty busy, after all, what with Hannah berating Brooklyn for buying that purple dress ("when you, like, *know* how aubergine complements *my* complexion"), and Brooklyn chewing worriedly on the end of her ice-blond braid, and Alexis totally zoned out because she hears some variation on that exact conversation at least twice a day.

"Jessica! Jessica, like from *The Merchant of Venice*!" Jeff Watkins called from a table with his sportsball friends (not Cam, unfortunately). "You've inspired me. I never realized poetry could be so . . . exciting!" He waggled his eyebrows at me, then stood on a chair and began an enthusiastic recitation of "I heard a Fly buzz—when I died—." The surrounding tables quieted somewhat, the popular kids' expressions ranging from baffled to bemused, and Vice Principal Yarmouth hovered nearby, clearly uneasy about the chair-standing but unwilling to discourage the American Romantic poetry.

After he finished, Jeff touched a hand to his Afro in a respectful salute toward me (cue additional baffle-/bemusement) and sat back down. Whisper-giggles assaulted my ears. I chanced a glance over at you three, who were neither baffled nor bemused. If I had to choose, I'd say either disgusted or nauseated with envy.

I got my pizza and started for my usual corner table, but when I passed the Creative Writing underclassmen, I slowed. Emily jerked her chin toward the empty seat across from her.

Cautiously, I approached. "Should I— Is it okay if I sit here?"

Drew's voice floated up from somewhere in the recesses of his hoodie. "You're like our boss, so you can sit wherever you want."

"I'm not your boss."

"No." Emily's lips quirked. "You apparently inspire jocks to memorize nineteenth-century poetry. So, really, you're more like a god."

MIGHTY-PEN-JESS
Sept 8

REASON #11:
It's my fault you have to eat your cafeteria pizza lukewarm.

Longtime observers of the Stone Bridge High School cafeteria will recall that the low counter along the back wall once held three microwaves available for student use. They are no longer there, and it's probably because of that one afternoon sophomore year when Chloe and I wanted to see what would happen if we cooked a fork for ten minutes on high.

(Spoiler alert: it involved flames.)

Today, I sat at that now-empty counter, wishing that Emily had my lunch on A-days. I'd turned my chair sideways so that I could see the table where you three sat with Chloe. She had her AP Physics book open and her earbuds in. She didn't say a word to you, but that was fine, since you were focusing on Brooklyn's attempts to toss bits of spit-soaked cafeteria napkin into my hair. Every time you hit me, Brooklyn, you'd peek over your shoulder at Hannah like you were waiting for a thumbs-up or a doggy treat. *Who's a good* bully? *You are, yes you are!* The best you ever got from your cronies was a superior smirk from Hannah and a sigh that screamed *I am so bored right now* from Alexis.

What does Chloe see in you?

I get that you're all in choir together, so you must have some things to talk about. And maybe the things you don't have in common complement each other. You know, Chloe's good to your evil.

Chloe and I used to be like that—not good vs. evil but a balanced team, Chloe's mathy genius and my creativity. It's why we won the sophomore-year STEM fair.

Admittedly, Chloe did most of the work for the Great Egg-Drop Experiment. She engineered the egg costumes (out of various combinations of Bubble Wrap, cardboard, duct tape, and crumpled balls of aluminum foil). She placed the ten-foot ladder on an even surface on her mother's driveway. She instructed me in how to release the eggs without accidentally applying a force other than gravity so that we could be sure that each repeated trial was identical.

But she was also the one who almost gave up after the first round.

Chloe pushed her chemistry goggles onto her forehead and stared at the final egg, whole and unfractured in its Bubble-Wrap-and-corrugated-cardboard cocoon. "They all work."

"Great!" My orthopedic shoes clanged against the ladder rungs as I descended.

"No. If they all performed equally, I can't determine the weakest design."

"But if they're all equal, then there *isn't* a weakest."

"They're not all equal." Her voice was loud, emphatic. "We aren't high enough to see the flaws."

"So we get higher."

"Can't. Tallest ladder we have." She shook her head, whispering, "Can't, can't, can't . . ."

Sometimes Chloe and I melt down at the same time—something causes huge emotions in both of us and neither of us can deal. Like the time we went to opening night for *Dreamgirls* at the community center and we were supposed to be thirty minutes early to get our favorite seats and use the bathroom, but the local theatre blog had listed the time wrong so we were actually thirty minutes *late*, and I couldn't stop crying, and Chloe was screaming at the alarmed box-office girl because *why hadn't they waited if they knew there was a mistake!*, and Dr. Barton had to take us back to the SUV until we calmed down.

Twin tornadoes. That's what Chloe's mom used to call those meltdowns. One storm, two frenzies of whirling emotions.

But I do not have any frenzied or whirling emotions about eggs and Bubble Wrap. So while Chloe was melting down, I was looking around for another solution. Chloe had already shot down my offer to climb the oak tree with the tire swing because it didn't overlap the driveway and "the uneven cushioning of the grass could skew the results of the experiment." But the only structure taller than the ten-foot ladder was that tree.

And, of course, the house.

I scooped up the Bubble Wrap–cardboard egg and left Chloe pacing around her stack of egg cartons. In Chloe's front hall (which Dr. Barton calls "the foy-*ay*" because she's fancy), I took off my shoes, per house rules, and also my socks, because I thought bare skin might have a bit more traction.

I knew I wasn't athletic enough to get onto the top roof, but the room above the garage (aka Dr. Barton's home office) was lower and had dormers. Dr. Barton was humming in the kitchen and cooking some amazing-smelling something or other (definitely vegetarian but also definitely not cabbage-based). I slid my feet along the fabulously textured carpeting up the stairs, and only hesitated for a second before entering the office. It was worth the trespass. This was For Science.

Chloe didn't hear the *shush* of the window opening or my mutters as I debated whether to exit the window head- or butt-first. I decided falling to my death backward would be more terrifying than seeing the ground rushing toward me, and with the edge of the egg's cardboard cocoon clutched in my teeth, I wriggled through the open window.

I maneuvered onto the roof, and then, still clutching the

window casement in one hand, I removed the egg cocoon from my mouth. "Chloe!"

It took her a ridiculous amount of time to find me above her. Her forehead crumpled. "You're on the roof."

"Yes."

"Why?"

"It's taller than the ladder." I started to wave the egg at her before realizing it wasn't a good idea to tempt gravity by shifting my balance.

"You're on the roof." She cocked her head to the side, waiting for her thoughts on this subject to settle. Then, "Wait." She ran inside.

Soon, she burst into the room behind me. "Do you have a free hand?" she asked. Her eyes were wide, lips pressed tight. She was loving this as much as I was.

I took the end of the tape measure she pressed into my palm.

"Hold tight," she instructed. I gripped the little silver nub in my fist as Chloe tossed the heavy end of the tape measure out the window and let gravity stretch it to the ground. Once she'd thundered back down the stairs and read the measurement at driveway level, I let go of my end of the tape measure and held out the egg.

I knew, from one of Chloe's many lectures on the topic, that the egg had inertia. In science, inertia can do two things: it can keep you moving or it can keep you still. Whatever you're doing, you'll keep doing it—until some force makes a change.

So, there in my hand was this egg, full of inertia, full of sitting still. Until I tilted my hand to the side, and then a force took over. Gravity tugged the egg down, down, until it smashed against the asphalt.

Chloe lifted her goggles and peeled back the egg's protective cage. "Fracture. Needs more cushion." She scribbled something in our notebook and marched back to the supply tub, the force of this new information propelling her in a new direction—full of inertia.

We are always full of inertia.

Inertia is what keeps Chloe from thinking of climbing on the roof while her brain is gliding down the need-taller-ladder track.

Inertia is what makes Brooklyn's silky Barbie-hair trail behind her while her pink-polo-clad body moves toward me.

Inertia is what keeps me sitting in my chair, waiting for another spitball to be flicked at my head, waiting for Chloe to look at me.

And when she does look up, sees Brooklyn toss the slimy wad, sees it strike my forehead and ooze down my cheek, sees, then turns away . . . inertia is what keeps me sitting there still.

MIGHTY-PEN-JESS
Sept 13

REASON #12:
I am a tattletale.

Julia has been home this week to take the LSAT. She'll go back to college tomorrow—unless she murders me first. I'm pretty sure UVA would consider murder a breach of the honor code.

It's not like I set out to get her in trouble. I wouldn't have told Mom about the party except she was interrogating me about my life again. She pretended like it was a friendly conversation, like I was her old BFF and we were catching up over dinner, but the more questions she asked, the more invasive it felt. Why was I spending so much time on the NYU application? And isn't VCU a more realistic goal? And what about UVA—after all, Julia will almost definitely get into the law school and then we'd be *together* (!)—and isn't that one of the schools Chloe is applying to, and she hasn't seen much of Chloe lately, and why is that, and what has she been up to, and how is that nice boy she was seeing, and what was his name again, and—

I had to change the subject fast, and only one thing came to mind.

I'm in my room as I type this, my weighted blanket pulled up to my chin with just my hands poking out to type on my laptop, in a position so unergonomic that it would probably give the Computer Lab staff aneurysms. Mom's downstairs on the couch waiting for Julia.

She's been doing a pretty good job of holding in her rage. When Dad still lived with us and Julia was in high school, Mom was super high-strung all the time. Back then, when I told on Julia about something involving boys or drinking, Mom flipped out at *me* for knowing about it and not telling her sooner, at *Julia* for doing it, and then at *Dad* for whatever after he got home. (I was usually in bed by that point, and I'd put my earbuds in so I didn't have to hear it.) But since Julia's been at college and Dad's been gone, Mom's been a little less explosive. Mostly she's just tired. She's always saying, *Jessie, I really just don't have the energy for this right now,* usually accompanied by sighing.

So maybe she just didn't have the energy to freak out about Julia when I told her about the frat party. She just said, "Okay. I'll pray for her to get home safely." But with Mom's track record, I'll bet her righteous rage is simmering just beneath the surface. I know how the confrontation will go down.

SETTING: "Town house" living room.

AT RISE: ANDREA sits on a rickety kitchen chair, facing the door, a chipped mug in one hand, a devotional in the other. A single lamp lights her stony face. The front door opens slowly. JULIA hangs her keys on the hook and starts for the stairs before she notices ANDREA. She stops short.

                      JULIA
I thought you were working tonight.

She tugs the hem of her dress, trying to lengthen it, but only succeeds in pulling it lower, exposing even more cleavage.

                     ANDREA
Obviously. Where were you?

                      JULIA
I . . . went to the library with—

                     ANDREA
That is a lie.

                    JULIA
          . . .

                    ANDREA
I work day and night to send you to college, yet in my absence you engage in sin—

                    JULIA
You just assume—

                    ANDREA
I know you were cavorting with loose men and heathens and demon-spawn. Jessica told me about the party.

                    JULIA
               (growls)
     Jessica!

Flames shoot from JULIA's eyes as she pounds up the stairs. The grinding of her teeth crescendos to a roar as she beats down the door to JESS's room and—

I may have taken some liberties at the end there. But I'm pretty sure there will be some broken nails for Julia and a few bruises and scratches for me.

It's only ten, but she's home. The conversation was softer than I expected, and I couldn't make it out. The stairs creaked as Julia came up. I held my breath, waiting for the angry knock, but all I heard was the soft click of her door at the other end of the hall.

MIGHTY-PEN-JESS
Sept 17

REASON #13:
I am in Drama Club with Noah.

This is not, strictly speaking, my fault. I volunteered to be treasurer for the Thespian Honor Society long before any of this happened, and THS officers are required to attend all Drama Club meetings. I had dropped Advanced Drama as a class since I really couldn't imagine facing him every other day, but I thought I'd be able to handle a once-a-month club.

If the last few months have proven anything, it's that the universe gets its kicks by undermining my expectations.

After a whole summer without speaking to him, maybe it was inevitable that he was the first person I encountered when I got to the Drama Room. I stopped dead in the doorway, and the kid behind me stepped on my heel.

He was sitting on the edge of the low stage, chatting with Carly and Dee, and when he saw me, he stopped talking and nodded somberly. Everyone else stopped talking, too. Carly started to lift her hand in a wave before a glance at Noah made her lower it again, her deep-brown forehead taking on a sheen below her headwrap. Dee's gaze darted from me to Noah, their fidget spinner's whir more restless than usual.

It took me longer than it should have to retreat to the hallway. A burning cold settled over my chest and the world's sounds blurred like I had my head in a fish tank. I leaned against a locker and sucked in air like I had just surfaced from a three-mile swim under an ice floe.

What was *wrong* with me? I assume that most of the human population can make out with someone or . . . whatever . . . without turning into a quivering blob of dysfunctional angst.

The late bell rang. I hated my options, too cowardly to wander the halls and risk a detention, too cowardly to reenter the room and face . . . everything. It wasn't until Vice Principal Yarmouth's wing tips squeaked around the corner that I made up my mind.

Noah was standing on the stage. The Drama Club meeting hadn't started. Nothing new there (we always run late), but the way everyone seemed to be glancing, or pointedly not-glancing, at me made me wonder if I was the one they were waiting on. Or maybe not me but the drama my presence portended.

He beckoned. From his perch, he was two feet taller than me, and I would've had to tilt my head back to even pretend to look at his face. I focused on his left elbow instead.

"Hey," he said. "I hope you don't think I had anything to

do with that blog. I didn't mean to start trouble for you. I'm just not okay with keeping secrets, and—"

"I know," I said. "It's fine." I ducked my head, brushing past rows of gaping-not-gaping theatre kids to take a seat in the far back corner.

I'd never sat in the back before. It gave me a whole new perspective on the Theatre Department, and you will be pleased to learn that although no one in the rest of the school cares about me and Noah (or your blog) anymore, the theatre kids seem to. They glanced at me on and off through Devi Sharma's monologue about dues and service hours. They never made eye contact, but they looked uncomfortable about it, like they thought they were supposed to be mad at me but weren't sure whether I deserved it. Or more likely, they wanted to ask me for all the juicy details but were afraid of being judged.

Emily was the only person unequivocally on my team. As soon as I sat, she abandoned her former seat and took the chair next to me, her purple head held high. Somehow that just made me feel worse. As a sophomore, Emily has to survive at Stone Bridge a lot longer than I do.

I made it through most of the meeting. When Noah stood up as VP to talk about earning THS points, though, I was done. I slipped out the side door through Ms. Otashi's office.

You want to believe that I'm avoiding Noah because I can't control myself. Because if I'm in a room with him—even a room with forty other drama nerds—I won't be able to stop myself from jumping him. That is not, and never has been, the case.

It's not that I don't like boys. I'd be lying if I didn't admit that seeing Jake Perkins strip his shirt off for the *R&J* sword fight caused some brief yet alarming sensations in the vicinity of my uterus. And that's in addition to the less-alarming fluttery feelings in my lungs every time he talked to me. I never told him I had a crush on him. I wouldn't even be admitting it now if he hadn't moved away last Christmas, because that would raise the possibility of it becoming something terrifyingly real instead of pleasantly imagined.

But since he is safely tucked away in Wyoming, I will tell you that I imagined a future with Jake Perkins. I pictured our children. I named them (Marlowe, Beckett, and Lin). I carved "Jessica Lanza-Perkins" and "Jess + Jake" into the baseboard in the corner of my closet behind the Rubbermaid tub of my Barbies.

But Noah Cunningham? What would our children be like? I can honestly say, it has never occurred to me.

MIGHTY-PEN-JESS
Sept 19

REASON #14:
I am weird and pretentious.

Noah pointed this out to me.

Is it hard to believe Noah and I were friends? It's hard for me to believe now, when just the sight of him sends me staggering into the hallway, but last year it didn't seem like a stretch. He was a theatre kid, I was a theatre kid. Of course we were friends.

Is it like that in choir? Or field hockey? Even if it is, it's not the same. You had to audition for Concert Choir and the field hockey team. You don't have to audition to be a theatre kid. I mean, you audition if you want an acting role, but to get involved in the show, all you have to do is show up and care. Whether you're the star of the show or a techie in the lighting booth, you're treated with the same respect.

The same goes for whatever social caste you come from. Yeah, Noah is hot and charismatic and popularish, and I'm doughy and awkward and invisible to the majority of the student body. Doesn't matter. We were both there because we chose to be. We were both working our butts off. And when the house lights went down, the show depended on us both.

The day Noah decided to psychoanalyze me, I was helping him run lines for *Into the Woods*. In case you didn't see it last spring, Noah was a pretty kick-ass Cinderella's Prince.

(I was the cow.)

"'I have on occasion wanted more,'" I said. "'But that doesn't mean I went in search of it. If this is how you behave as a *prince*, what kind of *king* will you be?'"

"'I was raised to be charming, not sincere.'"

We were the only ones on the little Drama Room stage—the only ones in the whole Drama Room, actually. Most of the actors were in the auditorium rehearsing "Last Midnight." Noah was lying on his back with his legs straight up in the air. I was sitting in a chair like a normal human.

"You really are perfect for this part," I said.

"Thanks. And you're a perfect cow."

I threw the script at his head. Missed.

"You should take some voice lessons over the summer. Then maybe you could have an actual role in *Grease* next year."

"There are no small parts," I intoned. "Only small actors."

Some choir girls (was it any of you?) skipped past the open Drama Room door singing *Phantom of the Opera*. Their voices reverberated off the tiles, like emaciated ghosts begging the empty hallways to turn their heads with talk of summertime.

I grimaced. "Andrew Lloyd Webber should be guillotined for that monstrosity."

"Longest Broadway run ever. Best Musical 1988."

"It is uninspired, melodramatic drivel disguised by high production value. *Into the Woods* won Best Score *and* Best Book. It deserved Best Musical. *Phantom* is overrated."

Noah let his heels clunk to the ground and rolled over. He propped himself up on his elbows and considered me. "I think you are the most pretentious person I've ever met."

I flushed, my leg beginning to jiggle. "Do you think I'm wrong? Name one song in *Phantom* that even comes close to Sondheim's—"

"I agree with you about Andrew Lloyd Webber. But you're so offended by his Tony wins that you want to condemn him to death. It's funny."

The heat in my cheeks fanned out to my ears. "Obviously I don't actually want him to die."

"You do, though." He laughed. "You actually hate him just because his music doesn't live up to your standards. And where do those standards even come from? It's not like *you* write musicals. You don't even sing."

"So I'm not allowed to have an opinion because I'm not talented enough?" Some emotion I couldn't name scrabbled from my gut to my throat. I stood, and my chair skidded back across the battered wooden stage.

"Chill out," Noah groaned, still half laughing. "There's already too much drama in this Drama Department!"

I loomed over him, not sure whether I should laugh it off or storm out.

He tugged on the leg of my jeans. "Sit down, dumbass. You know I didn't mean it like that."

I sat. "I didn't sleep well last night."

"Apology accepted."

I retrieved the script. "What scene do you want to work on?"

"Why don't you take voice lessons?"

"No sense in trying to make myself slightly less sucky at something I'll never actually be good at," I explained. He stared at me until I was tempted to poke him in the eyes. "Knock it off. What?"

"You are just a very strange person, Jessica Lanza. You would think that someone as snoberific as you would have a bit more self-esteem." He rolled over and stuck his legs back up in the air. "Page one seventy again. And can we at least agree that as eighties musicals go, *Phantom* is better than *Cats*?"

"Yes. But worse than *Into the Woods*. And *Sunday in the Park with George*. And *Dreamgirls*. And *Les Mis*—"

"Everything is worse than *Les Mis*," he said.

And even a snoberific dumbass like me couldn't argue with that.

MIGHTY-PEN-JESS
Sept 21

REASON #15:
I'm the one who ruined red M&M's.

Sunday is study day—the only day of the week Cam doesn't have sportsball. Of course, when you don't get to hang out with someone for the whole week, a good deal of "study time" gets spent chatting and seeing who can catch the most M&M's in their mouth after ricocheting them off the wall of the homework cave.

"Fifty-two," Cam announced, crunching down on his latest success.

"I quit." I dumped a dozen straight from the bag into my mouth. "It's easier this way."

"Why doesn't Chloe eat the red ones?" he asked.

I flinched a little at her name. "It's because she's weird and pretentious."

Cam laughed. "That, coming from you . . ."

"Oh, ha ha."

The true answer is that one time at a sleepover in seventh

grade, I made her watch *Carrie*, and we were eating M&M's at the time. Now, whenever we share a bag of M&M's, Chloe picks out all the red ones and gives them to me because they "remind her of the blood." Does she do that when she hangs out with you three? I've wondered if it's just something she does with me, a subtle reminder that she hasn't quite forgiven me for bulldozing her into watching a gory movie. (To be entirely fair, she bulldozed me into watching *Pitch Perfect*, but I guess that's not really the same. Also I'd be lying if I said I didn't enjoy it.)

My phone pinged.

"Is that the bullies?" Cam asked, snapping to attention.

"No, it's your friend Jeff." I waved the phone in his face. "Who apparently has been reading back through my archives and is very into costume jewelry now."

Cam glanced at the ridiculous photo of Jeff at the dollar store and rolled his eyes. "Well, if it's from your blog, it's clearly your fault."

A little puff of pride ballooned in my lungs. "Yup."

"I guess you're still blogging," Cam said around a mouthful of chocolate that wasn't quite enough to disguise an ominous hint of annoyance.

"You promised you wouldn't read it."

"I haven't been, even though it seems to be mostly about me."

"It isn't."

"You didn't tell the internet that I'm a slimy kisser?"

Whoops. "That is taken way out of context."

"Or that I chortle? What the hell is a chortle?"

"A wonderfully descriptive word to describe laughter."

Cam huffed. "I do not chortle."

"You do on my blog."

"So you just make up everything I say and do?" His voice had an edge I wasn't used to.

I shook a tingling anxiety out my fingertips. "I'm probably like eighty percent accurate. It's like when we watch a movie, and I can recite the whole screenplay back after."

"Hmm. Okay, fine, but in the twenty percent you totally bullshit, please make me less slimy and chortly. And whiny. Jeff says you make me sound really whiny," he whined.

"Stop questioning my artistic choices." I snatched the M&M's bag back with still-trembling fingers. "Why is Jeff Watkins even reading my blog?"

"He's a social media junkie. Your blog is his new thing. He's completely obsessed."

He was. I had three classes with him, and he kept daring me to steal things from the teacher's desk. I won't lie: it was tempting. "I think he wants to get me arrested."

Cam *hmph*ed, a not-quite-laugh. I flicked an M&M across the carpet, my anxiety buzzing. "Are you upset? About the slimy kiss thing?"

"No, I'm not upset," he said upsetly. "Knowing you, whatever you wrote, it was hilarious. Who am I to stand in the way of art?"

"Cam."

He sighed. "I'll get over it. It's not actually a big deal. Just..." He shook his head like a wet dog and gave me a tight smile. "Anyway, I'm surprised you're still posting. Jeff says he's like the only one reading it."

"There are two readers." I regretted it as soon as the words left my mouth.

His voice oozed pity. "You don't think the other one's Chloe, do you?"

"No," I lied. He gave me a look that screamed *bullshit*, so I added, "I hoped maybe she'd find it."

"Don't shoot the hot-shouldered messenger or anything—"

I lobbed an M&M at his nose.

"—but Jeff has mentioned it at least five times during AP Physics and she was sitting right there. If she wanted to read it, she would have. So if she hasn't reached out to you by now—"

"Don't say she's not going to."

"I was going to say you're better off without her."

"Well, that's worse. So don't say that, either."

Cam went quiet. The cliché cricket that lived under the TV stand chirped once, twice.

"I think you are better off without her."

"Cam. Don't."

"Because she's hanging out with those bullies, and still dating that asshole—"

"It wasn't his fault."

"It was at least half his fault, Jess. Why are you still defending him?"

"Why are you still refusing to acknowledge my terribleness?"

He rolled his whole head as though rolling his eyes wouldn't be dramatic enough. "I'm just saying, she's got some shit to figure out, so give her some space and move on with your life."

"And what would this hypothetical 'life' that I'm moving on toward involve?"

He threw his hands up. "I don't know. Get back into theatre. Hang out with that freshman, Emma. Come to my game on Friday and we'll go to IHOP after."

"Noah's in theatre. The *sophomore's* name is Emily. And I hate sportsball."

"It's football. And I don't really care what you do—I just think you should stop sitting here in the dark feeling sorry for yourself."

"Wow." I scooched into the far corner of the cave, pressing my back against the wall so hard it hurt.

"I'm sorry. I didn't mean that to sound so harsh."

"It's cool," I lied, staring at my knees. "I get what you're saying. I mean, you're wrong, but . . ." My attempt at a joke sank in the silence. I pushed my hands underneath me, hoping that if I stopped my fingers from quivering, my intestines would stop quivering, too.

Finally, Cam said, "I'm going to kill that damn cricket. Do you have a fly swatter?"

"Hall closet."

When he left, I could breathe again, no longer afraid of being judged, of being pressured to do something by someone I care about and don't want to disappoint.

And for the first time, I wondered if that's how Chloe feels now, without me.

MIGHTY-PEN-JESS
Sept 25

REASON #16:
I am a stalker.

I was thirty seconds late to Creative Writing today because I lost track of time crouching by my locker and sorting through the five pounds of M&M's I bought at 7-Eleven this morning. It took forever, and by the end of it, my hands were smeared in multicolored food dye, but it was necessary. To have any hope of Chloe accepting my offering, it would have to be perfect.

Class dragged, despite the laugh-out-loud comedy of Emily trying to constructively critique the heap of refuse I submitted for workshopping without using the words "bad," "terrible," or "dumpster-fire-of-incomprehensible-plot-development-and-unreadable-prose." Mr. Barton kept glancing over at our table incredulously. I don't know what I'd have said if he asked why my fiction suddenly sounded like something that came out of a Hallmark Channel writers' room.

                    JESS
Well, you see, Chloe isn't speaking to
me, which sucks, and her new friends are
kind of bullying me, which also sucks, and
she seems to be aware of it, but she's
not really doing anything about it, which
really, really sucks? So, could *you* maybe
do something about all that? You know, so
I can focus on fixing this dumpster fire of
a story? And that journal entry you've
been harassing me for? And maybe my Tisch
portfolio?

                 MR. BARTON
Oh dear! But . . . that doesn't sound
like my Chloe at all. Whatever could have
happened to prompt such un-Chloe-like
behavior? It must have been something
apocalyptically bad. And you're sure you
have no idea what it was?

                    JESS
Well . . . umm . . . you see . . .

                   HANNAH
                  (offstage)
Oh. My. God. Did that tattletale slutbag

  really just go running to Chloe's daddy to
  get her in trouble? After everything she's
  already done? What a psychobitch.

      CAMERON
      (offstage)
Hey, umm, maybe don't use the word "bitch"
because it's, umm, sexist and stuff? And
"psycho" is also kind of ableist, umm,
right? And I was thinking it would be cool
if we could be nice to each other. Like,
Chloe could forgive Jess for the, umm,
everything, and you all could be less,
uh . . .

      HANNAH
(extending her claws with a menacing *shing*)
She-demons . . .

  When the bell finally rang, I bolted out of the room and down the stairs. The extra five pounds in my backpack dug the straps into my shoulders. I focused on the subtle rattle of the M&M's in their giant ziplock bag as I followed the swarm of chatting students onto the breezeway.

  I had only braved the breezeway once before—during school hours, that is. At night, during rehearsal breaks, we theatre nerds routinely commandeer the open space. We sit on the raised brick planters, lean against the scrawny trees, and peer up through the screen to the starry sky. It's quiet, and it's empty, and it's ours at night.

During the day, it belongs to you normals, and except for one misguided attempt freshman year to take a shortcut through the throng, I had not set foot in it.

It was loud today. I wouldn't have thought it would be that loud since it was open to the sky and your voices could sail up through the screen and evaporate into the clouds. That's what I imagined would happen, anyway. Chloe could probably tell me why it didn't. Maybe the sounds bounced back and forth between the surrounding brick walls of the school. Or maybe there were too many of you. Or maybe the anxiety in my head had dialed up the control on my internal soundboard a few dozen decibels.

She was in the Senior Circle, sitting on the second step of the mini-amphitheater, unconcerned that the concrete might rough up her favorite purple suede dress. You three surrounded her, equally unconcerned about the effect of concrete on dresses—Brooklyn and Hannah behind her on the step above, singing something (or at least moving your mouths in unison), and Alexis next to her, listening to her talk. I knew I shouldn't eavesdrop, but I couldn't help myself. That's why I came so close, until I could hear her over the wall of sound.

". . . maybe regret it forever if I don't try," she said. "And if I go there, I'd be closing myself off to the option."

"Yeah, and I mean, college is about trying things, right?"

"I think it's more about going deep into debt and hoping you find a job that will eventually help you alleviate that debt. *Thank you, corporate America.*" She sang the last bit on a jazz riff that she probably invented on the spot. She does that—lightens something heavy through music. I just didn't realize she did it with you.

I must have made a sound of disbelief or despair because you looked up, Alexis. Sharply.

"Just a sec," you said to Chloe. She hadn't seen me, still mired in frustrations at the predatory business model of modern academia, no doubt. I think maybe you were trying to obstruct her view of me when you approached, arms folded across your corduroy jacket—goldenrod, the color of warning. Slow down, prepare to come to a complete stop. "What do you want, Jess?"

"I have something for Chloe."

The deep lines in your forehead softened somewhat, a slow breath easing the tension in your mouth. "She's gotten your notes, Jess. You can't make her read them."

"It's not a note." I dropped my backpack to the patio, scrounging inside for the bag of M&M's. "It's a gift."

As I pulled it out, I realized I'd done it wrong. It looked paltry next to all of you, in your dresses and stylish jackets, Puma Purple ribbons tied to your top backpack straps, glitter on your eyelids. It looked grimy and thrown together. Suddenly, the fact that I'd spent the whole morning picking out the red M&M's didn't even feel worth mentioning.

I think you knew, though, Alexis. You knew this was more than a gift. It was an apology—not just for what happened on Memorial Day but for *Carrie*, and for all the mistakes I've made in our friendship since that Cake-Dropping Incident in seventh grade.

You stared at the bag for a long minute, your teeth worrying one corner of your Puma Purple lower lip, before you took it from my hand. "I'm real confused, Jess. I'll admit I don't totally understand what happened with Noah or why you did it. And I know you say you're sorry, but . . . Look, I'll give her these, but if she wanted to talk to you, she'd have done it already. Stalking her isn't going to change her mind."

"I just want her to remember," I said, though I can't imagine how you heard my tiny voice over the hundreds of voices around us and the screech of despair that couldn't possibly have been confined to my head.

Your voice was so soft I almost couldn't hear it, either. "I think the real problem is the stuff she can't forget."

And suddenly, *I* was remembering: the prickly carpet fibers on the back of my arms, the lawn-mower drone outside Noah's window, his voice—*Why . . . ?*

And by the time the memory released me, the bell had rung. You were gone—all of you—and I was alone.

MIGHTY-PEN-JESS
Sept 26

REASON #17:
It's possible my relationship-suckage is contagious.

I wish I could forget Memorial Day.

No, that's not quite right. I wish Memorial Day had never happened—that I could go back in time with a giant pair of time-scissors and snip that one day out of reality.

You probably don't believe me. You probably think that I maliciously plotted in my under-stairs lair, crafting an insidious plan to seduce my perfect best friend's equally perfect boyfriend. I know nothing I can say will convince you otherwise.

But the truth is otherwise.

The truth is: I don't know how it happened. One minute we were working on our project, and the next . . .

Well, like I said. It doesn't matter. Whether I planned it or not, it happened. I could have stopped it from happening, but I didn't. Not soon enough, anyway.

Maybe that's why this whole thing has me so confused

that it makes my skin itch. Because not only did I not plan it, I'm not sure why I participated in it. Definitely not to steal Noah away from Chloe. I'm not particularly interested in dating. My parents cured me of that.

And no, surprisingly, it wasn't my mom's many lectures about the Consequences of Teen Pregnancy and Genital Warts. (If anything, those lectures made me wish I were *more* interested in sex, just to freak her out.) Instead, it's the worry that if I ever do have a relationship, it'll turn out like her and Dad's.

The day he left, my dad took me out for froyo. He explained at length about the new woman he'd met and (at greater length) all the ways my mom had driven him away—how she was never there for him, always working or volunteering at her church, never supporting him. I only got a few bites of frozen yogurt past the lump in my throat.

Afterward, my dad dropped me back at the apartment. As he peeled out of the parking lot, I wondered what I'd say to my mom. Should I try to console her? On the surface, it looked like Dad was the one doing the leaving, but the longer I stood outside the apartment door, key poised at the lock, the tighter the boa constrictor of truth clenched around my stomach and lungs. Dad was right. Mom had this whole life that didn't include him. If she wasn't at work, she was at the thrift store or a Bible study or the church soup kitchen or teaching someone else's kids religious education. Mom had always dragged me and Julia to church with her. I didn't really believe in it, but I had liked the ritual of it. For the first time, I wondered whether she actually believed it herself, or if it was just a way of avoiding Dad.

I pictured her standing in the kitchen, stirring a pot of something cheap and pungent. I imagined facing her in the narrow doorway and asking the questions that would probably result in a grounding.

Did you drive him away on purpose?

Why is nothing we do ever good enough for you?

Do you wish you'd never married him in the first place? Because you know that means I wouldn't exist. Would you have been happier that way?

The frozen yogurt sat heavy in my gut. I ran my tongue over my teeth and opened the door.

Mom wasn't home. Of course she wasn't home. She had gone to church, Julia told me. My sister was sitting on the couch, eating a slice of frozen pizza and watching *Ally McBeal*.

Maybe it's genetic, this soullessness of ours.

Smashed at her feet were the mangled remains of Dad's guitar.

MIGHTY-PEN-JESS
Sept 28

REASON #18:
I have an anger management problem.

I've finally learned to silence my phone before studying with Cam. That way, he doesn't know when Hannah's text-hate arrives.

Today's Sunday Study Session was at his house. Not in his room (his mom has Rules) and not under the stairs (where his dad has made a sort of ancient camera equipment museum), but they have a fancy carved-wood coffee table that makes an acceptable homework cave when I wriggle underneath it. I was holding a pen poised over my notebook (not writing anything, obviously, but *poised for miracles*). Cam was on the couch doing something mathy. And everything was fine.

Until he turned on Spotify.

Almost all music is a problem for me since Memorial Day. It's basically all about sex, and for some reason (probably guilt), that makes me want to puke. The current selection was a sappy guitar boy singing about people putting their bodies on each other (while playing the xylophone?). I tried to tune out the lyrics, but an underwater feeling overwhelmed me, and I started to feel dizzy.

"Can you turn the music off?"

"My house, my Spotify," Cam teased, turning the volume up.

The song pierced through the bubble of terror surrounding me, amplified in my panic-cocoon, echoing, *body . . . body . . . put that body . . .*

"Turn the music off *please*!"

Cam obeyed. "What's wrong?"

"I just really hate that song." I crawled from underneath the coffee table and wobbled to my feet. "I'll study at home."

"I'm sorry, Jess. I was just messing with you. No music, okay?" He was looking at me like I was an overtired toddler who might throw a tantrum at any moment.

"Sorry." I rubbed my temples. "I've just been on edge lately."

"You need to stop apologizing all the time. It's like you were kidnapped by aliens and given a personality transplant or something. This is not the Jess I know."

"Yeah, tell me about it."

"What does that mean?"

"I just mean—half the time I don't feel like myself anymore, either."

He was still looking at me like I was an uncostumed egg

wobbling on a precipice, so I scooped up my backpack and slung it onto his lap. He yelped.

"How's that? Convinced that I'm the real Jess?"

"Yes," he moaned, shifting the backpack off his crotch, "and I hate you."

"That's more like it." My heart was galloping, but I wasn't dizzy anymore. I needed something to force Guitar Boy and his weirdly sexy xylophone out of my head, so I grasped for the most mind-numbing topic I could think of. "Teach me math."

Cam shook his head. "Let's just chill for a minute. Have some Doritos?"

I sat beside him and accepted a generous handful. My jiggling legs shook the whole couch. I dug my toes into the soft pile carpet, willing my body to calm the hell down.

"Are you going to Homecoming next weekend?" he asked.

"Absolutely not."

"You went last year."

I ran my tongue over my teeth, tasting blood where a particularly sharp Doritos had nicked my gum. "Yeah, because Chloe begged me to come with her and Noah. Somehow that seems like an unlikely scenario this year."

"Are you still trying to get her to talk to you?"

I shrugged, pushing empty air from between my tight lips, because I didn't really have an answer. Because those things you said, Alexis, they were still screeching in my head. So, instead of giving the screech a chance to escape, I changed the subject. "Do you have a date?"

"Kate Heston."

"Nice."

"She is nice."

"I'll take your word for it." I am in the habit of assuming that anyone on the field hockey team with you three is equally abhorrent. You are a poor representation of your fellow sportsball-girls.

"I promise she's nice. And I'm sure she wouldn't mind if you tagged along with us."

"She might not be rude enough to complain, but I'm sure she would very much mind. I do not doubt that she is looking forward to some . . . *alone time*." My breaths were coming easier now. Ragging on Cam's dating life was comfortable territory.

"She's not going to get it. We're going to Tyler's afterparty and then we're coming straight home."

"Ah, but what is the point of having an ancient minivan if not to entertain the ladies?"

"We're riding with Jeff and his boyfriend."

"Then it's a good thing I'm not joining you. You'll have to make the most of the back seat."

He huffed his annoyance, fiddling with the edge of the Doritos bag. "You not coming to Homecoming . . . is it because of the music?"

I stilled, some unchewed Doritos shards melding with my tongue. "What?"

"Well, umm, you obviously have a problem with music right now. Is it too loud? Could you get some of those . . . umm, they're like headphones but with no sound? My cousin got some for her baby when they went to a wedding—"

"It's not too loud. I just can't . . ." The dizzy, nauseated feeling crept back. I sprang to my feet. "I have to go." I fumbled to shove my notebook back in my bag.

"I'm sorry, I didn't mean—"

"I just have to go." I staggered toward the door.

"I'm so sorry, Jess. I just want you to know you can talk about, umm, your issues or—"

I whirled on him. "By 'issues' you mean *autism*, right? Like, why can't I just be a *normal* friend who listens to music and doesn't shake the couch with her psychotic legs, is that it?"

"What? No, I didn't— I would never— I don't think you should call yourself psychotic."

"I called my *legs* psychotic. And I was reading *your* mind."

"No, you weren't. I wasn't even thinking about autism. *Is* it your autism—the music thing? Because you used to be able to listen to music, and if there's a way to help—"

"I don't need your help, Cameron. What I need is some space. So just back off." I stormed out the door, letting the pounding in my head squash down my guilt at the hurt downward pull of his lips.

It was 11:43 p.m. when I threw the first red M&M at Cam's bedroom window. I was trying to channel Rolf from *The*

Sound of Music (which I guess was my first mistake; Nazis aren't great role models), but my lack of athleticism let me down. I don't think I ever got one to hit the window itself, but the soft tap of candy on the vinyl siding must have been enough to alert Cam to my presence because eventually the door swung open.

"Fancy meeting you here," he said. Because he is a nerd.

I stood there staring at his Puma Purple sweatpants, the apology in my gut too heavy to make it up to my mouth.

"Don't worry," Cam said. "I am fluent in Jess-Silence. Shall I translate?" He made a puppet with his hand. "Oh, Cameron! I'm so sorry for yelling at you. I have come to grovel and beg your forgiveness now that I've realized you didn't mean to offend me and you're probably really sorry, too!" He quirked an eyebrow. "Did I get it all?"

"Yeah, pretty much," I mumbled. "Except for the *you* being sorry part."

"Well, I am sorry, and you'll just have to accept it." He stepped back with a wide gesture. "Come on in. I was thinking *Richard III*, but you could persuade me to watch that trippy *Titus Andronicus* instead."

"What?"

He grabbed my elbow and steered me toward the living room. "You, Jessica Lanza, are clearly failing at Senior Year Goal number one, and it is turning you into a miserable grouch-face, which means that *I* am not having fun, either.

So tonight, we are watching a movie to restore the balance of fun to the universe. *Richard* or *Titus*?"

"Those are the plays that scream *fun* to you?" A smile asserted its control over the corners of my mouth. "Regicide and cannibalism?"

"So. Much. Fun."

I let him cue up *Richard III*. Cam always went above and beyond on the friend scale. The least I could do was join him for some Shakespearean panzer tanks.

MIGHTY-PEN-JESS
Sept 29

REASON #19:
I am terrible at apologies.

When I was four, I knocked my dad's signed Kid Rock album off the wall and the record cracked. I told him it was the cat.

When I was six, I cut Julia's hair in her sleep. I told her I was sorry she wasn't fancy enough to appreciate the awesome new style.

When I was nine, I snuck out of the house to walk to Dairy Queen, and my mom thought I was abducted. After the police left, I locked myself in the bathroom and pretended to cry until she went to bed.

When I was ten, I mistook Kate Heston's blue Elsa lunch box for my blue Elsa lunch box and realized I'd eaten her lunch only when I went to put the lunch box in my backpack and found mine still there. Neither of us has mentioned it to this day.

When we were thirteen, I kicked a soccer ball into Chloe's neighbor's yard and smashed one of their patio lights. I hid behind her mom's SUV while she went next door to apologize.

Between June 4 and September 29 of this year, I texted Chloe 423 times, left 76 voicemails, threw 27 pebbles at (or at least near) the window of her dad's condo, sat on her mom's doorstep for a total of 19 hours across 7 consecutive Saturdays, pushed 3 apology notes into her locker, and delivered 1 ziplock bag of hand-selected brown, blue, orange, yellow, and green M&M's via Alexis on the breezeway.

    She still hasn't texted me back.

MIGHTY-PEN-JESS
Oct 11

REASON #20:
I have an overdeveloped sense of stranger danger.

Given my overall lack of social skills, it may not shock you to learn that I suck at meeting people.

I'd thought maybe Emily was as socially inept as I am since she's so quiet and (like me) never participates in group activities, like the Stage-Right Orgy Couch. But apparently she doesn't avoid the Stage-Right Orgy Couch because she finds interacting with other humans alarming and making out with them slimy and/or baffling, but rather because she has a girlfriend at another high school. A girlfriend who, for some reason, was "so excited" to meet me.

"Really?" I asked around a mouthful of cafeteria pizza. "Why?"

Emily tugged on the end of her October-orange ponytail. "'Cause you're my friend?"

My heart puffed up a bit at the word "friend," and since she'd said it like a question that needed answering, I said,

"Of course we're friends!" and found myself agreeing to meet a stranger.

At the mall.

I've always hated the Northstar Mall. It's loud, the fluorescent lights make me itch, and the neon store signs and lit-up ad boards give me a headache—and then, of course, there's the music they pipe in, which may or may not include guitar/xylophone sex-pop. But I'm always too on edge when someone suggests hanging out to voice an opinion about the location. It feels like I should just suck it up and be less weird (which Chloe's mom would say was "internalized ableism," but whatever fancy psychology name you give it, it doesn't feel worse than the stress of pushing back against the Allistic Lifestyle).

Last time I was at the mall was with Chloe and Dr. Barton. Dr. B had gone off to explore the nerdy T-shirt store, and Chloe and I had been lingering near the food court. Between sips of smoothie, Chloe had been explaining about this new design she had for a hypothetical not-destroy-the-world type of robotic prosthetic. Chloe's a loud talker, which is not uncommon among us autistics, but the lady who ran the perfume stall next to us was Not Having It. She kept shushing and glaring and finally muttered, "They're always so loud."

That got Chloe quiet. Silent, in fact.

I was enraged as we trudged down the tiled hallway to find Dr. B. "Does she really think it's *autistic people* who make this mall loud? Has she not heard these fluorescent lights? They're humming like at least ten hives of angry bees."

"I don't think it's about that," said Chloe.

"Not about bees?"

"Not about autistic people."

"You think she just hates teenagers?"

Chloe had shrugged and let the not-silence of the fluorescent lights and shoe squeaks and guitar/xylophone sex-pop replace the conversation.

Today, I wasn't eager to listen to sexy xylophones, angry bees, or hateful perfume ladies, so—in a stroke of genius—I brought my headphones. Not huge noise-canceling ones like Cam suggested (my old therapist insisted I get them, but I have never voluntarily worn them ever in my life), just some earbuds. But—and here's the genius bit—I put on a white-noise app. With the gentle shushing in my ears, I couldn't hear the music piping through the speakers.

My backpack weighed a million pounds because I'd brought a million notebooks. Okay, just twenty-six, but they're the big spiral ones. I dragged the old toaster-oven box where I keep them from my closet and separated out all the ones from seventh grade to now. When I packed them up, the zipper on my backpack strained like I was trying to get a pair of jeans onto an elephant.

Sitting on the bench across from the food court, waiting for Emily and her girlfriend, Nic, I flipped through the pages. Our handwriting evolved over the years, but mine was always messy, Chloe's always precise and multicolored.

Does Chloe make lists when she's around you? I guess she must. It's one of her major coping strategies. We both have "executive function deficits," which basically means our brains try to keep us from getting anything done. But while my brain sabotages me by dragging me off on tangents and refusing to let me focus on anything else, Chloe's brain sabotages her by showing her the Details. All of the Details.

Her lists help her categorize and prioritize the Details. That's why there are pages and pages of them—first a list of absolutely everything to do with a topic; then a list where she crosses off Irrelevant Details; then a list that ranks Relevant Details by importance or order in which they need to be addressed; then a list that color-codes the Remaining Details by some subcategory that helps her understand them.

On my bench, I flipped through notebooks full of Chloe's lists, interspersed with my stream-of-consciousness scrawl of stories and poems.

Chloe's lists for our first trip to the Outer Banks with her dad; my vapid story about a mermaid and reactions to the texture of sand on my feet in unpolished metaphors.

Chloe's lists for the start of high school: rules and expectations, new procedures to remember, new social conventions to study; my story about an immigrant arriving on a fictional island in 1890 only to discover that the people of the so-called paradise are embittered factory workers, suspicious of newcomers.

Lists for Chloe's junior-year science fair project, possible topics narrowed down to a single topic and dozens of carefully ordered tasks; two of my crappy starts for a fiction contest entry followed by a rough version of the piece that would win me first prize, the story of a soul separated from her body, slowly deteriorating until she takes refuge in another:

> It was warm in this body. Alma had forgotten what it felt like, the embrace of the living. But there was something else, something Alma had never felt in her own body, when she had her own body, before it was a barely breathing husk in the garden. There was a fullness here, not just the crowding of the air and throbbing of the blood, but a lack of space, something fierce and heavy that pressed Alma into the crevices between the girl's organs, flat like a skin around the veins.
>
> Alma let her own essence swell, squeezing against the veins that led to the girl's heart. The blood strained against the walls of its vessels, pressure building until the body gasped. And then came the cold—a blast, a bite, a nothingness.

Alma let go, releasing the pressure, melding once more with the girl's cells. The body's spirit whispered, "You cannot kill her. Without her, who would you be?"

Now, why couldn't I write like this anymore?

A stranger plopped down beside me on the bench, and I flinched, ice flooding my veins, heart thudding, until I saw Emily walking toward us, shaking her head.

"Jess! Jess, Jess, Jess!" The stranger bumped me with her shoulder. I recognized her now from the photos Emily had shown me after Homecoming last week: tall, pale skin, long blond hair, smile like a Rockette. This was Nic. She said something more, but between the white noise pouring into my ears and the fog of anxiety from meeting a stranger, I couldn't process it. I pulled out my earbuds and pasted on a smile, staring at her pink leggings while I waited for her words to settle in my brain.

"Give her space," Emily said.

Nic bounded up from the bench but hovered close.

"I'm so, so, so excited to meet you!"

An appropriate response would be . . . "I'm excited to meet you, too," I said, still smiling. My cheeks were warm. I was already failing at this. I busied myself with stuffing my notebooks back into my bag and wrestling with the zipper.

Emily crouched beside me. "You don't have to do that."

"You're suggesting, what, that I leave my notebooks here on the bench?"

Her lips quirked. "I meant, it's cool to just be you. You don't have to grimace like someone's pressing a gun into your kidneys."

Her words stoked my anxiety. My fingers drummed on my backpack. I glanced at Nic. She wasn't staring. I mean, she was looking at me but not in an *oh-my-God-what-is-this-crazy-girl's-deal* kind of way. She was beaming.

Kind of like she really was so, so, so excited to meet me.

Emily laced her fingers with Nic's and pulled her toward the food court. I sat a minute longer, still flushed, still fluttering. Easy for Emily to say *It's cool to just be you.* Emily already *was* cool. She didn't lose control of her body every time she met someone new.

Sometimes I hate me. Not the way *you* hate me—I mean, I don't hate *all* of me. I just hate that my brain won't do simple things like say "Hi" to my friend's seemingly nice girlfriend. Chloe would definitely be better than me at meeting Nic. I don't know why she's so good at masking, how we could be having a normal conversation, and then an allistic would walk up and suddenly Chloe had a smile that looked allistic and her voice was rising and falling, all her sentences ending in exclamation points. I'm lucky if I can get through a whole conversation without having a panic attack.

It was another minute before my body was regulated enough to stand. By the time I clomped over to the food court, Emily and Nic had gotten a table and three milkshakes. Emily slid one to me, and Nic proceeded to talk.

And talk.

She was so bubbly and open, so unlike Emily. By the time the first pangs of brain freeze set in, I already knew way too much about her three cats and their bowel movements. I hadn't said anything, but Nic didn't seem to mind. And though I never exactly relaxed, I let go of the fake smile, gave in to my jiggling knees, and did my best to "just be me."

"So, Jess, what do you think?" Nic said after a rare pause for breath. "Shouldn't Emily be stage manager for *Grease*? Wouldn't she be so, so, so good at it?"

I looked at Emily, surprised. She hadn't told me Ms. Otashi had offered her stage manager. Her ears had turned copper, and she shot Nic a mutinous look.

"I can't manage people," she said.

"Of course you can!" said Nic.

"I think you'd be really good at it," I put in. Emily was great on crew—organized, dedicated. She'd be kind of perfect. I made a mental note to tell her that when I was in a less chaotic setting and had more control over my voice.

Emily's blush blazed. She shook her head. Nic, on the other hand, was grinning. "Told you! I knew I'd like you, Jess. Emily has told me so much about you, and it just felt *wrong* that we hadn't met."

"Oh . . . Um . . . Emily told me about you." The words staggered out like stage crew after a cast party. "I'm sorry

I'm so . . ." I waved my hands to represent my inner mess.

"Oh my God, *no*!" She stopped herself before putting a way-too-friendly hand on my arm. "*I'm* sorry I'm so in-your-face. My mom says that I'm a blabbermouth."

"My mom calls you the girl who won't *shut up*!" Emily said, and they dissolved into giggles.

Isn't it strange how relationships change people? Actually, "change" is the wrong word. How they bring out something new. Like how some of Nic's bubbly joy tickled a giggle out of Emily's quiet voice. Like how being with Nic made Emily louder, brighter somehow.

Like how love is contagious, and when you're around it—even when you have a head full of anxiety and a backpack of memories digging into your shoulders—something inside of you starts to float.

MIGHTY-PEN-JESS
Oct 12

REASON #21:
I don't understand human relationships.

"Oh my God!" I said. Or that's what I meant to say. I actually didn't say anything because when I gasped, I inhaled half a french fry, and Cam had to pound me on the back till I coughed it up. I gulped some soda to wash down the bits of potato that were still clinging to my esophagus, then returned my focus to what had incited my near-fatal encounter with the fry.

Kate Heston had just come into the Five Guys holding Grayson Martin's hand and wearing his sportsball jacket.

Cam's back was to them. Now that I was no longer dying, he had returned his complete focus to wolfing down his two burgers and large cup of fries. Indecision gnawed at me. Should I tell him? Maybe Kate had already broken up with him. But if she hadn't... If she was cheating...

I'm sure you think that's rich coming from me, but at

least I had the decency to be ashamed of myself. I didn't make out with Noah on the counter at Auntie Anne's.

I was still wrestling with the complex moral nuances of the situation when Kate and Grayson wandered our way. Kate and Cam exchanged casual "Heys," and Grayson and Cam shared one of those hand-slap/handshake things sportsball guys do. Then Kate and Grayson settled down at a table not far from us. Cam turned back to his burger.

"I didn't know you guys had broken up," I said.

"What?" He looked at me like a ferret had just crawled out of my ear. "Kate and I were never together."

"But I thought... At Homecoming, didn't you and she—"

"Oh yeah, we went to Homecoming together," he said. "But we were never *together* together."

"Oh." I frowned. "Why not?"

He laughed at me. "You want me to date Kate Heston? Why do you care?"

"I just thought you liked her," I said, bristling. "You said she was nice, and she's obviously superhot, so why don't you want to date her?"

"We had fun at the dance, but . . . I dunno. I just don't like her that way."

Romance has always baffled me. It seems logical that if you get along well with someone and they meet a particular standard of aesthetic appeal that you should want to do more than dance. Maybe that's why making out with Cam was so confusing. I like him so much as a friend—and I genuinely do think he's gorgeous—that it seems ridiculous that I wouldn't like him *that way*. But I'm also pretty sure that when you make out with someone and the first word that pops into your head is "slimy," that's a pretty clear indication that you don't like them *that way*.

(P.S. Jeff Watkins, if you tell Cam I said any of that, I swear to God, I will smear so much ranch dressing on your windshield, it will take you a month to wash it off.)

"Anyway," Cam said, "between football and college essays and classes, I don't think I have the energy to sustain a relationship. Girls are very demanding."

"Popular girls, you mean."

"Of course. Look at them."

I looked. Kate was still wearing Grayson's jacket even though the restaurant had the heat on and it was like a million degrees. She was also wearing a glittery heart necklace, and I could guess where it came from. Grayson took a tiny bite of his burger and immediately wiped his mouth with a napkin.

"That's why friendships are easier than relationships," Cam continued. "I mean, you wouldn't care if I had a big blob of ketchup on my face."

"Of course not!" I assured him. "In fact, I wish you did. Then I could take a photo and remind you of it whenever you got too full of yourself."

"See? We can still sit here and eat burgers and insult each other, and I don't have to buy you cheap jewelry or give you my varsity letter jacket."

"I have my own varsity letter, thank you. Because yes, theatre *is* a sport, and *we* won our state championship last year, so hah!"

"We won our first championship game, too."

"Yes, but our winning performance was far more interesting than yours, and we came in second at SETC." It was the first time SBHS had made it to the Southeastern Theatre Conference, and I still felt kind of giddy about it.

"Technically, we also came in second in the quarterfinals, since we were only playing against one other team . . ."

"Ugh, sportsball. Are you going to eat all of those?"

"Definitely." He held the cup of fries over his head where I couldn't reach them. "You should come to our game on Friday."

"Hmm. Counterproposal: I *don't* sit out in the cold watching a bunch of sweaty guys throw balls at each other, and instead I stay home and do something fun."

"And your definition of fun is . . . ?"

"I dunno. Watch *Hamlet* or something."

"Which *Hamlet*?"

"Maybe all of them? Skip the game, and we'll have a *Hamlet*-fest!"

"Not as tempting as you think it is." Cam took pity on

me (either that or his arm got tired) and lowered the fries. I grabbed a handful before he could change his mind.

"If you're really just going to spend your weekends sitting at home watching TV," Cam said with the casual air of a scheming supervillain, "why don't you get involved in the theatre competition? Do you know what play they're doing?"

Exposure by Vishesh Abeyratne. "Don't know, don't care."

"Don't believe you." He hesitated, studying his burger with the intensity of a health inspector dining with Sweeney Todd. "Noah's doing it. That's it, isn't it?"

I stuffed the rest of my burger into my mouth, which didn't quite work since it was a double with all the free toppings and there was more than half of it left. Mustard oozed down my chin, and I reached for a napkin. Cam whisked them out of my reach, his half smile an apology for bringing up a forbidden topic. I gurgled my overall annoyance.

"I don't think you should let him stop you from doing theatre," he pushed. "Carly Hidalgo is in my Computer Science class, and she said they need another light tech for the Virginia Theatre Association competition. Some guy got sick."

I swallowed the last of the burger. "Who?"

"I forget. He has mono."

Hopefully not Ben Kendrick.

"Oh, no, I do remember. Ben something?"

Welp. Maybe no one would be going to compete at VTA,

because Ben Ken typically made out with at least half the cast and crew by tech week. I lunged over the table and ripped a napkin from Cam's hands.

"So Carly says they need someone who knows stuff about lights. She asked me to tell you."

I paused, napkin plastered to my chin. "Carly asked you to tell me?"

"Yeah. She thought you might be willing to do it."

"They must be desperate." I dragged a finger through the mustard splotches on the table.

"Maybe she misses you."

"I'm pretty sure no."

"*I'm* pretty sure she does. She keeps asking about you. She said you skipped Drama Club this month."

"I didn't skip. I was just . . . busy." I had spent Friday's meeting hiding in Ms. Otashi's office doing paperwork. I'd heard Carly asking where I was, but I didn't know why. I'd panicked, actually, thinking that maybe she had decided to be more militantly Team Noah and join the cyberbullying, even though that would have been totally out of character for my normally chill theatre-mate. But I guess she just needed a lighting tech.

"I don't think you should let Noah keep you away from all your other friends."

I rolled my eyes. Maybe last year Carly was my friend. And Dee. But I doubted they were anymore. I may have been hiding from them this month, but what about last month?

Had either of them been brave enough to even wave hello when Noah was in the room? Nope.

"Thanks for your input," I said, "but I can manage my own life."

Across the restaurant, Kate pushed back her chair, colliding with another girl and knocking her food to the ground. The girl assured Kate that she was very, very sorry as she scooped the mutilated burger back onto her tray, and Kate waved in regal forgiveness before looping her arm through Grayson's and walking away.

I really don't understand humans, but I'm learning to follow their rules.

MIGHTY-PEN-JESS
Oct 17

REASON #22:
It's only a matter of time before I accidentally call my creative writing teacher "Dad."

The Pubs Lab was way too cold for October. It is possible ice giants had commandeered the AC. Our Creative Writing class was spending only a half hour in the lab today (just to give the kids who were new to advanced creative writing, aka lit mag staff, the lay of the land . . . or the lay of the ancient desktop computers, overloaded power strips, and printer that jams only 63 percent of the time), but when January came around, we'd be in here the full ninety minutes of every Creative Writing class. If they didn't do something about the HVAC situation, we would all have frostbite.

The lunch bell rang before I'd finished demonstrating how to enter text in the design software.

"About damn time," Emily muttered. She'd spent the past ten minutes hopping up and down with her hands stuffed in her armpits. Drew, who had pulled his arms and knees inside his hoodie like an emo turtle, grunted.

I grabbed my bag and made to join the stampede of escaping student-cicles, but Mr. Barton called me back. "Do you have a journal entry for me today?"

I shivered, and this time not from the AC.

Mr. Barton's beaming smile slacked a little. "I'm trying to help you, you know. It's not uncommon to be intimidated by something like a college portfolio, and journaling can really help you break out of—"

"I'm working on it." I looked up in hopes that a rare effort at eye contact would make my lie more convincing. The fluorescent lights bounced off his glasses, sparing me the full effect of his scrutiny.

I could imagine it, though. It was the same look he'd given me at breakfast after an impromptu sleepover with Chloe when I'd said that my dad moving out the day before was really no big deal. His eyebrows had drawn together, and his lips had pulled back in a wince of understanding, and I'd realized that Chloe was wrong about his divorce from Dr. Barton. She'd told me that her parents never fought, that they just "grew apart," that her dad living in a separate bedroom from her mom since Chloe was in fourth grade was an amicable decision, and that the official divorce was just a notarized document to finalize the pain-free separation. But that morning, I saw in Mr. Barton's face that his divorce had had its share of pain and mess. He was just better at hiding it than my parents.

He was better at everything than my parents, really. Better

at seeing through my masks. Better at faking an interest—or maybe actually *taking* an interest—when I went on one of my theatre-themed rambles at the breakfast table. Definitely better at making Belgian waffles with blueberry compote while telling atrocious dad jokes.

"Are you really journaling?" Mr. Barton's voice dragged me back from the memory of his warm kitchen to the reality of the frigid Pubs Lab. "You don't have to lie, Jess. You're not in trouble. I'm trying to help you."

"I am journaling, in a way. There are just . . . some obstacles . . . to my brain, you know, working."

He tilted his head to the side. "What kind of obstacles? What can I do to help?"

I squeezed my eyes tight, the words struggling out. "Nothing. I just can't think. I have to . . . First I . . ." I opened my eyes. I'd been struck by a half-formed, almost certainly harebrained idea. "Actually, can I borrow your phone real quick?"

His frown deepened, but he pulled the phone from the pocket of his slacks. "My phone will help you overcome these obstacles?"

"Yeah. Well, probably not. But maybe." My fingers trembled on the screen as I keyed in the number I knew by heart.

If Cam were here, he could have calculated the odds that Chloe had her phone on during Robotics and that Mr. Granger would be cool about her answering a call from her dad, but I didn't actually need him to tell me that they were low. Low to nonexistent. But if Chloe wouldn't talk to *me*, I was going to have to pretend to be someone else.

It went to voicemail.

I turned my back on Mr. Barton as though that could stop him from hearing me. "Hey, Chloe. Sorry to do this, I just wondered . . . did you get that jewelry-heist musical I put in your locker? I hope it reminded you of . . . you know, how awesome and important you are. To me. And . . ." I took a shuddery breath and opted for honesty. "I just really need you to call me. It's kind of a life emergency. I can't figure out what's going on in my brain and— About Memorial Day . . . I don't know what happened. I mean, I know what happened, but not, like, how? Or if I–I just don't know. And I've been having these nightmares. And music is suddenly terrifying? So, basically, I'm a mess, and yeah. Call me. Please. It's Jess, by the way." The phone blooped as I ended the call.

I turned around. Mr. Barton frowned mournfully. He rubbed a hand over his bald head. "Jess—"

I shoved the phone into his hand. "Thanksbye." I ran from the room, sending a silent prayer to Lin-Manuel Miranda that the rogue AC would freeze whatever part of Mr. Barton's brain held the memory of that phone call.

Unfortunately, it didn't freeze the memory of Belgian waffles and corny jokes and a beaming dad that I kind of wished were mine.

MIGHTY-PEN-JESS
Oct 23

REASON #23:
I think my brain is dying.

"Maybe I won't go to college," I mused.

"If a crappy writer like me can finish the application, you certainly can."

Cam had a rare afternoon off from sportsball, so he was driving us home, and I was examining my latest Creative Writing failure. I'd suffered through two classes with Mr. Barton since the Phone Call. He didn't mention it, but I could tell he was thinking about it because every time I glanced in his direction, he jerked his face away and pretended to be fascinated by the *Get Out* poster next to the window. Which meant he had been staring at me. And that he wanted to ask what happened with me and Chloe.

Fortunately, I'd managed to snatch up my assignment and escape the classroom before he worked up the courage to confront me—about Chloe or my short story.

On the last page, Mr. Barton's purple scrawl read, *I'd*

like you to revise this. Stop telling the reader what your characters are feeling. Show us! Get out of their heads and give us some action and dialogue! Did you try journaling?*

I guess I could say these posts are somewhat like a journal, but writing them hasn't helped my fiction. Maybe it's because you three aren't a particularly inspiring audience. Or maybe the events of my life have become so soap-operatic that I've lost all sense of realistic story-building.

I suggested as much to Cam.

"Your blog is good writing," he said.

"I told you not to—!"

"I haven't been reading it, but Jeff says it's hilarious. Why don't you just use some of that for the portfolio?"

"Because it's a *blog*. It's drivel that I churn out in the middle of the night when my brain is barely working, and Jeff Watkins is probably the only person reading it." Most of my recent posts had two hits, but as much as I wanted to believe the other one was Chloe, I had begun to suspect it was just Jeff reading it twice. "I'm applying to *the Goldberg program*. My portfolio needs to be *exceptional*."

"I'm sure whatever you write will be great."

There is no point having serious conversations with Cam. He is way too chill.

Unfortunately, my mom is not.

And even more unfortunately, my first-quarter grades had posted.

She was sitting at the kitchen table when I trudged

through the door, so there was no way I could miss her. Her pink smiling-avocado scrubs cut a charming contrast to the steely fury on her face.

"Explain this." She held up her phone, open to the SBHS portal. Next to last year's litany of A's in Creative Writing and English were a pair of B's. And a B– next to Spanish.

"It's just a few B's." My erratic pulse spasmed through my veins, and my fingers began drumming the same wild rhythm against my thighs.

"A *D* in Math! A *C-minus* in Government!"

"I meant in the subjects that matter."

"And there isn't even a grade here for Physics. What does that mean?"

"I'm still working on a take-home test," I mumbled.

"Well, you certainly won't be leaving this house until it's finished and I've looked it over."

"I'm pretty sure that would be cheating."

My mom raked her fingers across her scalp like if she tore her hair out, it would somehow bring my grades up.

"Don't beat yourself up," I said, a low-level panic buoying my words even though my brain knew it was a terrible idea to speak them aloud. "At least you did all right with Julia." My sister may be a sex-crazed know-it-all, but at least she got good grades.

"Do you think this is funny?" My mom's lips had gone white. "Do you think NYU is going to accept your application when they see grades like this?"

The wave of hysteria swelling in my chest crested. "Well, in order for them to accept my application, I'd have to actually *finish* my application, which at this point seems unlikely, so . . ."

She puffed a long breath through pursed lips, and her gaze flicked down to my fluttering fingers. "I think we should schedule an appointment with an OT."

I forced my hands to still. "I don't need therapy."

"Jessie, it's okay to ask for help. You're clearly struggling—"

"It has nothing to do with being autistic," I said too loudly. "I'm fine. I cope. Dad says I don't have to go anymore. The end."

"Despite what your father believes, it's not *weakness* to see a therapist. He's not here, and—"

The wave crashed. "Yeah, he's not here because you drove him away by being a bitch all the time."

She gasped like she was on a telenovela. Her nostrils flared. "You're grounded."

"Fine with me." I stomped away.

"No more trips to the mall. No hanging out with Chloe and Cameron."

"I said fine." I thundered up the stairs.

Her voice followed me. "If you intend to keep living under this roof, you will finish that Physics test, and—"

I slammed my bedroom door. The bed frame squawked as I face-planted onto it and screamed into my mattress until I had no air left in my lungs. Then I lay there, my nose squashed into the sheets that reeked of my own BO. I really needed to do laundry.

This was all Julia's fault. I mean, I guess it was mostly my fault for sucking at school, but it was also partly Julia's fault for doing so well at school and making me look bad by comparison. You would think I'd get bonus points for not having anger management problems. For example, *I've* never gotten fired from my job for slapping a coworker I didn't like. Isn't it better to fail a Physics test than to beat up pizza waiters?

I hadn't taken off my backpack, and the corner of a textbook was skewering my kidney. Moaning, I shrugged it off and sat up. My phone was flooded with texts (thanks, Hannah) but none of them from anyone I particularly wanted to talk to (no offense).

I stared at it for a while; then I texted my dad: *Can I spend the weekend at your place?*

I had to wait only a few minutes for the reply. It was the one I'd expected: *Sorry, Jessie Bean, no can do. Working Sat and headed out of town Sun. See you for T-day?*

T-day and Xmas. The official Dad Days. This was why I always regretted texting him. I know the custody lawyer people sided with my mom, but does that really mean that I can never visit him? Or he can never visit me? It doesn't seem likely that my mom somehow convinced CPS that my dad's a serial killer who took a vow of nonviolence exclusively on cranberry-sauce-related holidays. Also, doesn't God do parental quality control? It doesn't seem like divine justice that one kid gets blessed with the dual awesomeness of Mr. and Dr. Barton while another is left to fend for herself with the infuriating mess of Rob and Andrea Lanza.

My fingers were fluttering again. I shoved my hands under my butt to stop them from moving and clenched my teeth against the torrent of curses gathering on my tongue.

The smell of boiling cabbage made its way up the stairs. I dug through my food stash for a protein bar. Then I opened my laptop. If the alternative to college was "living under this roof" another year, I'd better get writing.

MIGHTY-PEN-JESS
Oct 27

REASON #24:
I took credit for Chloe's genius.

I had an epiphany today as I sat in front of my blank computer screen contemplating the utter crapfest that is my life.

All this time, I've been thinking that I lost my ability to write because I'm distracted by the whole Noah-text nightmare/Chloe-and-Jess implosion. But here's the true story:

I never had the ability to write in the first place.

But, Jess, you're not thinking, *aren't you, like, a Future Tony-Winning Playwright?*

Nope. I only *thought* I was a Future Tony-Winning Playwright. In reality, all my best stories were ghostwritten by Chloe.

Some of her ghostwriting wasn't obvious. Like that piece that won first prize at the fiction contest about the two souls. When I wrote it, Chloe wasn't even in this state; she was up in DC with Mr. Barton and the rest of the Black Student Union for a field trip. But that's probably *why* I wrote it—because I was feeling a kind of pressurized absence, a lingering witch's spell, as Emily Dickinson might say. Without Chloe, I didn't feel complete, and it came out as that story. Plus, all that stuff about cells and blood vessels was totally inspired by the biology textbook Chloe had been studying for her CLEP exam.

And once I recognized Chloe's ghostly role in *that* story, it was impossible not to see her influence in everything else I've written. My lit mag piece about the renegade squirrel-demon was directly inspired by the squirrel's-eye view of the world I got while dropping eggs off Dr. Barton's roof. The story that got an honorable mention in the Writer's Eye contest at UVA couldn't have existed without Chloe's input on the physical capabilities of robots and what precisely it might look like if they decided to commandeer a Nantucket whaling vessel.

And then there was the play Carly, Dee, Noah, Ben Ken, and I did for the Spring Spectacle last year. The playbill said "by Jess Lanza," but Chloe was the indisputable mastermind.

If you've never been to the Spring Spectacle, congratulations. You have missed out on ninety minutes of narcissists and slackers putting on skits either to show off (the narcissists) or to pull up their abysmal grades in Ms. Otashi's drama classes (the slackers). Since you can also get extra credit by *attending* the Spring Spectacle, the audience is made up of even lazier drama slackers who couldn't be bothered slapping together a skit—as well as, of course, the narcissists' parents. But we nerds perform, too, because it's a chance to put on the kind of show that only desperate D students and unsuspecting helicopter parents would ever sit through voluntarily.

Shows like *The Maltese Electron.*

You know, like *The Maltese Falcon.*

But with electrons.

Yes, it was that good.

It was Chloe's idea that I should write a chemistry-themed noir mystery.

"Your main detective could be Iron because he's tough as nails," she'd said, sitting under her loft with the purple beads draped over her shoulders and her fingers fluttering as she got excited. "And the detective who gets himself killed could be Osmium. Because he's so dense." When I didn't react, she clarified, "Twenty-two-point-five-nine grams per cubic centimeter."

I blinked. "What language are you even speaking right now?"

"Osmium is the densest element, as in the physical property of density. But as a character, he could be *dense*, as in—"

"I get it," I said, scribbling Osmium's name onto my cast list. "I just don't understand why you thought a string of numbers would make that clearer." I tapped the eraser on the notebook, my tongue worrying my gums. "Okay, what will we name our femme fatale?"

After poring over the periodic table on the back of Chloe's bedroom door, we decided on Chlorine for our leading lady because it sounded like a girl's name and also kind of dangerous, and we picked Arsenic for the patsy she sets up to take the fall for her crime, partly because it sounded like a name, but mostly because it meant we could write this joke:

>   **CHLORINE**
> Oh, that's just Arsenic. He's harmless.

Most of the other jokes, Chloe came up with.

>   **FRANCIUM**
> Hey, babe. I've got an extra electron.
> Wanna do some . . .

> He waggles his eyebrows.

>   **FRANCIUM (CONT'D)**
> . . . oxidation reduction?

Don't worry. I don't get it, either.

Together we'd written eleven pages of comedy gold. *Gold.* (Though I was beginning to suspect that the five-minute time limit for skits was going to be a problem.)

"Why would Arsenic be so unwilling to cooperate if doing so could clear his name?" Chloe asked.

"Because it's the noir style. He has to be cagey. You know, like, 'You gotta lotta nerve. Of all the beakers in all the labs in all the world, you had to drip into mine. Well, there's only room for one of us in this research facility, and it ain't gonna be you, copper.'"

We both froze as the accidental genius of what I just said sank in. Then the giggles erupted. Once we'd gotten a grip—and assured Dr. Barton through the door that our strange, squealy hysteria was not the result of someone murdering us—I went back through all eleven pages changing IRON to COPPER.

"This is officially the best thing I've ever written." I shook the eraser crumbs from the notebook. "Well, cowritten."

"You are the writer. I am the consulting scientist."

"I don't think there's a spot for 'consulting scientist' in the Spectacle playbill."

"I don't need to be in the playbill."

You're probably surprised that I didn't argue. Or insist. I know from years of living with my mom and sister that I'm supposed to argue when another woman/girl says she doesn't need something. If I ask, "Do you need help?" and she responds, "No, I'm okay," I'm supposed to follow up with, "Please, I insist." If I don't, then later, when she's overwhelmed or something goes wrong, she'll blow up and shout at me for not helping and (if she happens to be my sister) deliberately turn the volume up on some weird techno music that she *knows* makes me nauseated.

Chloe is not an allistic with their bizarre social rules, so when she said no to being in the playbill, the conversation was over. But I wonder now whether this was another in my series of life-ruining mistakes. Because maybe that seemingly illogical social rule isn't about passive-aggressively entrapping autistic sisters in nets of guilt. Maybe it's about recognizing the value in one another and insisting people let us support them, even if they don't know they need it.

I can't really blame Chloe for ghosting me if I'm the one who let her become a ghost.

MIGHTY-PEN-JESS
Oct 30

REASON #25:
I went to a rehearsal for the one-act.

It turns out that "it will look good on my college application" is a miraculous phrase that will get you ungrounded for two hours on a Thursday afternoon.

I didn't want to be a light tech for *Exposure*. Through careful hallway maneuvering and occasional death stares, I'd managed to avoid my former theatre-mates thus far, but doing the show would put me in unavoidable proximity to all of them, including Noah, whose proximity still seemed to turn me into the human equivalent of *Cats*—overwrought and incoherent.

But I really, really wanted to get into college. If I didn't do at least one show, I'd be kicked out of Drama Club, and how would *that* look to Tisch?

Also, I missed theatre.

You may not understand, but there's a kind of magic

about doing theatre. Maybe it's how much of it happens in the dark that lends an extra sparkle. Or maybe it's the play itself—words performed by countless actors on countless stages, each time a little bit different. There's so much more *life* in a play than in some short story in an English textbook.

This semester, part of me has died. Truly. There's a gaping hole where some internal organ used to be. It aches when I see the *Pygmalion* posters and know that I won't be staying after school until one a.m. during tech week, won't be jumping up and down and squealing in the lobby on opening night, sweat-soaked and burbling with postshow euphoria.

And so, when I walked into the auditorium after school, it was in hopes of being healed.

Instead, I was eviscerated.

The theater was the same. The same ragged Puma Purple seats sloping down toward the stage with its regal velvet curtains. The same people clustered in the front rows, waiting for rehearsal to start. Ms. Otashi with her script and clipboard. Techies lounging on the stage, the lights flicking on and off as someone in the booth tested the lighting board.

And Noah. He was there. Of course he was there, in front of the stage, laughing, in full makeup, with his hair mussed to mimic bedhead, costumed in a baggy T-shirt and sweatpants he'd never be caught dead in IRL. Carly sat cross-legged on the stage wearing polka-dotted pajama pants, a silky purple bonnet over her locs. She said my name. I didn't hear it, but I saw her mouth move, saw Noah snap to attention, look out into the house, searching until he found me.

Scowling.

A roaring in my head drowned out the chatter. The room was receding, and I wasn't sure if I was passing out or running away.

When I came back to myself, I was in the lobby, knees clutched to my chest, eyes squeezed shut, rocking on the cold tiles.

I opened my eyes. Someone's fuzzy bunny slippers fidgeted in front of me. My body and brain felt sluggish, so it took me way too long to look up at the bunny-slipper-person's face. It was like a slo-mo pan in a horror movie. First the serial killer's fuzzy bunny slippers, then their embroidered kitten cargo pants, then their button-down rainbow unicorn shirt, and finally, after this appalling mismatch of species and clothing styles, Dee's face, somehow paler than usual, their eyes Looney Tunes wide.

"Jess. Are you—?"

"Don't worry." I struggled to my feet. "I'm leaving."

"Why?" They looked stunned, and I didn't have nearly enough energy to figure out whether they meant why was I leaving or why had I come in the first place.

"I came because I need to do a show for Drama Club; I'm leaving because I can't even do that properly."

"But Jess, you—"

"Look, you don't have to pretend to be friends with me, okay?"

I felt a little guilty as my words seemed to strike Dee full on the chest. They took a step back, tugging the fidget chain from their pocket and twisting it around their fingers. "I don't understand."

"I know you saw Noah's text."

"Sure, but—"

"So you know—" My legs tremored, and I nearly fell flat on the tiles. Dee grabbed my arm, but their touch was like lightning to my already electrified body. "Don't touch me. Just . . . stay away from me."

They dropped my arm. "I'm so sorry. What's wrong?"

I almost laughed. "So many things are wrong with me, Dee. Trust me, you don't need my mess. And Noah certainly doesn't."

Dee glanced toward the auditorium, almost reflexively, and I took the opportunity to lurch outside on gelatinous legs. Dee didn't follow. I'd been right when I told Cam that no one here wanted me. They'd all made their choice.

I sat on the front sidewalk, leaning against the flagpole, and texted my mom to pick me up. It was only four thirty in the afternoon, but it was cloudy and cold, and my skin was still hypersensitive, prickling at every breeze.

Spring of sophomore year, Noah, Chloe, and I had lain

by this flagpole long after midnight, waiting for our parents to pick us up from *The Wizard of Oz* rehearsal. It was the one time Chloe had done a theatre production with me, and really she'd done it at Noah's urging, to be close to him. But during rehearsal—which often lasted until midnight or later—Noah spent most of his time onstage scarecrowing it up while Chloe and I, with smaller roles and lots of down time, sock-slid down hallway ramps, rapped our way through the *Hamilton* cast recording, and "practiced" stage makeup on each other (which will come in very useful if either of us ever gets cast as a mummified clown prostitute).

As soon as rehearsal ended (and we'd gotten notes and changed out of costume and stored our props), the three of us would wait for our carpool, lying on our backs on the sidewalk, watching moths collide with the floodlights. Happy and stupid with exhaustion, we'd talked about everything, from which cast member would make the best POTUS to why cherry Twizzlers are called "cherry" when they taste nothing like actual cherries.

I closed my eyes. I could still feel it—imagine that the stormy fall afternoon was a cool spring midnight and imagine that my best friend and my theatre-mate lay beside me, giggling up at the sky. I could still feel the happy giggles in my lungs and the warm, contented lethargy in my limbs that closeness with Chloe—with both of them, really—had induced. But I knew if I saw Noah now, the roiling chaos in my body would be nowhere close to happy.

What's wrong? Dee had asked. I wish I could have said, "Nothing," but every day it grew more apparent that I'd broken more than friendships last Memorial Day. I'd broken something inside myself, too.

MIGHTY-PEN-JESS
Nov 5

REASON #26:
I know exactly who you are.

What are the odds that you would set foot on the sidewalk this morning at the *exact same moment* as me and Cam? Did you time it, Alexis? Did you wait in your car until you saw my emerald-green *Wizard of Oz* T-shirt out of the corner of your eye (or more likely, Cam's Puma Purple sportsball-jerseyed torso towering over me) before swooping over the crosswalk with a barely suppressed cackle?

"Hiya, Alexis," said Cam.

I gaped at him.

"Hey, Cam," you said. "Great game Friday. Shame about that field goal."

"Closest we've ever come against Northstar. Not that you'd know it if you'd heard Coach in the locker room after. Oh, hey, do you know Jess?"

My jaw dropped another inch and was now in grave danger of detaching from its sockets.

"Yeah, hey, Jess," you said, with a tight smile that wouldn't have fooled anyone less trusting and naive than Cam. We stepped across the threshold into the dingy, fluorescently lit lobby, which was somehow more ominous than the gathering storm outside. "Did you guys win that theatre competition this weekend?"

"I didn't go."

"Oh. I thought you'd be all over that."

"Well, Noah was 'all over that,' so . . ."

"Oh, yeah." Your face muscles slacked a bit, your forced smile wavering. "Well, hey, that's smart of you, you know? I'm glad you're taking a step back from . . . all that."

"I'll bet." That last was too sharp for even Cam to ignore. He paused, frowning.

You faltered a step, too, Alexis. "Well, it was good to see y'all." You hiked up your backpack, the Puma Purple ribbon on the strap flopping over your shoulder as you speed-walked away.

"What's with you?" Cam asked when you were out of earshot.

"What's with me?" I prodded his arm. "What's with *you*, being all friendly with cyberbullies?"

It was his turn to gape. "Alexis *Jones*? That's the Alexis who's been bullying you?"

"What other Alexis could I possibly have been talking about?"

"Alexis McAllister."

"Who's Alexis McAllister?"

"She's dating Tyler."

"Who's *Tyler?*"

"Our quarterback."

I looked right at his eyes to be sure his allistic brain picked up on my perfectly justified derision. "Why would some random sportsball-guy's girlfriend be bullying me? I obviously meant the Alexis that hangs out with Chloe. Where have you been all year?"

He had the decency to look slightly abashed. "I don't know. Not stalking Chloe, obviously." He scratched the back of his neck. "But Alexis Jones? I mean, she's so nice."

"To you."

"No, I mean to everyone."

"Not everyone."

"She actually seemed to be nice to you just now."

"It was an act. For your benefit. *I'm glad you're taking a step back,*" I mimicked. "Yeah, right. She's just glad I'm failing at getting Chloe to talk to me."

"Well, please don't hit me or anything, but I'm glad for that, too."

I didn't hit him. But he flinched at my glare.

"Not the failing part," he backtracked. "Just that you're having some space from Chloe. This whole bullying thing has been too much."

"Chloe isn't bullying me."

"Isn't she?" Cam scrunched up his face. "If they're her

friends, she's gotta at least know what's going on. I mean, if *Alexis Jones* . . ." He trailed off, frowning at the auditorium doors like they might hold the secrets of the universe.

Heat rushed to my cheeks. "Is this where you tell me that if Alexis Jones is bullying me, I must have done something to deserve it? Because I've never denied that I deserve it."

"You don't deserve it," he said automatically, tearing his gaze from the wall. "I'm just . . . I'm confused. You know when you think you know someone, and they surprise you?"

As we parted ways by the library, I realized that I didn't know what he meant. People don't surprise me. You will always be loyal to your little group, Alexis. It's in your popular-girl DNA. It is your inertia. Cam will always be trusting and a little bit naive. Noah will always be emotionally honest to a fault. Chloe will always defend that stark dividing line between black and white, right and wrong, truth and lies.

In fact, the only person who ever surprised me with who she really is was me.

MIGHTY-PEN-JESS
Nov 12

REASON #27:
Chloe and Noah are fighting again.

You already know this. It's all over school. Maybe you were the ones to spread the news. I notice you've given up on your blog, but judging by the rate at which Hannah shoots hate texts to my phone, you must still have a pretty efficient communication operation.

I wonder if that's why Dee and Carly were stalking me in Drama Club on Friday. They knocked on Ms. Otashi's office door before they came in, so I had time to scurry back into the racks of poufy '50s dresses she's collecting for *Grease*.

Carly called my name, tentatively. I held my breath. "He said she'd be in here."

I wondered whether "he" was Noah or Cam.

"Maybe she's absent? Or . . . I dunno, Carly, she told me to stay away from her."

"At rehearsal, not forever. And you said she seemed upset. She was probably just having a bad day."

"I dunno. She seemed super serious about it."

Even though I couldn't see anything through the layers of tulle, I could imagine Carly tugging the bottom of her headwrap. Then the door creaked closed, and they were gone. If they had been emissaries from Noah, they weren't very good at it.

Noah himself was much more effective.

He has German right before I have Spanish, which is very inconvenient. Most days, I manage to avoid him, but today, he was waiting for me.

"I'd like to talk to you," he said.

"I have to get to class." I tried to dodge, but he grabbed my arm. A wave of panic-lightning surged out from his fingers, shocking my heart.

"Since when do you care about Spanish?"

I swallowed. "I just don't want to talk to you."

"Oh, okay. I get it. You're not okay with *talking* to me. You're just okay pulling me on top of you and—"

I tore my arm away and covered my ears. "You know I didn't mean for that to happen. What do you want?" My voice sounded farther away than normal.

"I just want to know if Chloe's talked to you."

"She hasn't talked to me since June. Since you sent that text."

He leaned close, scrutinizing me, like he thought I was lying.

I flinched, pressing my palms into my ears so hard they burned.

"Jesus, you're jumpy." He huffed. "Okay. Well, if she talks to you, let me know what she says."

"Why?" I regretted it as soon as I said it. If I'd just said "Okay," the conversation would've been over.

He laughed, a harsh laugh. A rueful laugh. "Because in case you've forgotten, Chloe and I are in bad shape over *you*, so I'm counting on *you* to help me fix it."

He pried one of my hands off my ear. His fingers scalded my wrist, and my blood throbbed like it was about to burst from my veins.

"I love her, Jess," he said, his voice gentler, almost desperate. "It's like . . . when I'm with her, life makes so much more sense." He dropped my arm. "So I want you to talk to her. And then you'll tell me what she says."

It wasn't a question, but I answered anyway, my voice barely audible over the pounding in my head. "Yeah."

I slipped into the Spanish classroom, then slipped back out with a bathroom pass.

I wished I hadn't eaten the cafeteria sloppy joe for lunch. It burned more coming up than it had going down.

MIGHTY-PEN-JESS
Nov 14

REASON #28:
I finally got Chloe alone.

I waited for her outside the Science Hall bathroom.

I hoped Emily would forgive me for bailing on lunch early without explanation and also for surreptitiously pumping her for information about her brother's (and therefore Chloe's) Robotics class. They met in room 157. They had third lunch. Which meant as soon as the bell rang to end my lunch and start hers, she'd be heading to this exact bathroom to wash her hands. She was predictable.

With all the science classes surging into the hall, Chloe didn't see me lurking by the recycling bin. I probably wouldn't have seen *her*, what with the sensory overload, except that I knew where she'd be. I focused on the bathroom door, and when she marched inside, backpack bouncing against her chunky beige sweater, I followed.

She wasn't the only one in the bathroom, but I didn't know the other girl, so she didn't count. I knew exactly when

Chloe saw me behind her in the mirror because she froze. Like we were in a horror movie.

"I understand why you're avoiding me." I pitched my voice over the rush of the sinks. "There are so many reasons."

"I don't have anything to say to you." It was a flat statement. No exclamation point. No mask.

"Can you listen if I say something to *you*?" I asked.

"No." She twisted the faucet off, then flicked her hands. Water beaded on the cracked mirror. The other girl scuttled out the door.

"What happened was wrong," I said anyway, "and I didn't stop it, and now it's done, and you can't forgive me. It was unforgivable, wasn't it?" Right and wrong. Good and evil. Chloe and Jess.

The warning bell rang.

"I've got to go," she said.

I dodged in front of her as she stepped toward the door. "Can I please just tell you what happened? And then you can explain it to me, because I still don't understand *how* it happened. All I understand is that I'm so sorry that it physically hurts." It did. Everywhere. Like my lungs were full of fire, igniting every nerve in my body.

Chloe's forehead scrunched so low it nearly closed her eyes. "Do your words mean anything anymore? Aren't they all stories? You tell a story where I date the boy you tell me to, and still you're the main character." She clutched the bottom of her sweater, keeping her hands from flapping.

"Hannah says you're writing blog posts, trying to rewrite the story of me and Noah with yourself at the center like some sort of antihero. But you're not the antihero—you're the villain, and the story of you and me is over."

Every matter-of-fact word was a thorn poking into a different part of me, slowly deflating me until I was barely standing, a limp husk that she brushed past to reach the door.

And then the final barb as the door closed behind her, your word in Chloe's voice:

"Slut."

MIGHTY-PEN-JESS
Nov 18

REASON #29:
I am a coward.

Hannah, do you remember the summer before seventh grade when we did swim camp together? Do you remember that one day we ended early, and you, Kate Heston, and I walked to your house to wait for our rides? We sat on the dining room table and ate stale Cheetos and gossiped about your fellow popular girls. You laughed so hard telling us how Pearl Wu's voice cracked on a high note during choir and she blushed so much you could see the red through the two inches of foundation she had slathered on her face. And I laughed, too. Because it felt so good to be included in the conversation. Like I was one of you.

But the next day, when I saw you at Sweet Frog with all your friends and you looked past me like I was a ghost or a speck of dust in the sunlight, it was my turn to blush. I wasn't even wearing foundation.

Brooklyn, do you remember Hannah's ninth birthday party? I was there. I'm sure it was just because Hannah's mom insisted she invite all the girls in our class, even the cringe ones. But I was there in the basement when Hannah laughed at your pink dress and long blond hair and called you Barbie. I laughed along, but inside I felt gross. Because I could see how hurt you were, your cheeks pink, your words too fast and too high and too thin.

I couldn't understand why, though. Isn't it good to be a Barbie? It must be better than being a—what did you call me yesterday?—a cave troll?

Alexis, we were never friends. But we could have been. We had Chloe in common. We both get A's on AP Lit papers, and we both laughed when last year's prom committee chose the theme "Perchance to Dream" because we knew that line in *Hamlet* is a reference to hell. And according to Cam, you're nice. *To everyone.*

But we aren't friends. And we aren't friends because you chose them over me. And being polite to my face doesn't make up for trashing me behind my back.

So, I'm sure you all can imagine why tagging you in these posts brings a little thrill to my fingertips and curls the edges of my lips in a faint but satisfying smirk.

But every time I start to tag her, my smirk fades and my fingers freeze. Every time I think of her, it feels like someone is gouging out my intestines with a spork. And this morning, when I peered out my kitchen window through the gelatinous raw-egg muck dripping down the pane and saw her Volt tearing out of the parking lot, the half-digested oatmeal in my stomach hardened into cement, and an invisible drawstring pulled tight in my throat.

And I tagged you instead. Because in the deepest, most secret part of myself, I am a coward.

And it's easier to hate you than to admit I should be mad at her, too.

MIGHTY-PEN-JESS
Nov 27

REASON #30:
Despite your best efforts, I am still kind of thankful.

I texted Julia to remind her that Dad invited us for Thanksgiving. I knew she wasn't planning to come (she hadn't visited Dad once since she turned eighteen), but I still text her every time, just to be sure she feels the appropriate stabs of guilt.

I think my jaw actually dropped when I saw her waiting at the foot of the stairs wearing a stylish yet appropriately modest burgundy sweater.

She looked up from her phone. "What?"

"I didn't think you were coming," I said.

"I'm not." She slipped the phone into her bag and shrugged into her peacoat. "I'm going to Albert's."

"Who's Albert?"

She rolled her eyes. "The guy I've been dating for a year and a half. Geez, Jessie, get online once in a while."

I didn't bring up the fact that we'd lived together all

summer and she hadn't mentioned this Albert. (Or maybe she had mentioned him. I will admit: I was kind of distracted this summer.)

Now that she'd brought it up, I realized I had seen a lot of this one guy on her social media.

"Is he kind of tall? Asian?"

"Very good. You do know how to use the internet." She made as if to pat me on the head, but I dodged. Her phone dinged. "I'm out."

"What about Mom? Are you just leaving her alone?"

She stopped in the doorway, scowling at me. "No. *You're* leaving her alone. I only made plans with Albert *after* she told me she was working." She swept out. I followed as far as the doorway to get a peek at Albert but was disappointed. The windows of his SUV were tinted. Julia paused at the car and waved. "Be sure to tell Rob I said go to hell!" she called cheerfully.

"Julia says hi," I told my dad as I slid into the passenger seat of his midlife-crisis-red Mustang convertible.

"Good to see you, Bean." He planted an awkward kiss in my hair as I fumbled with the seat belt.

"Can you turn the radio off?" I asked automatically.

His thick eyebrows lowered over his aviators. "Why?"

I flushed. "Oh, uh. No, you don't have to. I just . . . you know, Christmas music already, right?"

"Yeah? Okay." He switched the radio off. "How's school?"

"Okay. How's work?"

It was the magic question. He spent the next ten minutes elucidating me on his latest business venture ("get-rich-quick scheme," Julia would say) as we zoomed down the tollway. I found myself distracted by the way his beard bobbed as he talked. It was new, and it moved awkwardly in the wind, like it was too thick and matted in some places. I wondered if he dyed it to keep it so black. Mom's hair went gray a few years ago.

"So, what do you think? Is it a winner?" he shouted over the wind.

"Uh, I guess?" I shouted back. "I mean, I can imagine that someone who has a lot of cats might want a Jacuzzi for them."

"People are wild about their pets."

"Yeah. Um . . . Would a cat be willing to get into a Jacuzzi? Don't they hate water?"

"That's a myth, Bean. Don't be so gullible." He pulled off at a different exit than I was used to.

"Did Rachel move?"

"We're not going to Rachel's. This year, it's just you and me." He tossed a handful of coins into the toll basket. "Damn antiquated system. Who the hell has exact change anymore?"

"I think it said you could get one of those pass things."

He grunted.

Dad not living with Rachel threw a wrench in some of my plans. Rachel liked me, and her house was in the Northstar High School district. Since my disastrous conversation with Chloe, it had occurred to me that maybe distance from Chloe wasn't the problem. Maybe *proximity to Chloe* was. Maybe what I really needed was to switch schools, find a new theatre department, find a new life. Yes, it would mean no Cam and no Emily and no Mr. Barton and I wouldn't be head of the lit mag anymore and probably a bunch of other changes I'd hate, but it would have to be better than my life right now, wouldn't it? "T-day" was my chance to broach the subject with Dad.

We passed a gas station with half the lights out and turned into a run-down apartment complex with too many letters fallen off the sign to make out the name. We definitely weren't in Northstar territory, but it might have been Jefferson High. I decided to stick with the plan. Just as long as it wasn't Stone Bridge.

Dad pulled into a spot marked 902. A second spot marked 902 housed a gleaming Harley (also midlife-crisis red).

"I've never been to your place before. It's exciting!"

"Yeah? Yeah, it sure is!" He motioned me up the stairs and unlocked a weathered green door.

I think he'd made some effort to clean. It was mostly clutter, not actual filth. Dishes dripped in a drying rack. Several laundry baskets lined one wall. It kind of resembled my bedroom, actually.

I started clearing the mail off the kitchen table and stacking it on the floor (there really wasn't another surface available). "Do you need help in the kitchen?"

"I thought we'd do something special this year." Dad opened the fridge and pulled out a paper bag. "Jade Dragon!"

He'd gotten egg rolls and sweet-and-sour chicken because "I know it's your favorite, Jessie Bean." It was. In kindergarten. The whole meal felt a little bit like my five-year-old self's dream Thanksgiving: special time with Daddy, eating deep-fried chicken dipped in sugar syrup off paper plates.

He and Rachel must have split up. He couldn't have ever brought her here. I shuddered to think what the woman with a display of meticulously dusted ceramic pottery on a credenza in her dining nook would think of the overflowing trash can and peeling particleboard furniture.

"Are you still working at Walgreens?"

"Nah. I couldn't stay there. No chance of advancement, you know? They keep bringing in these corporate stooges for the management jobs when they were damn lucky to have me. Too damn lucky."

"So, where are you working now?"

"Not at some nine-to-five. I'm putting my time in on the Kit-Cuzzi. This is the one, Bean. By Christmas, you'll be looking at a rich man!"

"Can't wait!" There was no way it would happen. He'd said that exact thing like a thousand times. But pointing that out might have soured him on the idea I was about to propose. My knees were jiggling, shaking the table, but the Chinese-food nostalgia stoked my courage enough that I got the words out. "Any chance I could come live with you?"

Dad's plastic fork hovered halfway between his plate and his beard. An ooze of neon-pink sauce dripped from the chicken onto the tabletop.

I plowed on. "It's just, things are rough at school."

Dad lowered his fork. "Boy trouble?"

"More like, um, all-humans trouble?" My face was on fire, and the Chinese food in my stomach felt less like courage and more like a sack of rocks.

"Look, Bean, you know I'd love to help you."

Here came the *but*.

"But . . ." He gestured around us. "This isn't a big apartment."

"I don't need—"

He shook his head with finality. "It's a one-bedroom. And it's my office, too, these days. I just don't have room for you. I'm sorry."

"It's okay," I said, pushing past the slight teeter in my voice.

My dad continued expounding upon the many benefits of the Kit-Cuzzi, and my pulse slowed its sprint to a jog. Maybe it was because the answer hadn't been surprising (in fact, I might have dropped dead from shock if he'd said yes). But actually, the emotion I was feeling came closer to relief, which was weird.

I tuned out most of my dad's Kit-Cuzzi prattle over dinner, turning the question over in my mind: Am I *happy* at Stone Bridge?

I think maybe I am. As much as I hate AP Calc, I love having it with Cam. I love seeing Emily and Mr. Barton in Creative Writing. I love being in charge of the lit mag. I love that I know all of SBHS's nooks and crannies from years of late-night rehearsal breaks. It feels like home. It feels like *mine*.

Sure, sometimes life sucks, mainly when I run into one of you. Or Chloe. Or Noah. Or if someone somewhere turns on a radio. Or—

Not the point. The point is that despite what I have to believe have been your best efforts to make me miserable, most of the time, I'm not miserable. In fact, most of the time, I'm mostly happy.

So, happy Thanksgiving. And if I might offer a suggestion: Since it hasn't worked so far, why not give it up? I'm sure you could find a more productive use of your time.

MIGHTY-PEN-JESS
Nov 28

REASON #31:
I am a car thief.

It's beginning to look way too much like Christmas. Everywhere, Santas are mocking me. They grin and ring celebratory bells and quiver on people's front lawns like the giant fans up their butts are doing something decidedly inappropriate.

The music is worse. I never realized how many Christmas songs are about love—like sexy love, not God love. Why? Christmas is about either Baby Jesus or Santa (depending on your religious/political affiliation), and neither one is especially sexy. I mean, who looks at a four-hundred-pound man in a red sweatsuit and says, *Let's get it on!*?

No, wait, don't answer that. That's a porn site I definitely do *not* want to know about.

Anyway, I left the radio off today when I stole my mom's car.

I say "stole," but I fully intended to bring it back, because unlike you three, I don't have a driver's license yet. Possibly ever. I failed my behind-the-wheel test, and I'm not sure when I'll get the courage to try it again. (And I'm so sorry, Ms. Franklin, that I "hesitated" at green lights. I suppose you'd prefer if I blew through them without checking for other cars so that we could be T-boned and spread out on the asphalt like strawberry jam?)

But I technically *know how* to drive—and if anything, I'm *too defensive* of a driver—so I felt only slightly guilty about breaking the law to drive to Chloe's mom's house.

I wasn't planning to stop. Thanksgiving had me feeling nostalgic, so I just wanted to see the garland wrapped around the porch railing and the white reindeer grazing on the front lawn. I nudged the car right up against the sidewalk in the cul-de-sac and shifted into park. (Continuing to drive while staring at Christmas lights is a definite no-no for the overly defensive, unlicensed driver.)

The Christmas decorations were a bit of a letdown. It was eleven a.m., so the lights weren't lit, although I could see them nestled amid the garland, sun glinting off their plastic coverings. It was plain green garland this year. Chloe and I used to put it up together, wrapping the garland, then tying on pinecones and clusters of fake berries at mathematically specified intervals that Chloe calculated to achieve Maximum Realism and Aesthetic Appeal. Maybe it was too big a job for one person.

I was about to shift the car back into drive when the front

door opened. I slumped in my seat—or tried to, nearly severing my neck on the cross-body strap of the still-buckled seat belt. I gagged, wriggling back up, then squeaked in dismay as someone knocked on the passenger window.

At first, I was shocked that Chloe was smiling at me. Then I realized that, of course, it wasn't Chloe.

Have you met Dr. Barton? She's basically Chloe's older twin. But there are differences if you know them well enough. Dr. Barton's warm brown skin is a shade lighter, her freckles a few more numerous, and of course there's the silver stud in her eyebrow. She wears her hair in short Sisterlocks that bounced around her head when she pumped her arm to get me to roll down the window.

My mom's car is too old to have working windows, so I had no choice but to unbuckle, open my door, and shuffle sheepishly around the car. Dr. Barton was wearing "work clothes," which for her are jeans and a blazer over a hot-pink SCIENCE IS REAL T-shirt. She held her arms wide and crushed me in a hug before I could object. Her briefcase thumped against my back.

"It's so good to see you, Jess. I'm glad I stepped out of the house at this exact moment! God is good."

It took me a minute to process her words. "Umm, okay?" She released me from her bear hug, and I wrapped my arms around myself. I hadn't brought a jacket because it hadn't seemed that cold when I left my apartment.

"Come inside. We need to talk."

The chill bit through my skin, right to my lungs. "Aren't you going to work or something?"

"I'm not in a rush." She started across the lawn. I debated leaping back into the car and tearing down the street, but I was suddenly feeling super dysregulated. Knowing my luck, I'd probably crash.

Walking into Chloe's house was like walking into the past. I wavered in the foy-*ay*, filling my senses with the pattern of the wood floor, the aroma of slow-cooker veggie curry, the warm updraft from the heating registers in the floor. I wondered if this was how Hamlet felt when he returned home from Wittenberg to find everything and nothing the same. Did the castle still feel like home once he realized its king had betrayed him?

"I've got orange soda, if you want some."

I followed Dr. Barton's voice to the kitchen. The oak bench squawked on the tile as I took a seat at the farmhouse table across from her. She slid me a cold can.

I ran my tongue over my teeth. "My mom is expecting me back."

"Your mom didn't know you left."

The chill from outside must have followed us to the kitchen because my whole body froze, right down to my blood vessels. "But—"

"I texted her. She knows you're okay, and she's getting a ride over to pick you up. And the car." Her voice softened. "You're lucky you didn't get pulled over, honey."

"But how did you know—"

"Jess, your mom and I still talk, even if you and Chloe don't. I know you don't have a license. I also know you're failing some classes."

"Not failing." My knee started jiggling, my tongue scrubbing at my gums.

"Look, your mom's been bugging me to convince you to come into the center to talk with one of our therapists." She reached across the table and popped the tab on my soda can. "But I'm not going to do that."

"She . . . You're . . . not going to convince me?"

"Nope." She took a swig from her water bottle.

I always feel a little weird around Dr. Barton, partly because she's really cool, but mostly because she's a therapist. She's never been *my* therapist, though. I'm not sure if the psychologist I used to see at the Autism Center is still there, but I stopped going before I met Chloe. By like third or fourth grade, I'd figured out how to mimic other people just enough to seem . . . "normal" is definitely not the right word, but normal *enough*. I hid my weirdnesses: kept my drumming fingers under my desk, stifled the urge to rock until I was safely hidden in a bathroom stall, nodded and smiled and fought my way past the distracting noises to understand what people were saying to me. I blended, and my dad (who had never believed I was autistic in the first place) said I could stop going to therapy.

"It's okay to regulate," Dr. Barton said.

"What?"

She nodded at my hands, which were attempting to hold down my jiggling knee. "Flap, tap, clap, rap—whatever you do to regulate, it won't bother me."

I pressed harder on my knee, though the desire to move it shuddered through me. "I thought you weren't going to therapize me."

"I'm not, but while you're here, I do want to convince you that it's okay to let yourself be autistic."

"Umm . . . I mean, I can't really help it?"

"Uh-huh. And you're not fighting a losing battle with your left leg right now?"

I flushed and released my knee, letting it jiggle with wild abandon. "Happy now?"

"Always." She took another swig of water. "Do you let yourself regulate at school?"

"When I can't help it."

"Why do you need to help it? What harm would it do?"

"You know what's super fun? Having everyone stare at me and laugh about me behind my back. Suuuuper fun."

"Sounds like their problem, not yours."

"Really, though? *Is* it their problem? Because other people have *no* problem making fun of me. It doesn't hurt them to do it, and if you say something here about sticks and stones, I am leaving."

There was a long pause. "I'm sorry, Jess. I didn't mean to make light of bullying. Heaven knows I see my fair share."

I remembered the day Chloe's dad had driven us over to Dr. Barton's house after school to find her scrubbing the N-word off the garage door. We'd all helped—Mr. Barton, too. My stomach turned again at the memory. "I know I shouldn't complain. I can blend in, and I know you . . ." I trailed off. *You don't know*, Chloe would have told me. *You have compassion, but you don't* know.

"You're right that it's not the same as racism, but I was actually referring to the bullying that autistic people face. I've seen a share of that, too. Chloe's told you her uncle is autistic?"

I nodded.

"When we were kids, no one believed James was autistic because he was Black. Never mind he had all the traits. If he couldn't focus on a task, they told him he was lazy. If he spoke bluntly, they told him he was rude and angry. I went into neuropsych to make sure kids like James and Chloe and you got the same treatment as the white boys."

"I'm not Black, though."

"No, and it will always be harder for people of color like Chloe and James. But you girls, and trans and enby kids—you *all* have to fight to be seen, to have your autism seen."

My fingers fluttered against the soda can, tapping an uneasy rhythm in the condensation. "I think I'd rather be invisible."

"Are you invisible, though? Or do people just demand that you be someone you're not?"

I filled my mouth with soda to avoid answering. The refrigerator hum seemed louder in our silence.

Finally, she said, "I gather school sucks?"

Dr. Barton is not one for subtlety.

When I didn't answer, she added, "I can't get Chloe to tell me what went down between you two."

I studied the tabletop.

"Guess you're not going to tell me, either."

I almost smiled. It was the way she said it. Not in a defeated-guilt-trip way. Not in a demanding-interrogation way. Just casual, matter-of-fact. "Sorry not sorry?"

She laughed as the doorbell rang.

"Judgment day." Her bench scraped back. "Prepare your excuses."

I slumped.

"I'll put in a good word for you." She paused in the kitchen entryway. "And Jess, whether you decide to come in to the center or not—"

Not.

"—I hope you'll remember that it's okay to expect that people accept you for who you are—to demand that. And it's okay to ask for other things, too. Extra help on an assignment, a study buddy for a test, patience, forgiveness—ask for what you need, okay?"

As she walked from the room, I scrutinized her body

language, looking for clues that she knew what happened on Memorial Day, that she was lying when she said Chloe hadn't told her what I'd done.

But she opened the door with her usual laid-back cheer and let my irate mother into the foy-*ay*.

MIGHTY-PEN-JESS
Nov 29

REASON #32:
I suck at all relationships—not just friendships.

Even though my mom had done more hugging and *Thank-God-you're-all-right*-ing than yelling, the Car Theft Fiasco got me grounded for the rest of Thanksgiving break, which meant no escape from Julia the All-Knowing and her aura of superiority. I was lying on the couch going down an autistic rabbit hole on my phone (as in a rabbit hole *about* autistics, not a rabbit hole *because* I'm autistic, although if I'm honest, maybe a little of both) when Julia returned from her boyfriend's. Her keys jingled in the lock, but she didn't open the door. I almost went out to see what happened to her. Five minutes later, she came inside wrinkling her nose.

"Why did Chloe Barton and some Kylie Jenner clone just leave a bag of what appears to be dog shit on our front mat?"

"Welcome to my life," I muttered.

"Well, if you're planning to incite any more people to

throw shit at you, at least have the courtesy to wait until after I leave tomorrow so I won't have to smell it."

"I'll do my best." I pushed myself off the couch and headed for the front door.

"I already threw it in the dumpster."

"Oh." What an uncharacteristically altruistic gesture. "Thanks."

She handed me an orange soda from the fridge. "So what happened with you and the BFF?"

"Like you care."

"If I didn't care, I wouldn't ask. But whatever. Be an asshole." She grabbed a soda for herself and slammed the fridge so hard all the condiments clanked together. As if she was annoyed at *me* for not welcoming her to pry into my personal life. "And I had a great Thanksgiving, by the way, not that *you'd* care." She swept past me and up the stairs.

You'd think that having known me my entire life, Julia would have figured out by now that I don't make small talk. I guess I could have asked about this alleged boyfriend she spent Thanksgiving with. But honestly, if I can't get excited about making out with the hottest guy at school—and if having almost-sex with SBHS Drama Department's leading man turned me into an autistic meltdown incarnate—I probably can't convincingly fake an interest in whatever Julia does with some guy I've never met.

I sat on the couch and held a sip of soda in my mouth

until I could feel my teeth beginning to dissolve. I counted the people who hated me. Chloe. Noah. Julia. You three and probably anyone who is friends with you and/or friends with Chloe. Who else is Chloe friends with now? Certainly some choir girls. She's definitely mentioned Pearl Wu. They probably hang out more now. Did they hang out before?

How could I have been her BFF for so long and know so little about her life? I'd read enough blog posts by autistic Black women in the last hour to be 100 percent positive that Chloe has experienced hate she never mentioned to me. And why would she bring it up? I'd probably witnessed some of it without *seeing* it, like she and I were operating on different planes of existence. Only just today did it occur to me that the Angry Perfume Lady at the mall may have been making a racist comment when she accused Chloe of being loud. It stands to reason I missed other things, too. I'd never thought to check if she felt safe at school or ask about what being autistic was like for her or who she hung out with while I was at theatre rehearsals or what she liked to do without me.

Maybe we'd been growing apart for longer than I realized. Reciting Tony Award winners and staging English-class jewelry heists is fine when you're a kid. She's an adult now, as of 8:13 this morning. Any other year, we'd have spent the morning together, shoving Dr. Barton's vegan chocolate cupcakes in each other's faces. It's the first birthday in five years that we've been apart.

And yet, even with you three and Pearl Wu at her disposal, she spent at least part of her birthday bringing me a bag of dog shit.

Maybe we're still closer than I thought.

 PRIVATE
Dec 1

REASON #33:
My trash tends to travel.

I'm not sharing this post with the cyberbullies. Or Jeff Watkins. Or whoever the two readers of my blog are.

I'm not planning to share it with *anyone*.

I knew something was up as soon as I walked into Mr. Barton's class after Thanksgiving break. He should've been in the teachers' lounge getting a granola rock from the vending machine, but he was at his desk. Not *sitting* at his desk—standing behind it with his fists pressing down on either side of his planner, his shoulders hunched like he was preparing to give a sumo wrestler a piggyback ride.

When I came in, he looked up, then immediately back down at the desk.

This was not going to be good.

I eased myself into a chair, pulling my notebook and pens from my backpack like I was a hobbit trying not to wake a dragon. In my peripheral vision, I watched Mr. Barton opening and closing his mouth, trying out words. I couldn't read his lips without looking directly at him, and I wasn't about to do that. Everyone who watches fantasy movies knows that if you look the dragon in the face, it will awaken.

He finally straightened. Finally turned his head toward me. Finally opened his mouth to for-real speak.

And Emily walked into the room.

And Mr. Barton walked out.

"Where's he going?" Emily asked, pulling her newly dyed evergreen hair into a messy bun.

I shrugged. "Granola bar?"

The class filtered in, and the late bell rang. I knew I couldn't escape whatever conversation Mr. Barton was plotting, but I held out hope that he wouldn't accost me during class. The deadline for lit mag submissions had been before Thanksgiving break, so we now had a lot of work to do: sorting through those submissions and making sure everyone in the class got an equitable number to read and understood the rating scale. As senior editor, I should have been very involved in that process. In charge of it, really. Indispensable.

And yet . . .

"Jess, may I talk to you in the hallway?"

Everyone stopped chatting and stared at Mr. Barton's tense frame in the doorway. They hadn't missed the awkward in his voice. No one could have any delusions that this was just an editor/teacher-advisor consultation.

I slunk after him into the empty hall. He looked around

to be sure we were alone, which was bizarre because surely he could berate me about my abysmal grades even with an audience. Actually, he had never looked this uncomfortable while talking to me about grades. Mr. Barton never looked uncomfortable about anything. He was a totally laid-back human. So, whatever this was, it was very, very not good.

But then he pulled a crumpled piece of notebook paper from his slacks pocket, and I knew it was worse than not good. It was Armageddon.

"That's not mine," I said instinctively, though I knew it was the poem I'd thrown away before break. The poem I hadn't wanted anyone to see.

"It's your handwriting."

My scrawl was unmistakable.

Lying
To you.
To me.
To him.
    With him.
        Under him.

My heart stuttered. "You read your trash?"

"No, but I do read papers I find wadded up under the desks. Because sometimes they contain brilliant works of art."

"And sometimes they contain something really personal that you don't want your teacher to read." Breath shuddered into me like my lungs were experiencing an earthquake.

"Is the 'you' in this poem Chloe? Is that who you're talking to?"

My breath quaked back out again. "*I'm* not talking in the poem. It's the *speaker of the poem*, not the poet. Do you need to take your own class?" My voice was louder than his because I couldn't control it. It careened out of me, bouncing wild off the wall tiles, battering back against my ears.

"I'm not . . ." He paused, his jaw working as he chewed the inside of his cheeks. "I just want you to know, it's okay if it's about Chloe. You can write about anything, even people close to me, and it won't affect your grade."

"Fine. Can I go inside now?"

"No. I, ah . . ." He tugged a handkerchief from his pocket and dabbed at the top of his bald head, and for the first time, I wondered whether the primary purpose of hair might be to absorb anxiety sweat. "The topic of this poem. It sounds like . . . Were you . . . I don't want to assume I'm understanding your poem—"

"Then don't." I snatched it back. It sliced through the skin of my fingertip. I fixed my stare on the tiny red bloom soaking into the notebook paper.

And knowing
            I wasn't—

I couldn't under-stand.

But you. If you could under-stand—

My heart was galloping, gaining so much speed with each passing moment that I knew it would soon burst from my chest. This was how I died. Alone in the Language Arts Hall with no one but my favorite teacher and the trash-can ants to mourn me.

The door creaked open. "Mr. Barton?" Emily murmured. "Can we have Jess back? She needs to divide up the submissions."

"Why don't you go ahead and do that, Emily," Mr. Barton said.

"Me?" Her voice was a mouse squeak. "I—I'm not qualified—"

"Sure you are. You're a born leader, just like Jess. Tell you what: give it a try. We'll be in to help in a few minutes."

I glanced at Emily, whose eyes had widened in a combination of terror and regret.

"Okay," she whispered, more to herself than to us, as she eased the door shut.

I turned back to the wrinkled, bloodstained poem.

"You have some heavy stuff on your mind, Jess." His voice was uncharacteristically thick. "Are there more poems like this?"

The paper in my hand blurred. I closed my eyes, shook my head.

"I wish there were. Not so I could read them. Just so I could know that you're . . . I worry about you less when you're writing."

My eyes twitched behind my eyelids. "Why do you worry about me?"

"Well, before I found this poem, I worried because I didn't see you around the condo anymore; you showed up at class at the last second; you missed assignments—and the ones you completed didn't sound like you at all. Now . . ." His lungs suffered an earthquake of their own, the breath huffing from his body uneven and pained. "Now I think I understand a little better, but I'm worried a little more."

"I don't think you do understand."

"If the 'you' is Chloe, is the 'him' Noah?"

My eyes flew open, lava leaking from their corners, my whole face volcanic. "Do you really want to talk about this? Do you really want me to tell you how I had almost-sex with your daughter's boyfriend?"

He flinched, which sent a perverse stab of satisfaction to my already bleeding heart. But his voice was measured when he said, "That's not exactly how I interpreted this poem."

"Then you interpreted it wrong."

"Okay."

"That's it? *Okay?* You read a private poem that I obviously meant to throw away, you come to all kinds of bullshit conclusions, and then when I correct you, you just say *okay*?"

"You know your poem better than I do. You get to tell me what it's about, not the other way around."

My body imploded, crunching down to the floor, my head hiding between my knees. I squeezed them against my ears until it hurt and hoped I wasn't saying aloud the refrain that was shouting in my head.

I don't know what it's about.

Or maybe the not-knowing *is* what the poem is about. All the questions I couldn't answer—*Why did I? Was it really me in that room? How did this happen? Did I want it to? Was it my fault?*—they swirl in my head and never resolve into a clear yes and no, right and wrong, truth and lie, and the only person who is guaranteed to make sense of this, guaranteed to see the line between good and evil and where I fall, is Chloe. And she won't tell me.

Except, she did tell me.

Slut.

Only it doesn't seem like the right answer.

The door creaked again. I couldn't make out Emily's whisper, only Mr. Barton's kind but firm assurance that we'd be back soon. I pulled my head from between my knees as the door clicked shut.

Mr. Barton was sitting beside me, his legs out straight in front of him, his neon-green argyle socks poking from the tops of his Pumas. He waited until a pair of curious sophomores had shuffled by before asking, "Do you want to talk about it?"

"No."

"Do you want to write about it?"

"No. It . . . it hurts. Thinking about how I . . . I just can't write about it."

"I get that." He fixed his eyes on the door opposite us, probably to spare me the humiliation of having him look at my undoubtedly blotchy, tear-streaked face. "But keeping all that hurt inside can cause more damage. At least that's what I have gleaned from spending over a decade married to a psychologist."

"It must have been awful being married to Dr. Barton."

It was an honest (and obvious) statement on my part, but it surprised a laugh out of him, a low burst that cooled the air between us. "Sometimes it was. We . . . weren't the best fit. She's a great person, understand."

"But she can read minds."

His lips quirked. "She can, can't she? That wasn't it, though. We just made each other worse people somehow."

We sat, listening to the hum of the HVAC, the murmur of English teachers from the closed doors around us, and the increasingly raucous din from the classroom we had abandoned.

"I had an epiphany over Thanksgiving," I told him.

"Oh?"

"Yeah. I'm happy. Like, happy with my life most of the time. Maybe seventy percent of the time."

"Seventy percent, huh? So your happiness is getting a C?"

"Exactly. Average. I'm average happy."

"That's good." His jaw worked like it wasn't sure whether it should let the next words out. "But this poem . . . I suspect you wrote it because you *had* to. Because some part of that thirty percent of you had to make itself heard."

"It was torture," I confessed. "Writing this." *Feeling* this.

He nodded, still staring across the hall. Sweat beaded on his brow like this conversation was as much a workout as a 5K. "Writing can open wounds. It can also heal them. In fact, sometimes you have to open a wound before you can heal it. Otherwise, it might get infected, and—hmm, that metaphor is getting a bit graphic." He swung his head toward me, his deep-brown eyes meeting mine for an instant before I dropped my gaze. "Do you understand what I'm trying to say, though?"

"You're saying that you want me to torture myself so I don't die of gangrene."

"Not— Kind of. I just keep thinking . . . you titled the poem 'Lying,' but it's the most truthful thing you've written all year."

That was the truth.

"The best writing connects us to emotional truths. They don't have to be big truths or even serious truths. They just have to be true."

"Truth sucks."

"Not all truth sucks. That piece you wrote last year about the chemical elements—it was full of wordplay and subverted tropes. I'd say the emotional truth of that play was that pulling the rug out from under our expectations is hilarious and delightful."

"Chloe wrote that."

"Jess." Mr. Barton's eyebrows rose high on his forehead. "I love my daughter. But she did not write that play. She may have helped, but the voice was yours."

I scuffed the heel of my orthopedic shoe across the tile. "She *mostly* wrote it."

"Hmm." He pulled a purple pen from his shirt pocket and tugged the poem off my lap. When he handed it back, there was a giant A across the top. "I'll put this in my grade book to replace one of your missing assignments."

I nodded, afraid that if I opened my mouth to utter a thank-you, the tears would start flowing again.

"And for next week, I want another truthful piece. It doesn't have to be about *this* truth if that's too hard. Maybe find a truth in your childhood and build a story around that. Nonfiction or fiction, poetry or prose or scripts. I just want you to keep writing."

I nodded again.

"And in the interest of truth . . ." He hoovered a giant breath through his nose. "I'm not a psychologist."

"Umm . . ."

"I'm not done. I'm not a psychologist . . . so I don't know what's the right thing to do."

Ants of anxiety scurried under my skin. "What do you mean?"

"I'm worried about you."

"I'm average happy," I reminded him, my voice rising a few pitches with each word.

"I need to talk to Mr. Goodman about this conversation."

A new army of anxiety ants hatched in my throat. "I don't need a counselor."

"I can't hold this alone, Jess. I need to make sure you're taken care of. And I honestly think—whatever it was that happened—you shouldn't hold it alone, either."

"Please don't talk to him." I hugged my knees, crushing them against my chest, smushing the crumpled poem against my solar plexus.

"You can come with me if you want."

"No."

"I hope you'll forgive me."

When I didn't answer, he pushed himself up with a groan. I fixed my eyes on his Pumas, which paused outside the classroom door.

"You don't have to come in until you're ready. You can go splash some water on your face if you need—"

"Don't-tell-him-about-the-poem." My words came out in a rush, tangling with one another in a nearly unintelligible blob.

"I won't." His deep voice reassured some of the many ants still scrambling inside me. "That's your private writing. And I understand that you don't want to talk about it with me. I'm always here if you change your mind, but I won't bring it up again." He hesitated, his long, slow breaths audible in the silent hallway. When he spoke again, his words tangled, too, urgent and awkward. "I have to ask. I have to. Would Noah— Is Chloe safe with him?"

My head snapped up, propelled by sheer surprise at the question that had never even occurred to me, the answer to which was so automatic, it left my mouth before I had a chance to think about it. "Of course."

He let his breath out in a whoosh, bobbing his head, either convinced by my assurance or trying to reassure himself. But I suddenly wasn't sure of anything. The whole hallway tilted when he opened the classroom door, the squeak of the hinges whispering, *Is she safe with him?*

I was still groggy with surprise thirty seconds later when Emily poked her head out. "Everyone okay?" she asked, her eyes darting away from my blotchy face and deepening frown.

"Yeah," I said, and wondered if it were true.

                                        Lying
To you.
To me.
To him.
                    With him.
                                        Under
him.

And knowing
                    I wasn't—
I couldn't
                                        under-
stand.

But you.
If you could
                                        under-
stand—

if you remembered
                                        lying
                                        under
the loft on purple shag,
light dancing through beads
                    and you
goddess,
            friend,

patches for my
patchwork brain—

if you remembered,
there I'd be:
                                                    lying
                with you,
                                                  under-
standing
(finally)
how it can be
                                            the truth

that I didn't choose it
didn't do it,
didn't move,
couldn't breathe
couldn't be, even
                though, I am   lying,
                I was   lying
                                      under.

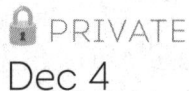
Dec 4

REASON #34:
I have mounted my final offensive.

I crumpled the poem a thousand times.

Crumpled, then smoothed, then crumpled—until the pen marks started to rub into dust.

So I rewrote it.

Then crumpled it again.

I'm not really mad at Mr. Barton for talking to Mr. Goodman (even though it meant I had to spend an hour in the converted-janitor's-closet-that-is-his-office listening to him spout nonsense about emotions and teenage hormones). Mr. Barton was just doing that thing all of us do when we have worries—or really any feelings—that are too big to contain: passing some of it on to someone else. Diluting through oversharing.

And I think he may have the right idea.

And that's why I wrote the poem again—typed it, actually, and printed it on a crisp sheet of white paper in the Computer Lab during lunch. I folded it as neatly as I could and printed Chloe's name on the back in careful letters.

Because if you want a wound to heal, you have to drain the pus.

If you want your direction to change, you have to apply a force.

So I didn't let my hands crunch around the paper, didn't let my feet turn the other way, and marched myself right up to her locker—my final march, the deciding battle that will let me know once and for all whether there is any hope of reclaiming lost ground—and slipped my truth inside.

MIGHTY-PEN-JESS
Dec 5

REASON #35:
I am a hypocrite.

Two Decembers ago, Chloe and I watched the Greta Gerwig *Little Women* together on a Friday night, huddled under a quilt on Dr. Barton's couch. It was really, really good. Especially Florence Pugh. I mean, she almost made me like Amy.

Almost.

"I would never have forgiven her," I said as Laurie pulled Amy from the hole in the ice and Jo kissed her cold, wet forehead.

Chloe frowned. She yanked off her glasses, cleaning them on the front of her shirt with three quick wipes. "So, if Julia burned our notebook, you'd let her drown?"

"Absolutely."

"I don't believe you."

Chloe never believed the worst in me. Maybe that's why it was such a blow when she found out what I'd done. Maybe that's why the apologies wouldn't take. Maybe that's why the truth wasn't enough to earn me a second chance.

When I opened my locker this morning and the confetti that had been my notebook—what should have been *our* notebook—fluttered out onto the tiles, the first thing I thought of was that night at her mom's house. Saoirse Ronan and Florence Pugh. The smell of the popcorn and the bits of kernel my tongue kept finding as it ran over my teeth.

Chloe was at the end of the hall, and before Hannah hurried her into the bathroom, I saw her gnaw at her lip.

And that was when I knew exactly how much of a hypocrite I am. Because it had only happened two seconds ago, and I had already forgiven her.

She wasn't even drowning.

Dec 7

REASON #36:
Even my (current) best friend thinks I'm a horrible person.

Sunday's study session with Cam needed to be epic because if I failed the Calc midterm, my mom was going to ground me. Possibly forever. Possibly literally, in a wooden box six feet under.

We'd stocked the cave under the stairs with a cooler full of orange soda and (the ultimate study jolt) Monster. We had our Calc books, our graphing calculators, scratch paper, half a dozen sharpened pencils, and several binders of notes.

We made it through one page of the study guide before we got bored.

"I saw that friend of yours. The sophomore with the green hair," Cam said.

"Emily? Where?" I slammed my Calc book shut.

"Mario's. She and her girlfriend were on a date, I think. I was there with the team to celebrate the end of the season."

"That *is* something to celebrate."

"Yes, ha ha. Does she always talk that soft? I had to, like, bend halfway over to hear her."

"That is because you are a giraffe."

He didn't banter back. In fact, his face was alarmingly frowny. "She told me about your notebook."

"Ah." I opened the Calc book again, letting my eyes run over the blur of numbers and symbols on a page that may or may not have been relevant to the test. A blizzard of shredded paper swirled through my memories.

"I'm so sorry. It wasn't Alexis Jones, was it? That really doesn't sound like her."

I sighed. "No, this wasn't your precious Alexis Jones. This was definitely the work of Chloe Barton." No one else could have known so well how to hurt me. Also, no one else knew my locker combination.

"Oh." Cam tugged at the strings of his hoodie, worrying the knotted ends between his fingers.

"It's not a big deal actually, since all my writing this year has been crap. It's not like I lost anything valuable."

"Oh. That's good, I guess."

"Yup." I flipped a page, pretended to scrutinize it, wondered what an "indefinite integral" was.

"And it's good you're moving on from her, since she, you know . . ."

"Is officially one of the Barbies now?" I felt proud of my voice, the way it tossed the words out like they weighed nothing at all.

Cam's hands stilled on his hoodie strings. There was a long pause before he said, "Brooklyn's in my AP Physics class."

I squinted at him. "And you're announcing this because..."

"I'm just saying, it's not fair to call her a Barbie. She's smart."

"Okay, Slutty Scientist Barbie."

"Seriously?" His face twisted, incredulous. "You—of all people—are going to call someone a slut?"

I flushed, but before I could decide whether I was angry or mortified, he groaned. "No, Jess, I'm not saying you *are* a slut. I'm saying I can't believe you're judging someone else that way. Are you saying she's a slut 'cause she's hot? Or 'cause of what she wears? Or who she dates?"

"I can't believe you're defending her."

"I'm not defending the way she's treating you. The things she's been saying about you suck. But in fact, that's kind of the point I'm trying to make."

"Oh my God, Cameron. If I want a lecture, I'll talk to my mom. Teach me math or get out of my house." I tried to keep my voice light, but it crackled.

A suffocating silence filled the cave. Every flip of a page, every scratch of pencil on paper, found my nerves like a gunshot. The inch of space that separated our bodies was a canyon. Unbridgeable.

"Do I need to know this integral thing?" I had begun to

rock gently, my body taking it upon itself to calm my skittering heart. "I think calculus is my Aaron Burr: smart, enigmatic, and destined to destroy me."

"Maybe if you spent more time on your math homework and less time listening to musicals, it would be less likely to shoot you." It might have been a joke, but he was still frowning.

"Or maybe if *you* spent more time teaching me and less time running off to your sportsball things—"

"Football."

"Whatever."

"No, not whatever." His tight voice sliced through the air. "I play football every fall and baseball every spring."

My tongue was suddenly a desert. I tried to smile, though it came out as a wince. "They're all the same. Throwing things. Hitting things. It's impossible to keep track." My shoulder blades bounced off the wall as I rocked harder.

"Last spring you did *Into the Woods*. You were Milky White the cow." His voice was quiet, controlled. Furious. "In the fall, you were on stage crew for *Paper or Plastic?*, which won the VTA competition and came second at SETC. You also did *Romeo and Juliet* as a Capulet sword fighter. The year before, Auntie Em in *The Wizard of Oz*, ensemble in *Antigone Now* for VTA, and stage manager for *The Importance of Being Earnest*. Freshman year, I wasn't even at this school, but I still know you were a techie in *Little Shop of Horrors* and an offstage voice in *The Miracle Worker*."

"You've made your point." My voice careened out of me. "And I agree. Theatre is *much* more interesting than sportsball."

He tensed before grabbing his books and crawling out of the cave.

"I was joking," I called, rocking back so hard that my head audibly cracked against the drywall.

The front door creaked open. "I know you *think* you were joking. But the reality is that I play two sports—the same two sports every year—and you don't care enough about me to even *pretend* to care about what I do."

I wish he had slammed the door. The soft click had a more disturbing finality than the close of a coffin.

I rocked under the stairs for a good ten minutes before crawling out and wandering to the kitchen, unsure whether I was hungry or thirsty or tired or just done. Maybe I should have put away the jokes, talked to him honestly for once.

JESS

```
The way my brain works . . . once I start
caring about something, I really, really
care about it. Like, if I started learn-
ing about football, I'd have to learn ALL
about football—the rules, the teams, the
players, the history, the everything. My
brain might quite literally explode from
```

the pressure of all this new information.
I have enough obsessions as it is, you
know?

Except...

                    CAMERON
           (quietly, a conviction)
I'm not asking you to care about football.
I'm asking you to care about me.

PRIVATE
Dec 8

REASON #37:
I Am a Coward, Act II

I am proud.
> I am judgmental.
> I am impulsive.
> I am quick to blame.
> I am slow to forgive.
> I am a bad student and a worse friend.
> I am lonely.
> I am exhausted.
> I am just so *done* with all of this.

But now you'll never know because I've gone through these posts and set them all to *private*.
> Because *privately* is how cowards admit that we're wrong.

🔒 PRIVATE
Dec 11

REASON #38:
I screwed up the best relationship in my life, and I'm not sure I can fix it.

To the boy in the parking lot scraping snow off the minivan:
a prose poem

I'll be taking the bus again this week.

It will be cold waiting at the stop. Cold avoiding the eyes of the other dozen kids from this apartment complex who don't know who I am. Or who do know who I am. Which is worse.

In Calculus tomorrow, it will be cold in the back corner by the crack in the window. Cold watching you not-watching me.

It will be cold coming home, seeing your van already back, knowing that if I knocked, your mom would give me a mug of hot cocoa and a slice of gingerbread, whether you wanted her to or not. That will be the coldest: the warmth that I'm too afraid to ask for.

Years ago, I wouldn't have been alone in the snow. My dad would be here, and Julia would be here, and we would squeal and run and pelt each other with snowballs. We had to go out as soon as it snowed because if we waited too long, it would turn to mud and slush. It always turns to mud and slush, faster than you think it will. Suddenly.

There's mud and slush now, under your boots while you circle the van, scraping white off white. But it's still snowing. Millions and billions of tiny flakes, and they'll stack and stack until everything is covered. And it won't matter anymore. Not the mud, not the slush, not the words from three days ago.

What if I made a snowball and threw it?
Would you catch it?
Would you want to?

Re: Prose Poem
From: Eli Barton
To: Jessica R. Lanza

Hi Jess,

This is another A. Keep it up! Get me two more pieces by the end of the month and you're caught up for the semester. Can you include this in your portfolio for Goldberg, or does it need to be a narrative? Have you thought about revising some of last year's pieces?

Mr. Barton

PRIVATE
Dec 12

REASON #39:
I talked to Noah today.

We both have first lunch on A-days. (So do the cyberbullies. So does Chloe. In related news, I hate my life.) I've always tried to avoid the bullies because the sight of them makes my stomach turn, but ever since Cam pointed out my own judgmental terribleness, I've been feeling guilty about the mean things I said about them publicly on my blog. Now the drive to avoid them is urgent and all-encompassing.

I thought that everyone who hates me went out the main doors of the cafeteria, which is why I always slip out the side by the Fine Arts Wing. But today, I'd barely pushed the door open when Noah called from behind me.

"Hey, Jess!"

I jumped and bashed my elbow into the doorjamb. It hurt so badly that he was already next to me before I could flee.

"I need to talk to you," he said. "I'll come by your place after school."

"I don't think that's a good idea."

"It's important."

I was having trouble thinking of an excuse, so I busted out one of my mom's helpful suggestions about what to say in the event of peer pressure. "I'm not really comfortable with that."

He huffed. "You're not comfortable with me coming to your house? What do you think is going to happen? I hate to break it to you, but everything that is going to happen already has. And you seemed pretty comfortable while I was—"

"Okay!" My face was burning, and I had my hands over my ears, like if I could just stop from hearing him, it wouldn't have happened. "Okay, you can come over."

"I will," he said, his new Chucks squeaking on the tiles as he jogged up the short flight of stairs that separated the Fine Arts Wing from the rest of the school. The bell rang, and I was still standing by the cafeteria. My legs just weren't responding.

"Jess, are you okay?"

It was Carly, her face scrunched in some allistic expression I didn't have the bandwidth to interpret.

"I'm not feeling well," I whispered. "Excuse me." I staggered to the bathroom by the auditorium, and I stayed there, just sitting in a stall, for the rest of third period. I wonder if Ms. Vasquez even noticed.

The whole bus ride home, my knees were jiggling, my tongue scrubbing my gumline. I prayed to Lin-Manuel Miranda. *Please let the kids at the stops before mine have their backpacks bust on the way down the aisle so we have to wait for them to collect their stuff. And let us miss the exit off the traffic circle. And let there be traffic on Commerce so that it takes at least an hour to make that unprotected left onto Maple. Maybe by that time, he'll have thought better of it and left.*

I was not so blessed.

As soon as I stepped off the bus, I saw his SUV in my mom's parking spot. He got out and followed me to the door. My heart tap-danced as I fumbled with the keys.

When we got inside, I tossed my keys at the kitchen table and squared my shoulders, staring at a stain on the carpet to the left of his shoe. "What do you want?"

"Chloe."

"And I can help you with that how?"

"Tell her it wasn't my fault."

I let my breath out in a whoosh. Of all the things he could have wanted to talk about, this at least was straightforward. "I have sent her texts, emails, voicemails, notes, and even short plays to that effect. She didn't want to hear it."

"Try again."

He leaned against the front door, not quite lazily, as though he were covering my escape route—or possibly preventing a rescue party from breaching the entrance.

"It won't help. She won't listen to anything I have to say." I trudged into the kitchen. "Soda?"

He followed. "How can you be so casual about this?" He shook his head to refuse the soda.

"Believe me, I'm not," I said quietly. "I'm devastated. But I can't make her listen to me."

"Well, you're going to have to fucking try."

His anger had swelled so suddenly, I took a step back and cracked my head on the refrigerator.

His features twisted, hurt—or maybe disgusted. "What, so you're scared of me now?"

"No. I just . . . I don't remember how it happened last time, and I don't want it to happen again."

"Trust me, once was enough." He stalked to the door.

I followed. "You know I didn't mean for any of this to happen, right? I'm not even—" I swallowed, my voice lowering of its own accord. "I'm not really interested in sex."

He spun. "Is that what you're telling yourself? Because I was there, and trust me, you were plenty interested." His jaw tensed. "Some advice, Jess: get laid. Find some hard-up freshman—or is that jock friend of yours single?—and get him to fuck you sideways. Maybe if you weren't so repressed, you wouldn't have jumped someone else's boyfriend and ruined his life."

The keys on the table rattled as the door slammed. I set my soda can carefully on the bottom step before I curled into a ball and wept.

🔒 PRIVATE
Dec 13

REASON #40:
I am gullible.

It's her first day home for winter break, and Julia already wants to murder me.

It's not entirely fair that she blames me for her being grounded. Technically, I'm grounded, too (as a result of this morning's heated debate over the correct positioning of an animatronic Santa decoration that ended with me spitting in Julia's coffee and Julia dumping said coffee on my head and also the living room rug), but it's definitely more of a punishment for Julia, since she actually has friends to hang out with. Emily has been super busy with family stuff (apparently Christmas shopping is a group activity; not sure how surprises work), and Cam isn't speaking to me. Or maybe I'm not speaking to him. Regardless, "grounded" isn't so much a punishment as my current state of being.

Julia's anger was the main reason I was still crammed into the kitchen with her, smushing butter with a wooden spoon. Another, smaller reason was my deeply rooted desire to taste my great-grandma's candy kiss cookie batter. But the primary motivation was an annoying younger sister's innate desire to do and say things that piss off her older sister.

"Are you coming to Dad's for Christmas?" I asked.

Julia snorted.

"You haven't seen him in years. You might at least text him."

"He doesn't deserve a goddam text."

"That's the Christmas spirit."

The oven screeched as she opened it. "Move. These are done."

I sidestepped just in time to avoid being seared by a hot tray. She began shoveling cookies onto the flattened paper bags we'd laid out for cooling.

"We didn't go to Rachel's for Thanksgiving," I said. "I think they split up."

"Shocker."

I retrieved some eggs from the fridge. "I don't see why you can't at least be civil to him."

"Because he's a cheating bastard."

"I know he should have broken it off with Mom before he started sleeping with Rachel—"

She laughed. Guffawed, really. "And what about Jennifer? Or that blond when he was working at Costco?"

I gaped at her, the cracked egg in my hand oozing through my fingers into the bowl below. "Jennifer . . . his cousin?"

"God, Jess, are you that gullible? He was cheating on Mom before they were even married. And do you still believe that bullshit about him getting laid off? My money is on him grabbing some intern's ass and getting fired."

"But how . . ." My brain ached. "Mom never told me."

"She didn't tell me, either. I'm just not quite as gullible as you. I figured it out and told her that if she didn't throw his lying, cheating ass out, I would."

"But . . . why didn't she leave him sooner?"

"Because she's Mom," Julia said, softening a bit. "And she loves him, and she loves us, and she thought everyone would be better off if she bit back her own misery and dealt with it. Martyrdom was fine in ancient Rome when your best-case scenario was to make it to fifty before you caught cholera or got speared by a Visigoth. Mom deserves better." She leveled her spatula at me. "Especially from you."

I washed the egg off my hands and made some excuse about needing the bathroom. Upstairs, I burrowed into my bed, pulling my weighted blanket up to my chin. Could Julia be lying? Julia was many things, but as much as her all-knowing smugness infuriated me, she did often notice things that I didn't. Could Dad really have been parading his girlfriends in front of me all these years and I hadn't seen it?

The mysterious "cousin" Jennifer who we'd never met and never saw again.

Christine (Christina?) from Costco.

The lady with black hair who met us at the park every time Dad took me to soccer in fourth grade.

That college-age girl who thanked him for helping with the plumbing in her apartment. Plumbing. Oh my *God*, ew.

All the times he ducked out of the house when his phone rang? The miscellaneous "coworkers" and "old friends" who looked inexplicably embarrassed if I was the one who answered the door?

And what about the divorce? He told me he was the one who left. Lie, according to Julia. Did he also lie about custody? Dad said that he got me for Thanksgiving and Christmas because that's all Mom would give him in the custody agreement. Was that true? Or could Dad just not be bothered with me on the day-to-day?

I just don't have room for you, he'd said at Thanksgiving.

Bile crept up my throat. Mom would be home from work in an hour. How would I face her? How would I face *Dad*? I was supposed to see him for Christmas in a couple of weeks. What would I even say? I imagined the scene.

SETTING: ROB's apartment. A cheap plastic
             wreath hangs crooked on the
             inside of the door. The trash can
             overflows with discarded paper

                    plates, and the room smells
                    faintly of sour milk and the
                    theatre guys' dressing room.

AT RISE: ROB wipes the counter as he waits
                    for the rotisserie chicken to
                    reheat in the microwave. JESS
                    clears two spaces at the table,
                    relocating the heaps of junk mail
                    and take-out containers temporar-
                    ily to the floor.

                              ROB
How's school, Jessie Bean? Still top of
your class?

                              JESS
What happened with you and Rachel?

                              ROB
Well, you know how relationships go, Bean.
Sometimes people just grow apart. Like you
and that boy you were seeing. What was his
name?

                              JESS
I've never dated anyone. Did you cheat on her?

ROB freezes. The microwave beeps. He ignores it.

                    ROB

Jessie—

                    JESS

Did. You. Cheat on her?

                    ROB

Yes. We were growing apart, and men—all people—have needs, not just physical, but emotional, and—

                    JESS

Is that what you tell yourself? Is that how you make it okay?

                    ROB

. . .

The microwave beeps again.

                    JESS

How many times?

ROB

What do you mean?

JESS

How many other women did you sleep with while you were with her?

ROB
(softly)

Are we still talking about Rachel?

JESS

. . . No.

The microwave beeps again. ROB yanks it open, then slams it. He pauses with his hands braced on the grimy cooktop. Heaves a sigh. Doesn't look at her.

ROB

I don't know, Jessie. And that's the honest-to-God truth.

JESS
(softly)

You lied to me.

                    ROB
              (turns to face her)
Look, Bean—

                    JESS
My name. Is Jess.

                    ROB
Jess. I'm not good at relationships. Worse than not good. I fuck them all up—every single one. But your mom is the only woman I married. And I loved her. You have to believe I loved her. And I regret my mistakes, but one thing I can't regret—and I'm sure your mother doesn't regret it, either—is that I married her. Because if I hadn't, we wouldn't have you, Jessie Bea—Jess.

He crosses the kitchenette and stops with a hand on JESS's shoulder. She tenses but doesn't pull away.

                  ROB (CONT'D)
Say you'll forgive me, Jess, huh? I can't bear the thought of you hating me. How about it?

JESS

I didn't know what happened next.

I didn't even know if the scene was fiction or truth.

I pressed my palms into my eye sockets and let the scene cut to black, trying not to wonder whether the Jess in my imagination (or the Jess in real life) would forgive him.

🔒 **PRIVATE**
Dec 15

REASON #41:
I have never before tried to understand my mother.

<u>MY TURN</u>
<u>A (MAYBE) FICTIONAL MONOLOGUE</u>

ANDREA

I'm leaving you.

Don't give me that smile. I am sick of your lips and the way they twitch and curl like they're so much smarter than me, like everything I say is cute, and everything I think is wrong, and everything you are will always be more.

More than me.

More than us.

More than this life we have—had—together.
Well, now you're going to sit in that chair
and listen, for once in your life, listen
to what I am feeling, because I need you to
know. I need you to understand why it's over.

The girl was yours, Rob, wasn't she? You
shuffled her and her mother out the door so
quickly, you probably thought I didn't have
time to see her eyes.

Your eyes.

But you were wrong. I would know those eyes
anywhere. They are the eyes that first drew me
in that night in the coffee shop where you
were pretending to have a soul and an interest in my nursing degree. I will never forget
those eyes.

I might have followed her out the door if I
hadn't had a baby on my hip and another at
the kitchen table with her crayons.

My girls.

Our girls.

You didn't come back for hours, so we ate alone, and when you came back inside and went up to your room—our room—without saying a word, I was glad that I'd already put the girls to bed so that they didn't see me cry.

I'm not crying now, Rob.

After two decades of excuses and disappearances—two decades of lipstick on your collar and brandy on your breath and perfume lingering in the back seat of the car—I have dried my tears. I have swallowed them back into my soul, which is drowning.

But I am ready to let those tears go.

Don't think that I'm crying over you, Rob. Don't let yourself believe that lie. The tears I will cry tonight and tomorrow are tears I will cry for me. For the years I've lost. For our girls.

My girls.

Who have spent their childhood sharing a house

with a man who has such contempt for them
that he didn't even take out their car seats
before he screwed his mistress in the minivan.

No smile now, Rob?

How does it feel to be nothing to us? How does
it feel to be a ghost in your own house, where
the people you thought belonged to you see
through you, brush past you, trample over you
because they know you aren't worth noticing?

You don't need to tell me. I know how it
feels.

And now it's your turn.

> Re: Monologue
> From: Eli Barton
> To: Jessica R. Lanza
>
> Hi Jess,
>
> Your use of language in this piece is pure
> poetry. Thank you for sharing what I know

must be a personal piece. You know I'm always here if you need any support.

Mr. Barton
P.S. This is an A.

PRIVATE
Dec 16

REASON #42:
My life is so clichéd that my sister can read my mind.

Being grounded with Julia would have been bad if we were fighting. It was somehow worse when we weren't. I lay on the couch, watching her watch her phone in the corner armchair, both of us knowing how much I suck.

I've always known I sucked (it's the main theme of this blog), but Julia's bombshell about our parents made me sink lower in my own esteem. I asked Mom last night at dinner whether Dad had cheated on her before Rachel. Her face told me everything I needed to know. Julia was angry at me for blaming Mom for the divorce, but I was angrier at myself. And a little bit angry at Julia for not telling me sooner, and at Mom for not telling me at all.

I'd finally gotten up the courage to text my father to let him know I wasn't coming for Christmas. I didn't tell him why. *I just found out you've been lying to me my whole life, and I'm not sure I'm ready to see you right now* felt kind of heavy for a text.

So I'd just settled on the vague *something came up* excuse.

But I think he saw through it because all he texted back was *Ok Jessica.* I cannot remember the last time he called me Jessica. I'd been avoiding my phone all day in case he decided to call and interrogate me. I really can't handle any more confrontation in my life.

Which is why every synapse in my brain began to wail when Julia the All-Knowing—who I'm finally accepting might actually be a better person than I am, or at least a better daughter—suddenly put down her phone and asked, "Are you ever going to tell me what's going on with you and Chloe?"

I stiffened. "Unlikely. Why?"

"Just wondering if I should be expecting any dog-shit deliveries over Christmas."

"I would recommend mentally preparing yourself for such a contingency."

She snorted. "You talk like the dean of the law school."

"Which one?"

"All of them."

I shifted, brushing crumbs off my stomach before grabbing another cookie off the plate on the coffee table. "Is Albert applying to law school, too?"

She looked up from her phone again, a small surprised smile lighting her face. Five points to Jess for remembering his name. "No. He actually graduated from undergrad last year. He's an econ guy. He works for Capital One now."

I nodded like I cared. And maybe I did. A little. "So, will I ever get to meet him?"

Her smile blossomed into a full-blown beam. "He'll be here this weekend."

"Oh." I frowned. I couldn't remember Julia ever bringing a guy home to on-purpose meet Mom before. What I *did* remember were the great lengths she went to in high school to keep Mom from finding out she had a boy in her room. "Is he staying here?"

"Just for a couple nights."

"And Mom's okay with that?"

Julia's smile faded. She looked at me like I just crawled out of a dumpster. "Mom treats me like an adult. You need to stop thinking the worst of her."

"But . . . she's okay with you sleeping around?"

"Oh my God." Julia stood, her phone sliding from her lap to thud onto the carpet. "First of all, you have no idea whether Albert and I are having sex, frankly because you never asked or showed any interest in our relationship whatsoever. And second of all, even if Albert and I *are* having sex, that wouldn't be *sleeping around*. We're in a relationship. We have been for almost two years. So get off your goddam high horse. From what I've heard, you're not such a spotless virgin yourself."

The world tilted. There was a roaring in my ears, and I couldn't see anything, could just feel my heart pounding, my muscles taut like a trampoline.

I don't know how I got upstairs. But when I came back to myself, I was lying on my bed, all crunched up around my pillow. My chest was screaming, and I realized I was holding my breath. I let it out in a shuddering rush. Trust Julia to set me off like that. It was a special talent of hers.

"Are you okay now?"

I flinched. I hadn't realized she was in the room with me. Did she help me up the stairs? She must have. Oh *God*, how humiliating. "I'm fine."

"Well, no. Obviously you're not fine," she said with a dose of very un-Julia-like tenderness. "Tell me about it?"

"You can go now."

"I'm not going anywhere," she said, again in that strange tender voice. And when she put her hand on my shoulder, I started to sob. Like, from nothing to great wracking, snuffling sobs in less than a second. Julia wrapped her arms around me and pulled my head into her lap and kind of rocked me like I was a baby or a kitten or something.

"Please go away," I sobbed.

"Do you really want me to?"

I didn't answer.

When I had finally emptied my body of all excess moisture, my head was pounding. Julia brushed the wet, sticky hair back from my face and lowered my head to my pillow.

"I'm going to pee," she said. "Can I get you anything while I'm up?"

"My dignity?"

She smiled. "Be right back."

She returned with a Gatorade and a box of tissues. She sat next to me on the bed and wriggled her feet under the quilt.

"Why is it always so goddam cold in your room?"

I took a swig of the Gatorade.

"I'm going to tell you some things I heard and some things I guessed," she said. "If it's true, you don't have to say anything. But if I'm wrong, you should tell me. Deal?"

I blew my nose.

"That girl who delivered the dog shit with Chloe was Hannah Brewer, right? I saw Mia Brewer at Starbucks, and she told me you had sex with Chloe's boyfriend."

I said nothing.

"But I'm guessing that's not exactly what happened."

"You're wrong," I said. "That is what happened. Well, more or less." She stared at me for a long time. I have always prided myself on my ability to glare at Julia for prolonged periods, despite her height advantage and beauty advantage and confidence advantage. But just then, I couldn't look at her, not even in my peripheral vision. I traced the ribbon of green and red roses that snaked in and out of circles on my quilt with a ragged fingernail.

"More or less how?"

"We didn't completely . . ." I started feeling dizzy again. "I can't talk about this."

Julia took my hand. "Whatever happened, did you want it to?"

"I guess. I don't know."

"Did you ask for it to happen? Did *he* ask before he touched you?"

"I– It was complicated."

"Was the word 'yes' involved in that complication? And if so, was it freely given or pressured?"

I dug my forehead into my knees. There's no point arguing with Julia when she wants to be pedantic. She'll be top of her class in law school.

"Jessie—"

"Don't."

"—I think you may have been—"

"Don't!" I shouted, and my voice shattered. "You think you know absolutely everything, but you don't. You weren't even there. Why are you always butting into my business? Why don't you put on a tube top and go drink some vodka and screw your hot boyfriend already?"

The hand on my shoulder twitched, but she didn't remove it. It was a long moment before she said, "We don't have to talk about it if you're not ready."

How I possibly had more tears left in my body, I don't know. Julia hugged my shoulders until I stopped crying. Again.

"He wasn't . . . I was just . . . confusing. He's a good person."

"I don't give a shit about him," Julia said. "Don't you worry about him, either. Or Chloe. If she's blaming you for this, that's her problem. Let's just find a way to help you be okay again, yeah?"

She sat with me until I finished the Gatorade—and the box of tissues—and she promised to tell Mom I wasn't feeling up to dinner.

"Hey," I said as she was leaving. "I'm really sorry about what I said. About you and Albert."

"Which thing you said?" she asked, but she was smirking.

"All of the things. Really. I'm excited to meet him."

"He's excited to meet you, too," she said, and pulled the door closed behind her.

Half an hour later, my mom knocked. The instant I saw her face, I knew Julia had told her. I knew, knew, *knew* I shouldn't have talked to Julia.

Mom put a plate of steaming leftover kielbasa on top of my Calculus book and sat on the edge of my bed. She wrapped her snowflake cardigan tight across her chest, then squeezed her crossed arms, too, like she was creating a protective barrier for the world's most uncomfortable conversation. "Julia said you were . . . dealing with . . . something."

"I really don't want to talk about it."

"You don't have to talk to me about it. But would you . . ." She pulled a business card out of her pocket. "I know you don't want to go back to the Autism Center, but would you consider seeing a regular therapist? I've been going since

Dad left, and there's this new lady in the group who's supposed to be good."

I took the card, rubbing my thumb along the thick paper. The slightly raised letters tickled my skin. Maybe it was the post-meltdown daze or the incontrovertible evidence that I wasn't able to cope or the fact that we'd just entered some parallel universe where Julia and I actually get along, but for some reason I said, "Yeah, okay."

"Yes?"

I nodded.

My mom squeezed my arm. "I'll call right now. If they have any cancellations, maybe you can start this week."

And then, mercifully, she left, closing the door softly behind her.

PRIVATE
Dec 18

REASON #43:
When my emotions are too big for me to handle, I take it out on my sister.

When I was five and I spent a day in the woods pretending to be a Wild Thing and got so much poison ivy that I couldn't go to the state fair, I screamed and threw such a violent tantrum that my dad didn't take Julia, either. He went by himself. Or more likely, now that I think of it, with some other woman.

When I was eleven and I didn't get a speaking role in the children's Shakespeare production at the community center, I snuck into Julia's room and stole her makeup case and hid it in a hollow tree. I forgot which one. It's probably still there.

When I was thirteen and I got a D on a math test, I told my mom about Mia Brewer's Homecoming after-party. Mom grounded Julia until New Year's. She also called Ms. Brewer and got Mia grounded, too.

The night before my first therapy session, I accused Julia of drinking too much at dinner, and she accused me of being a judgmental dickhead, and we shouted at each other for a full ten minutes before she stormed up to her room. It was the first time we'd fought since before my big meltdown.

I'd be lying if I didn't admit it felt kind of good.

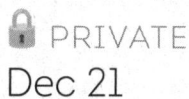 PRIVATE
Dec 21

REASON #44:
My previous conception of reality was largely fiction.

Merry Fake Christmas.

If you have a hospital nurse for a mother, Fake Christmas is the date that you choose to celebrate Christmas because it's a day when your mom doesn't have to work a twelve-hour shift. Fake Christmas is usually the twenty-third or twenty-seventh or something, but this year we decided to celebrate it a little earlier with Albert.

He arrived yesterday morning, twenty-four hours after my first session of therapy with Alyssa, possessor of the world's highest heels and most unnatural tolerance for awkward silence.

ALYSSA

. . .

JESS

. . .

ALYSSA

. . .

JESS

. . .

For an hour. An *hour*. I seriously regret saying yes to this nonsense.

Unfortunately, the awkward silence seems to be a disease that lingered into this morning, preventing me from making small talk with the stranger who is dating my sister. I contributed exactly seven words to the conversation while we strung lights and hung ornaments, and four of those words were "yeah."

We had lunch/dinner (linner? dunch?) around two in the afternoon, and after stuffing ourselves with Mom's turkey and brussels sprouts and Albert's (!) Vietnamese yam soup, we retreated to the living room to open presents and subsequently collapse in various stages of food coma. Mom fell asleep in the recliner, and Julia was reading one of her new books, and Albert was watching Julia. It was the way he was looking at her—like she melted his insides and made his face all soft and sleepy—that made me queasy. I excused myself to the bathroom.

It's not that I don't love Julia. It's just that I don't do a good job of it. I've known her my whole life. Literally, my whole life. It's easy to see her rough edges because they're jagged as broken glass and I'm constantly getting cut on them.

I wonder what it's like to see her as Albert sees her.

When I came out of the bathroom, he was leaning against the wall. He straightened when he saw me.

"All yours," I said.

"No, that's okay. I wasn't really waiting. I wanted to talk to you, actually. Not like I'm a stalker or anything. I just wanted to know . . ." He raked a hand through his hair, drawing his black bangs back from his forehead. "How do you think I'm doing? Okay?"

"Yeah," I said, a little weirded out.

"Yeah? Good. Good. So, do you think your mom liked the soup?"

"Well, she didn't have to cook it, so, yeah." He looked unsure, so I added, "And it was delicious. She loved it."

He bobbed his head like he was auditioning for the role of a chicken. "Cool. Cool. And Julia—do you think she liked the book?"

I narrowed my eyes. "You're really freaking out about this, aren't you?"

He was. A blush warmed his cheeks. "I just want to make a good impression."

"Impression made," I assured him. "You're awesome. And I can tell Julia really likes you."

"Yeah? Thanks. That means a lot—especially coming from you. I know how much Julia respects your opinion."

I laughed, then realized he wasn't joking. "Seriously?"

"Yeah. She's always talking about how smart you are."

Total gut punch.

I slunk back to the living room. My super-smart sister (who apparently thinks I'm super smart?) looked up from her book and smiled. I smiled back, then picked up my phone. Photos of Julia and Albert saturated her social media—all happy, though I guess if there were any sad photos, she wouldn't have posted them. It was more than happiness, though. She looked content. Fulfilled.

I scrolled back to November. There she was at Albert's place. Nice big dining room. Two—no, three—brothers, parents, and Julia laughing and actually eating pie. When did she start eating desserts? College, I guess.

I scrolled back further. No annoyed Julia. No frowning Julia. No cursing Julia. No angry Julia. No bitch-slapping-pizza-waiters Julia. Only happy, joyful, relaxed, peaceful, pleasant Julia. And there were a lot fewer pictures of partying Julia than I thought there'd be. Almost none, in fact. I'd expected thumbnail after thumbnail of Julia grinding up on miscellaneous men, but they're just not there. Julia on campus with friends. Julia dressed up for Halloween. Julia and Albert holding hands. Julia, Mom, and Albert at the park over the summer. Julia at Albert's graduation last May. I had to go all the way back to last New Year's Eve before even one red Solo cup made an appearance. If social media is to be believed, Julia's life looks a lot different than I thought.

Maybe it's not Julia's temper that causes us to fight.

Maybe it's been me all along.

🔒 PRIVATE
Dec 28

REASON #45:
It's Christmas vacation and I'm super excited to be doing homework.

It was weird not seeing my dad on Christmas, but not seeing Mr. Barton on the twenty-sixth was definitely weirder. I've spent December 26 with Chloe and her dad every year since eighth grade. It's my favorite holiday tradition, partly because it's so dependable. Even if Mr. Barton was dating someone (and he must have dated someone at some point over the past five years, right?), he never brought him/her/them to Christmas. It was just Mr. Barton, Chloe, Chloe's grandmother, and me.

Jjajja Barton always gave us both handmade Christmas socks. They were lumpy and warm and wonderful. Mr. Barton played the piano and we sang Christmas carols like a hokey family in a Hallmark commercial. We all had a sip of eggnog because it was traditional and several mugs of hot cider because it was delicious.

This year, my mom worked both the twenty-fifth and

twenty-sixth. Julia went with Albert to his parents' house. Cam was still in North Carolina visiting his grandparents, not that he was speaking to me anyway. I spent part of Real Christmas on my phone, liking Emily's photo of her baby cousin dressed as a Christmas elf and Jeff Watkins's photo of himself tossing half a dozen Christmas cookies in the air (and ignoring like five DMs from him harassing me about where my blog went and when I'll start posting again). Then I decided to stop procrastinating and buckle down on my portfolio.

I'd decided to revise two old pieces (the demon-squirrel play and the twin-heart story), but I needed one more piece. Another play, and not a comedy. At the top of my page, I typed out Mr. Barton's advice. If I couldn't be with him in person, singing Christmas carols and drinking hot cider, at least he'd be with me in spirit through his many clichéd, kind-of-contradictory-but-admittedly-helpful principles of writing.

> *Make it personal. Write what you know!*
> *Use your imagination. A writer isn't bound by reality!*
> *Less is more. Give your reader the chance to make connections herself!*
> *Details are your friend. It's the little things that make your written world real!*

I wrote for hours in my homework cave. All day, actually, my body rocking back and forth, propelled by an abundance of ideas that thrilled me. When my mom got home from work, I realized I'd forgotten to eat lunch. And dinner. The pages and pages I'd written were crap, but that wasn't what mattered. Because that giant creative writing turd was at least vaguely shaped like a coherent narrative.

And after another day of revising, that turd had come very close to resembling a play I could actually submit to the Goldberg program.

Maybe some of Mr. Barton's cheesy writing adages are actually true: "A crappy first draft can fertilize something wonderful."

RESTRAINT
A PLAY IN ONE ACT

CAST OF CHARACTERS

JOSEPHINE, a bird
AMY, a toad
Four VICES/VIRTUES:
    BOSSY/INTELLIGENT, a crow
    VAIN/BEAUTIFUL, a butterfly
    SHREWISH/CONFIDENT, a porcupine
    SENSITIVE/COMPASSIONATE, a rabbit

SETTING: A forest.

AT RISE: JOSEPHINE stands atop a stool. The VICES surround her in a semicircle (downstage), their backs to the audience. Labels on the back of each costume identify them as BOSSY, VAIN, SHREWISH, and SENSITIVE. They each hold a rod, forming the bars of a cage around JOSEPHINE. AMY sits center stage, blindfolded, picking at something on the ground in front of her.

                    AMY
    Dry and shriveled, all of them.

She holds an invisible fly to her blindfolded eyes.

                    AMY (CONT'D)
    Hardly worth eating.

She pops the invisible fly into her mouth.

                    JOSEPHINE
    Why do you, then?

A beat.

                    JOSEPHINE
    I eat bugs, too, you know. I find them
    delicious.

                    AMY
    You would, of course.

                    JOSEPHINE
    Of course.

A beat.

                    JOSEPHINE (CONT'D)
Why do you say that?

                          AMY
                     (exasperated)
Because you're not down here in the mud,
are you? You're up in the tree where the
flies are healthy and crunchy, and I'm left
with the old sickly husks.

                       JOSEPHINE
You should come up here, then.

                          AMY
Don't act like you know what's best for
me. You don't know anything.

                       JOSEPHINE
I know quite a lot of things, actually.
But likely nothing that you want to hear.

BOSSY slowly rotates their cage bar from
vertical to horizontal—the top rung of a
ladder—and turns to face the audience. The
label on the front of their costume reads
INTELLIGENT.

                    AMY
I have excellent hearing. My eardrums are
on the outside of my head. That's another
thing you didn't know.

She eats another fly.

                    JOSEPHINE
            (pushing against a cage bar)
I wish I could come down there.

                    AMY
You don't. You'll get dirt on your
feathers.

                    JOSEPHINE
I don't mind the dirt. Rolling in dust
helps me clean my feathers. Or it would,
if I could get down there.

                    AMY
                (grunts)
Huh.

                    JOSEPHINE
What, "huh"?

                    AMY
Just, you spend a lot of time worrying about
your feathers is all.

                    JOSEPHINE
    Is that wrong? They're part of me.

VAIN slowly rotates their cage bar to form
the second rung of the ladder while turning
to face the audience. The label on the front
of their costume proclaims them BEAUTIFUL.

              JOSEPHINE (CONT'D)
    This is wrong, this cage.

                    AMY
You sound so sure.

                    JOSEPHINE
                (passionately)
    I *am* sure. This shouldn't be here!

                    AMY
Don't be angry.

JOSEPHINE

I'm not. I should be, though. I deserve to be.

SHREWISH slowly lowers their cage bar to form the third rung of the ladder while turning to face the audience, becoming CONFIDENT.

AMY

You're so angry all the time.

JOSEPHINE

Stop saying that.

AMY

Relax.

JOSEPHINE

How can I? I can't even stretch my wings.

AMY

Then move someplace else.

JOSEPHINE

That's impossible.

                    AMY
Anything's possible if you try. You just
enjoy wallowing.

                  JOSEPHINE
I'm trying to help you see.

                    AMY
You want me to pity you.

                  JOSEPHINE
Not pity. I wish you would care.

                    AMY
              (sarcastically)
Is that what you call it? This obsession
with cages? Not whining but *caring*?

                  JOSEPHINE
Some things need to be cared about.
Especially those that are hard to see.

AMY frowns, her hands stilling on the ground
in front of her. SENSITIVE slowly lowers
their cage bar to form the final rung of

the ladder. They turn to face the audience, becoming COMPASSIONATE. JOSEPHINE contemplates the ladder.

                  JOSEPHINE
I could come down now, I think. I could try.

A beat.

                  JOSEPHINE (CONT'D)
Would you care if I did?

                  AMY
    (in a small voice, her body tense and still)
I won't pity you.

                  JOSEPHINE
I know.

                  AMY
                  (hesitantly)
Does it feel good?

                  JOSEPHINE
What?

                    AMY
Always seeing. Always *knowing*?

                 JOSEPHINE
I don't know everything.

                    AMY
You know more than me.

                 JOSEPHINE
It helps to start seeing things—seeing the
world and the creatures that live in it.

                    AMY
That's impossible.

JOSEPHINE climbs down from the stool. She
approaches AMY from behind and tenderly
removes her blindfold. AMY gazes out at the
audience in rapture.

CUT TO BLACK

🔒 PRIVATE
Dec 30

REASON #46:
I have more than I will ever deserve.

I sent *Restraint*, which was shaping up to be my third portfolio piece, to Mr. Barton yesterday and got back an email with an absurd number of exclamation points and emojis.

> Yes! That's more like it! Go, Jess!! Look out, Tisch, here you come! <3 :D :-P 🎂🎉😋🏍

(I think that last emoji was a mistake.) He had some comments, and I made some changes, but by this morning, I was stalling. I'd changed three words, deleted a comma, added the comma back in, then changed two of the words back to the way they were before. It was time to submit my applications and get it over with.

Mom and Julia both wanted to be present when I clicked the button. My instinct was to say no, since it wasn't a big deal, and I didn't want them to turn it into a Thing. But in the end, I didn't argue, probably due to my residual guilt at having been a terrible daughter/sister. Or maybe just due to laziness.

All in all, it was somewhat anticlimactic. Mom had Spotify on some weird station with chanting nuns, which added an appropriate aura of tension and foreboding, but the button-clicking itself took a fraction of a second, and then the screen shifted to say that my application had been successfully submitted. Julia and Mom cheered, and I rolled my eyes. Then I clicked the button to apply to a handful of state schools to keep Mom happy.

When it was all over, Julia poured us all some sparkling cider (though hers was slightly less yellow than Mom's and mine, and I suspected she had secretly helped herself to some of the cheap André champagne she had hidden in the produce drawer). It was a surprisingly celebratory moment for the three of us. It had only been a few taps on a trackpad, but it felt like a huge relief. Like one of the weights that had been dragging behind me all year had been lifted.

Maybe I could shrug off some others, too.

I waited a whole hour after Cam's parents' sedan pulled back into the parking lot before I knocked on his door. His mom opened it almost immediately. She was wearing leggings and the three layers of tank tops/sports bras that she always wears when she's going to some trendy exercise class. Her blond hair towered in a messy bun and her makeup was inexplicably flawless given that she'd just spent like five hours in the car.

"Jessica! So good to see you! Come in."

The aroma of baking gingerbread embraced me as I stepped inside. It was almost enough to ease my revulsion at the sounds of Johnny Mathis singing from the iPad on the counter. Mrs. Lewis had wasted no time getting back into the holiday spirit after their road trip.

"Let me get Cameron for you." She jogged upstairs, and I had to look away because her leggings were *way* too tight for a mom. On the coat tree in the hall, I hung my jacket next to Cam's sportsball—*football*—jacket and Mrs. Lewis's fluffy marshmallow coat.

Cam came down the stairs in a Puma Pride T-shirt and sweatpants. My heart swelled a little. The only way I'd survived the last nineteen days without him was by distracting myself with my trainwreck of a life. But now there was no distraction. Just Cam, a tentative smile on his face, his arms folded protectively across his chest.

"Hey," he said. "Merry Christmas."

"I am so, so sorry."

"'S okay."

"No. It's not. You were one hundred percent right about everything. I've been so—"

"Jess, it's—"

"No." I put out my hand to stop him from taking another

step closer. "Let me finish saying this. I've been practicing for like a week."

He stopped and leaned against the wall. "You don't have to. I already forgive you."

"No. You can't yet. Stop talking." I took a shaky breath and started over. "You were one hundred percent right. I have been very judgmental about a lot of people, not even just Brooklyn or Alexis Jones and all of them but my sister and my mom, and I've been totally unfair to you, and I've taken you for granted, and I should care about your sports, and I suck."

He tugged a hand through his tangled hair. "Wow. That was quite an apology."

"It was. You can forgive me now. If you still want to."

His mouth twitched. "I do. But listen, I'm sorry, too. I was out of line. I know you get overwhelmed by details when you have too many things to pay attention to—"

"It's overwhelming but not impossible. I went to all of Chloe's robot-y things. I should go to your sporty things. Football things. I want to care about your football things." I punctuated the last with an emphatic nod that I hoped conveyed the fullness of my resolve.

Cam's mouth-twitch broadened to an amused smirk. "Well, thank you. Though football is over for the year, so you're off the hook."

"Oh." I cast about for something to prove my commitment

to this new friendship endeavor. "What about . . . movies? Are there football movies?"

"Are there . . . ?" His jaw went slack, like the shock of this suggestion was just too much for his face muscles. "Why did I never think of this!"

He took my hand and tugged me toward the living room, and I tried to ignore the shivery warmth that radiated up my arm from where his fingers linked with mine. After about ten minutes on Wikipedia, Cam decided that the ideal football movie to introduce me to what was apparently a substantive subgenre of film was *Friday Night Lights*.

And I am kind of amazed to report that it is actually a good movie. Like, it makes that whole football thing look kind of exciting and fun. And it was probably the melodramatic sports movie and the gingerbread sugar rush, but lounging on the couch with a friend who cared about me despite my suckage—it was almost enough to make me believe in miracles.

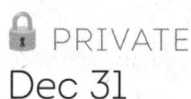
PRIVATE
Dec 31

REASON #47:
I apparently don't know how my own brain and body work.

Mom had to work the overnight shift New Year's Eve. As soon as she left, Julia pulled the André out of the produce drawer and poured us each a generous glass.

"This is illegal," I told her.

"Damn right."

I took a sip of the bubbly liquid and immediately spat it into the glass.

"Ugh. Why?"

"Because it's cheap!" Julia raised her glass in a mock toast and took a disgustingly large swig. "It's an acquired taste."

"I'm good with my existing tastes, thanks."

She shrugged, drained her glass, and grabbed a couple of mugs from the cabinet. Five minutes later, we were sitting on the couch, sipping steaming hot chocolate.

"What did you tell Mom?" I asked. It was the first chance I'd had to talk to her alone.

"Not much," she said. "Just that I thought you were having a hard time at school and might need someone to talk to. Professionally."

"So you didn't tell her about . . ."

"I didn't mention boys. But she's not totally clueless, so she may have guessed."

I nodded. Mom was less naive than I had previously suspected.

"I can't listen to music," I confessed. "I mean, real music. Anything about love or—you know, anything physical. Or if a sexy ad pops up on YouTube or something, I just kind of freeze. It feels like someone dumped a bucket of ice water over my head and I'm suddenly drowning in it."

"I can't go to pizza places. You know why I got fired from Mario's, right?"

"'Cause you slapped some guy."

"Punched him, actually. He was one of the waiters. He was always hitting on me, making jokes about wanting to screw me—'jokes.'" She grimaced, putting the word in air quotes. "Then one day, he stuck his hand up my skirt, and I lost my shit."

My jaw fell so far that I may have turned part cartoon character. "But why did they fire *you*? Didn't you report him? You were like sixteen! That's got to be illegal."

"He said, she said. Anyway, whenever he made his

'jokes,' there were always other guys around, and they always laughed. I mean, what's the point of reporting something when everyone else obviously doesn't think it's wrong? And I hate the way they look at me if I complain—like I'm being too sensitive, or can't take a compliment, you know? Just because I object to some skeezy thirty-year-old drooling over my breasts." She took a long drink from her mug. "Basically, men are gross."

"Albert seems pretty great," I offered.

Her face softened into a very un-Julia-like smile. "Yeah, he is pretty great."

I hummed the first few bars of "Here Comes the Bride." She swatted me on the back of the head, and hot chocolate sloshed on my lap.

"Hey," I said, sopping it up with my sleeve.

"Sorry." She paused, then asked, "What about you?"

"What do you mean?"

"Is there anyone in your life?"

"I can't even listen to music. Can you imagine what would happen if I went on a date? I'd probably go into cardiac arrest."

She didn't laugh. Or smile. Just nodded. "Was that—bad experience—the first time you'd . . ." She trailed off, which somehow made the question more awkward since I wasn't sure exactly what she was trying to ask.

"I made out with Cam once?"

"Cameron next door? Oh my God, *he is so hot*. I mean,

definitely too young for me, but *so* hot." When she had recovered from her lust, she asked, "But you guys aren't dating?"

"No," I said. "I mean, we're really good friends, but I don't know."

"They say you should marry your best friend," she said. "But I tried dating my best friend once and it was a total shit show."

"Were you and Albert friends before you started dating?"

"Not really. We had mutual friends, but mostly we started getting to know each other by going on dates."

It was kind of surreal, sitting on the couch with Julia, drinking tepid hot chocolate and talking about dating. We'd never talked about dating before. The four years between us was enough that we hadn't been at the same school since I was in first grade. By the time I started getting curious about the topic, she was heading off to college.

"Do you think I could be broken?" I blurted. "Like, can people's dating instincts have faulty sensors or something?"

She looked vaguely alarmed at this abruptly intense conversational turn, but then she let calm lawyer-face take over. "I think it's very normal to *feel* a sense of brokenness after something like what you experienced, but—"

"No, not about that. Well, I mean, obviously, something about me is screwed up from that, but I mean, in general, before that. It's like, I feel things sometimes, when I'm around hot guys who are also super charming and funny and stuff, but it's always like this brief shot of lightning-type feeling and then it's gone?"

Julia had abandoned all attempts to maintain calm lawyer-face and had settled into unblinking fish-gape, her hot chocolate mug hovering in her statue-like grip halfway to her mouth.

I plowed on, my face hotter than—and likely the same color as—molten lava. "Like with Cam, sometimes I feel butterfly feelings for him, so I thought he'd be a good person to make out with, and it felt really nice to be snuggled up with him, but then as soon as he kissed me, I was suddenly less into him. It was like we had this emotional connection, and it just snapped as soon as we started sucking face and all I could think about was how weird it is to spit inside of someone else's mouth."

Julia choke-laughed. "Yeuch. You make it sound so gross!"

"It *is* so gross!"

She set down her mug. "Do you think you might be asexual?"

"I . . ." I paused, giving my brain a second to crunch itself around this possibility. "No? Like I said, I feel things sometimes. You know, like, sexy things and dreams and whatever, so . . . Do ace people feel things?"

"Well, I think . . ." The confidence rapidly siphoned out of Julia's voice. And even though my face was still well past the boiling point, she looked so panicked that I burst out laughing.

"Wow. Have I just witnessed the exact moment when you realized you don't know everything?"

"Shut up." She swatted the air in front of my face. "But okay, you're right, I don't actually know. We could google it."

"Isn't it a bad idea to google anything with the word 'sex' in it? Won't Russian hackers commandeer your phone or something?"

"That feels extreme. But if you don't want to google it, doesn't Stone Bridge have a GSA?"

"Yeah, but it's at the same time as Drama Club."

"Isn't *Drama Club* a GSA?"

"Fair." I thought for a moment, my ears still burning from the embarrassment of saying these things out loud, to Julia, of all people. "But how do I talk to someone about this if I don't even know what word describes me? And I mean, I still haven't ruled out the possibility that I'm a hundred percent hetero, allo, whatever."

"I think— Yeah, I don't know that, either." Julia tugged at her earring. She used to do that all the time, when she was in middle school—her nervous tic. It'd been so long since I'd seen her do it that I felt the past in my whole body, like I'd actually time-traveled or something. "Okay, so maybe other people have had trouble putting words to their identities at first, too? Like, maybe some of your queer friends, so if you talk to them, they might understand that you're not sure?

But also, could it maybe just be a sensory thing, and not an identity thing? Like, I wonder if some other autistic people don't enjoy sex stuff? I don't know. I also wonder if it might be harder to figure out while you're still processing the shit with that guy. So maybe some procrastination wouldn't hurt? Again, just guessing. If it feels urgent that you figure out your identity, I'm not saying don't do that, because I obviously don't know what that's like— Are you even listening to me right now?"

I lowered my mug after licking the last drops of hot chocolate from the inside. "I've invented a new drinking game. I was planning to take a sip every time you admitted you didn't know something, but then there were so many things you didn't know that I ran out of hot chocolate."

She threw a couch pillow at me. Fortunately, my mug was empty or we would have been facing a lifelong grounding on account of upholstery stainage.

"But," I said with great magnanimity, "some of your guesses could be right. I'll think about it." It probably would make sense to wait until the whole melt-into-a-puddle-of-unhappy-goo-when-someone-mentions-sex thing resolved itself before probing too much into my sexuality.

That was fine. Procrastination is an area in which I excel.

🔒 PRIVATE
Jan 5

REASON #48:
Because of me, the Senior Hallway smells like dead dolphins.

It's weird being back at school after the holidays. It's a new year, but it's the same year. I've applied to college, but I'm still in high school. We're still in the same marking period, technically, although both my AP classes had their midterms before break, and I could not give less of a crap about Physics or Government.

I deliberately didn't check my locker before winter break because I didn't want any gift the cyberbullies (and/or Chloe) might have left me. But I regretted my life choices today when I opened the locker to the stench of the pouch of tuna they'd squished in through the vents. I mean, did none of the custodial staff smell that this morning? Maybe they did and just left it to me, as my penance. At least I know Chloe wasn't involved in this one. Her tender vegetarian heart would never tolerate such a nefarious use of a previously living creature.

"Ew, what died?" Over break, Emily had dyed her hair

a festive blood red. She buried her nose in her sleeve as I scraped the dried tuna out of the vent with a ruler.

"Fish. Possibly also dolphins, tragically."

Emily laughed.

But then Hannah's voice cut through the levity of the moment. "The stench! I mean, does she even bathe? Is that something people like her can't handle?"

I snapped my head up, flashing hot, eyes prickling. But the heat turned to ice when I saw the person Hannah was talking to.

Chloe had frozen, too, hands clenched on her skirt to keep them from flapping, smile so tense it wasn't fair to call it a smile anymore. Brooklyn and Alexis were just as still, their gazes darting from Hannah to Chloe.

People like her.

"Hannah," Alexis said, her face contorted in nervous incredulity, but the Queen of the Cliques was already swaggering toward the bathroom. Brooklyn, who'd been looking downright terrified throughout the whole exchange, gnawed the end of her braid before—with an apologetic glance at Chloe and Alexis—she scurried after Hannah.

"Uh-uh." Emily shook her head. "Nope. That's too much. We need to report this."

But I couldn't move. Not when Chloe was still an ice sculpture. Had Hannah said it on purpose? Was she that cruel even to Chloe?

Or could she genuinely not know that Chloe is autistic,

too? She does mask really hard at school. But . . . my stomach twisted. I'd mentioned it on the blog back when it was public. Guilt plunged into my chest like several daggers, and the blog articles I'd read about being "autistic while Black" paraded before my eyes like the apparitions in *Macbeth*.

I'd never stopped and thought about why Chloe masks so hard. Her mom is the director of the Autism Center, after all, and "let yourself be autistic" is basically Dr. Barton's mantra. (I wouldn't be surprised if she'd had it tattooed on her body somewhere.) But maybe letting ourselves be autistic is just another white-person luxury. And if Hannah had read any of the early posts of my blog, I may have outed Chloe to her.

Chloe's finger twitched. I knew the pressure building inside her, so strong she couldn't move or speak, so strong she should have been self-regulating, but she wasn't, and I'm not sure what was keeping her from shattering.

Some invisible magnet pulled me a step closer.

"She wasn't thinking," Alexis murmured, pulling Chloe into a tight side hug. "I'll talk to her."

"Jess," Emily prompted. "That was not okay. We need to report it."

The ice in my body was melting, giving way to a warm weight that made me want to puddle on the floor.

"It's not okay," I said. "But I don't want to tell the principal."

"But—"

"No." I tore my gaze away from Chloe and Alexis. "It's not the worst thing she's said about me."

"That isn't the point."

"If I go whining to the administration, it might just make her worse." To me and to Chloe.

Emily set her jaw, looking for a moment less like my quiet sophomore friend and more like a superhero about to save humanity. "If we don't hold them accountable because we're afraid of their power, then they'll always *be* in power."

I've never seen that on a bumper sticker, but she said it like it was one. Like it was a mantra or an incantation or the final words before the music swells in the climax of a Jimmy Stewart movie.

"I'll think about it," I said.

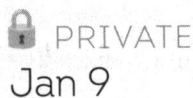
Jan 9

REASON #49:
I still make terrible life choices.

I have now had three whole sessions of therapizing from Alyssa, the fancy-lawyer wannabe. We have covered topics ranging from Chloe to the cyberbullies to Why She Won't Just Prescribe Me Some Medication and Let Me Quit Already.

Unsurprisingly, I have yet to see a positive change in my overall mental well-being.

In fact, talking about Chloe might have actually led me to make *worse* life choices. Because when I saw her get in the salad line in the cafeteria today, I hurried to get in line, too.

She was wearing her Puma Robotics sweatshirt from two years ago, the year they won the AI competition. I stared at the blinding purple, shuffling along behind her until I worked up the courage to ask, "Are you okay?"

She startled and turned. "You don't care."

"I do. I heard what Hannah said."

Chloe shivered. She tried to disguise it by turning back

to the salad bar and scrutinizing the cherry tomatoes, but she must have known I could see through that. "She said it to you, not me."

"Still."

Someone tapped me on the shoulder. I flinched, expecting it to be one of the cyberbullies, until they said, "Jess! Is it okay if I say hi?"

I stared at Dee for a second, like they were a cucumber that had just started talking. Their sparkly kitten-themed T-shirt was approximately the same color green. "Um . . . yes?"

Their eyes were wide, wary. "It's just—at rehearsal that time, you said stay away from you, and I wasn't sure if you meant, like, forever?"

"Oh. Um, not forever. That was just . . . not a great day."

"Oh, good." Their face relaxed into a smile. "That's what Carly said, but I wasn't sure, like, if you were mad at us for not standing up to Noah more."

I glanced at Chloe. Her mouth was set in a hard line.

"I—"

"Because we totally should have. It's not your fault Noah's being such a diva."

Beside me, Chloe flinched.

"He's not lying," I said softly.

"I didn't say he was a liar; I said he was a diva. That *text*! He sent that thing to everyone in his phone, like his life is a prime-time drama that we all need to be tuned in to. He is way less interesting than he thinks he is. And, like, why should we care about his sex life? Everyone in the Theatre Department has made out with everyone else at some point, am I right?"

"Um . . ." The air rushed past as Chloe abandoned her tray and darted out of my field of vision.

"Carly and Ben Ken have this lunch, too. You wanna sit with us? We really miss you." Their smile was so hopeful—and a little anxious—that I couldn't say no.

They tugged me away from the salad bar. "You don't really want to eat this crap, right? Come with me for pizza. And seriously, don't let Noah get to you. That drama queen just doesn't know when to stop."

 PRIVATE
Jan 14

REASON #50:
I didn't stop him.

Last May, Noah and I were paired together for our final drama project. We had to work out two contrasting scenes in an American play, and we chose *The Crucible* by Arthur Miller. (Because it is awesome, and '90s Daniel Day-Lewis is hot. I watched the movie five times. For Research.) We would be playing husband and wife John and Elizabeth Proctor, first in act 2 when they're fighting about John's affair, and then in their final goodbye in act 4 before John's execution.

Noah is a good actor—I mean, a seriously good actor. When he took my hands, begging me to understand why he would lie and confess to witchcraft, he brought tears to my eyes. I poured out my (Elizabeth's) heart not just because I was following the script but because his acting made me *feel* it.

"Whatever you will do, it is a good man does it," I said. "It needs a cold wife to prompt lechery."

"Enough, enough—" His hands were trembling.

"Better you should know me!"

"I will not hear it!" He dropped my hands and turned away. "I know you!"

I grabbed his hands and pulled him back toward me. "You take my sins upon you, John—"

"No, I take my own . . ." He paused, for dramatic effect, I assumed, and I barely had to act. The deep lines etched in his face that I knew meant grief, love, and regret—it was all so raw and real that I could feel it. We weren't on his bedroom floor anymore. We were crouched in dirty straw on the floor of a Puritan jail cell. My stomach did a flip because I could see how much he loved me, and I loved him, too, and he was about to die. He leaned toward me, and I lowered my forehead to his, as we had blocked the scene that afternoon in the Drama Room.

Then he tilted up my chin and pressed his lips to mine.

I froze. He was ad-libbing. We hadn't practiced it this way. A chaste moment, foreheads together, to highlight the purity of their love. That's what we had decided on.

He licked his way into my mouth, easing me back on the rug, on top of me.

My limbs weren't working.

My brain wasn't working.

I was feeling everything and nothing, hearing a zipper, my jeans.

His hand

I couldn't

"I don't . . ." My voice sounded strange, not my own, cotton balls stuffed in my ears. "I don't . . ."

He stopped. Scrambled away.

"I don't. I don't." The words echoed in my head, out of my mouth. I wanted to cover my ears, but my hands wouldn't move. Couldn't breathe. Prickling eyes shut tight, warm cheeks. "I don't. I don't. I don't."

It still felt like he was

"Oh my God." Noah's footsteps shook the floor, pacing the room. "Why didn't you stop me?"

My sluggish hands found my face, cold on my burning cheeks. No tears, but my eyes were on fire. My brain on fire. The buzz of a lawn mower outside, a pickax in my head.

"What will Chloe say?" he moaned. "I was caught up in the scene, and then we were—"

I pressed my hands over my ears. I wanted him to stop talking. Stop pacing. Just stop.

"Why didn't you stop me?"

Why didn't I stop him?

 PRIVATE
Jan 15

REASON #51:
I am stupider than Andrew Lloyd Webber's worst musical travesty.

When I finished telling her what happened, my therapist just watched me for a while. While I talked, she had kind of shifted in her puffy armchair, the twin of the one I was sitting on, and she had leaned forward, her elbows on her knees and her chin braced on her folded hands. I wondered if I should say "The End!" or give a big "Ta-da!" with jazz hands so she'd know the story was over.

It was my fourth session with Alyssa, and in the first three, I'd done my best not to talk at all, just stared at the sage-green wall behind her head and parried her attempts at conversation as best I could. But ever since I'd started eating A-day lunches with the drama crowd, my reality had been shifting. The way they talked to me, the way they talked about Noah, it was like they were seeing a kaleidoscope version of the world I was looking at. Or maybe it was *my* eyesight that was distorted.

On Tuesday night, I'd been so disoriented that I actually sat down with my laptop and typed out what happened on Memorial Day. Or as much as I could without my lungs imploding. There were gaps, images I couldn't let myself re-create because they threatened to tug me back into a black hole like what happened over winter break with Julia.

I'm pretty sure there were gaps in the story I told Alyssa today, too, although if I'm very honest, I don't remember much of the session. At least not the part between telling her about the drama project and the moment where I realized I was silent and she was staring at me like a vibrating wineglass that might be about to shatter. In retrospect, I should have just given her access to my blog so she could read about the mess of my life without my having to say any of it out loud.

"That's a lot to have been keeping inside all this time, Jess. I'm honored that you chose to share it with me."

I tried to shrug, but my shoulders were already hunched up by my ears. In fact, my whole body had crunched in on itself—my arms wrapped tight around my torso, my knees pulled up to my chest, like I was preparing to cannonball into the fluffy beige carpet between us.

"Sorry," I whispered, forcing my feet back down to the floor in defiance of my screaming muscles.

"What are you sorry for?"

"I dunno . . . bad posture?" My gaze flicked up to her face in time to catch the slight twitch at the corners of her mouth.

"You can sit any way you feel comfortable. You don't

even have to stay in that chair if you'd be more comfortable on the floor."

"It's okay." I tried to unwind my arms from around my body, but they protested.

"How does your body feel right now?"

"Tense."

"Mmm."

She waited, but I didn't have anything else to say. I studied the creamy green walls, the ivory bookshelves, the floor lamp's soft glow. In the corner, I found a spider and watched its rapid scramble toward the carpet.

"What were you feeling a moment ago?"

The spider disappeared behind a dehumidifier. "Tense."

"Mmm. And how about emotionally? What feelings were you experiencing?"

My arms tightened around my body again. "I don't know."

Alyssa kicked off her red stilettos and tucked her knees to her chest, wrapping her arms around herself, a mirror of me. "What does it look like I might be feeling right now?"

"A desire to cannonball into the carpet."

Her mouth tugged up at the corners. "I can tell humor is one of your strengths, Jess. It must serve you well when you write your plays."

Heat rose to my cheeks. "Sometimes."

"If you were writing an action for one of your characters . . . What is the word for that?"

"Stage direction."

"Thank you. If you were writing a stage direction for one of your characters, and you had them protect their body like this, what emotion would you be trying to show the audience?"

Fear. The thought came instantly, automatically, obviously. It was the stance of Toby hiding in the cellar, knowing that Mrs. Lovett wants to slit his throat. Of Audrey waiting to be beaten by that no-goodnik boyfriend of hers, Orin Scrivello, DDS. I was a Broadway cliché. A victim, cowering in the face of . . . what exactly?

"That's so stupid," I murmured.

"What's so stupid?" Alyssa asked just as quietly.

"Being afraid of the past. It's worse than stupid. It's like . . . it's *Cats*. The *film adaptation* of *Cats*, even."

"Mmm." She paused. I familiarized myself with a particular strand of fuzz on the carpet. Then she said, "Feelings are feelings. They're not really stupid or smart, good or bad."

"This one feels bad."

"That's a good point." She paused again. "What do you think of when you hear the word 'trauma'?"

War. Car accidents. The ER.

I shrugged, an unconvincing shoulder jerk.

"I know you're very bright, so I'm going to share some information with you that I didn't learn until I was studying psychology in college but that I wish I had learned sooner."

I waited.

"Our emotions are tied to our bodies. They're caused by chemical changes in our brains, and they cause physical reactions in our bodies. Like when I see a spider, my pulse speeds up, and my body freezes for a second. That's what my fear feels like."

I glanced over to the corner where the spider had disappeared a moment ago. I decided now would be a bad time to bring it up.

"But sometimes when we experience a big, frightening event, our brains and bodies get stuck on that fear. And even much later, when nothing scary is happening, we can have some of the same fear feelings in our bodies. That is *trauma*."

My pulse sped up. "But that's not what happened to me. I wasn't— I mean, there wasn't any big, frightening event."

"Ah, I see. How would you describe that event?"

"I—" I searched for a word other than "frightening" but couldn't find one. "What are you saying? Like, a boy kissing me and . . . like, sex is so scary it makes me curl up in a ball of terror? That's not a thing."

Or maybe it was. Is that what it means to be ace? But then wouldn't I have also felt frightened when making out with Cam?

"Mmm."

"Stop *mmm*ing! If you have something to say, just say it."

Alyssa's voice was much calmer and softer than mine. "I'm sorry, Jess. I sometimes use sounds like 'Mmm' or 'Uh-huh' as indications that I am listening to you. That's a habit of mine, and maybe not such a great one. I was trying to encourage you to go on."

"Oh. Well, I'm done. I don't have anything else to say." I had already shared one deep, dark secret today. I wasn't about to let Alyssa into my whole Am I Asexual or Just Overly Sensitive to Tongue Texture Conundrum.

"Okay," she said.

The silence in the room was almost suffocating. My toes felt like tiny ice cubes. My leg jiggled like it was going to jackhammer through the floor.

"Would it be okay if I summarize what I'm taking away from what you've said? I want to make sure I'm hearing it the way you want me to hear it."

"Okay."

"A moment ago, you said you felt 'afraid.' You had feelings of fear surrounding the events of Memorial Day. But you also feel that fear isn't the right emotion to attach to those events—that they shouldn't have been scary and you shouldn't still be feeling afraid of something that happened in the past. Did I understand correctly?"

"I guess." I hated the way it sounded in her voice. It was like Chloe restating one of my ideas in the simplest terms and thereby revealing it as illogical nonsense.

"I get really frustrated when I can't figure out *why* I'm feeling something," she said. "You'd think that after six years and two degrees in psychology, I'd be better at that."

"Yeah." Not particularly encouraging that someone who

studies emotions for a living doesn't understand their own.

"I think I like to understand *why* I have certain emotions because it makes me feel like I have more control. But sometimes when I'm searching for a *why*, I lose track of *what* I'm feeling. If I think I *should* feel one thing in a certain situation, I have trouble recognizing that I'm actually feeling something else—because it doesn't seem to make sense. Those *should*s really set me back."

I said nothing.

"Do you ever feel that way—like you *should* be having a different emotion than what you're really feeling?"

"I don't know."

"Okay."

"It's not okay, really."

There was a pause before Alyssa asked, "What isn't okay?"

"Feelings. These feelings." I scrubbed a hand over my eyes, which were alarmingly warm and watery. "I shouldn't be feeling afraid now about something that happened a long time ago. I shouldn't have been afraid *then*, because how was that scary?"

"When I think about the story you told me, I can imagine that I might have felt fear in a similar situation."

I half expected to see a mocking smile, but her mouth was a relaxed but undeniably serious line. "Really? Why?"

She wet her lips. "I'm not as good of a writer as you, so bear with me because I'm going to try to use a metaphor here... It reminded me of a time when my car skidded on ice on the highway. It was unexpected, and everything was out of my control for a time. That was a very frightening feeling."

I could imagine that, the feeling of skidding on ice, my hands clenched on a steering wheel, my stomach plummeting to the dirt-streaked car mat beneath my feet. And in my imagination it wasn't too different from what I'd felt when Noah kissed me.

Except.

"Except it wasn't out of my control. As soon as I said something, he stopped. And if I'd said something sooner, he'd have stopped sooner, and it wouldn't have happened."

Alyssa started to *mmm* but caught herself.

"So that pretty much pulverizes your trauma theory."

Her lips quirked. "I like how you think therapy is a competition. It keeps me on my toes."

"Then I guess I'm winning," I muttered.

"Our session is almost over for today, and I want to say again how honored I am that you chose to share these things with me. I hope that this week you'll check in from time to time with your emotions and your body. You don't need to decide if it's good or bad or right or wrong—just notice what you're feeling. Sometimes just giving a feeling a label helps me feel less confused and more in control of my life."

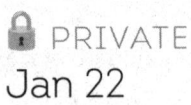
Jan 22

REASON #52:
I'm going to be famous (for a good thing this time).

"I don't want to be famous," I told Dee. The chaos of the cafeteria was making my brain sluggish, but that hadn't stopped me from understanding what they were asking.

"I didn't mean *famous* famous," Dee said. "It's not like that many people actually go to the Spring Spectacle. It will just be theatre kids."

And there was the crux of my anxiety. Noah *always* did the Spring Spectacle. I don't even think he cared about the extra credit for Drama class. He was one of the narcissists; it was just another opportunity to be onstage.

"And you can direct us," Carly said, tugging at the bottom of her yellow headwrap. "Think of it: a world premiere, directed by the playwright. Tisch will be impressed."

"I already turned in my application."

"They'll still be impressed. And anyway, the play is *amazing*. It's going to change the world! Or at least the school!"

Not for the first time, I regretted showing Dee and Carly the script for *Restraint*. My heels drummed the tiles, my tongue scrubbing at my gums. "I don't think I can do it."

"Is this still about Noah?" Dee asked. "Because Ben Ken has threatened to beat him up at least twice this year. You could ask him to go through with it."

I turned to Ben. "Why do you want to beat up Noah?"

He chewed slowly, pulling off his newsie cap and raking a hand through his dark curls as he mused. "Can't remember, actually."

"Because he's *Noah*." Dee waved a hand. "He's always doing *Noah* things and being generally *Noahish*."

"Oh yeah," Ben said through a mouthful of pizza. "I definitely wanted to beat him up when he made that freshman bring him vending-machine dinner backstage because he was 'too emotionally drained' to make it to the cafeteria."

A giggle startled out of me. "Does he still do that thing where he lies on the floor with his feet in the air?"

Carly raised her hand with a flourish. "Because it helps the blood flow to the brain, Jessica! Brain blood is key to the development of an actor's craft . . . and shit . . ."

We all lost it. I was laughing so hard I actually had to grip the table to keep myself from floating away like Uncle Albert in *Mary Poppins*. And when the laughter finally died back and I reopened my eyes, which were now slightly blurred by tears of ecstasy, I saw Chloe. Two tables away. Watching.

You want to know what emotions I felt, Alyssa? All of

them. Every possible emotion at once, like a fireworks show of feelings. Shame, anxiety, sadness, anger . . . but happiness, too, sitting at the table with three friends who hadn't rejected me, who reminded me of other friends who'd stood by me the whole time: Cam, Emily, Julia, even. And somehow—somehow after everything—still love for Chloe, for this person who was once a part of myself and whose memory now literally hurts me. My phantom limb.

The emotions crackled through me, each so loud they drowned out the chaos of the cafeteria, and it wasn't until a long pause had passed that I realized Carly had spoken, had asked again if I would let them perform *Restraint*.

I fiddled with the crust of my pizza, closing my eyes and trying to focus past the explosion of emotions, past the buzz of conversation and jarring clatter of forks on trays and squeaks of shoes on tile, down to the specific emotions surrounding my play—a very personal play about my own judgmental terribleness—being performed onstage in front of some of the same people who've been judging me all year. Somehow, even though it was fiction, it felt much more personal and vulnerable than any of these blog posts that used to be public. It might be exciting, but it would definitely be embarrassing. And would it actually change anything?

I opened my eyes. Two tables away someone was tossing M&M's in the air and catching them in his mouth: Jeff Watkins, football star who now knew at least five Emily Dickinson poems by heart.

"Yes," I said.

"Yes!" Dee echoed, slamming a fist on their tray and shuddering the whole table.

"Yes to letting you perform the play, but no to being the director."

Once that play got on the stage, it wouldn't be mine anymore. The actors would each bring something to the roles. The designer would set the tone. And the whole thing would be shaped by a director, someone brave who could bring their own vision to the words that I'd put on the page, turning it into something unique and new.

And I had the perfect person in mind.

Jan 29

REASON #53:
The narrator of my life is an a-hole.

"Do you think the characters know they're in a play?" Alyssa asked.

It was our second session since I'd told her about Noah, and so far she hadn't brought it up again. Last time, we went through the emotions I'd recorded in my notebook and talked about strategies for regulating emotional and sensory overload. (They were "strategies" rather than "solutions" because at least 70 percent of the time they didn't work.)

This week, apparently, we were talking about theatre.

"Not in my one-act," I said. "But when the playwright or the director calls attention to the fact that the play is a play—it's called 'metatheatricality'—sometimes the characters are in on it."

Alyssa leaned down to scratch her ankle where the strap from her ridiculously high heel chafed her skin. (The shoes were gold this week. With sparkles. *Sparkles.*) "You're saying the playwright can create characters that know they're in a play?"

I dragged my gaze from her shoes to the scuff on the wall next to her head, my normal focal point. "Yeah, like in *Into the Woods*. The characters figure out that the narrator isn't really part of the story and they kill him off. In the play. Not in the movie."

"Do you have a narrator?"

"In *Restraint*?"

"In your head."

Silent alarms flashed in my brain. Alyssa's mouth was relaxed in her calm-therapist smile, which I had come to realize was her game face. She was on the offensive. "I don't hear voices, if that's what you're trying to ask."

"No. Many people have an internal monologue or dialogue in response to things. For example, if I leave the milk out on the counter all day, when I get home, I might think, 'Well, that was stupid, Alyssa.'"

"Oh. Yeah, okay," I admitted, ignoring the immediate feeling that such an admission could be a tactical error.

"So, when you say that you're anxious about your friends putting on your play, what kinds of things is your narrator saying?"

Ah, we had arrived at the Point. "Like, *this is a bad idea* or *it's only going to make things worse.*"

"Make what things worse?"

"You know, the cyberbullies. Not that they'll see it. But Noah . . . Noah will be there."

And if he sees it, he might tell the cyberbullies. And more important, he'll see it, *and I'll have to face him and maybe talk to him, and then I'll have a panic attack and/or puke on the stage and–*

"Would you like a cup of water, Jess? Or some tea?"

I shook my head, took a deep shuddering breath, and blew it out through pursed lips.

"The blanket next to you is weighted if that would help."

I dragged the blanket onto my legs, then up to my chin. I let the pressure seep into my body, grounding me, let my tongue rove over my teeth.

Maybe ten minutes passed before Alyssa asked, "What would be helpful for us to talk about right now?"

"I don't know. Whatever you want."

"I don't have a preference. We could talk more about your play, we could talk about what your narrator was saying a moment ago, we could talk about musicals—whatever you're comfortable with right now."

"I'm not sure I can go to my play's premiere," I said, "if even just thinking about it makes me freak out."

She nodded slowly. "Choosing not to put yourself in a situation that might trigger a panic attack is a perfectly valid choice. Do you think your friends will understand?"

"Yeah." I sighed. "I just . . . I really want to see it onstage, you know?"

"Is there another option? Could we brainstorm ways that we could make going to the play a safer choice for you?"

"I don't know." I tugged the blanket up a little higher. "I guess I could bring one of these. It's just so stupid that I can't be in the same room with him without losing my mind."

"Mmm. When I hear you say 'it's just so stupid,' I wonder if that's your narrator talking."

"Just because it's my *narrator* or whatever, that doesn't mean it's not true."

"If I were the one experiencing a panic attack, what would you say to me? Would you say I was being stupid?"

"I'm not that much of an a-hole."

"Would it be true, though? Would I be being 'stupid' for having a panic attack?"

The blanket slipped off one of my shoulders when I shrugged. I wouldn't give her the satisfaction of admitting that the answer was no.

"Are there other things your narrator has to say about Noah or your emotions surrounding him?"

My head spasmed in something between a headshake and a nod. The heat kicked on, a low hum that oscillated at rhythmic intervals, like the lowest, droning pitch in my mother's chanting-monks music.

"You're responsible! You're the one to blame! It's your fault!" I sang quietly.

"Your narrator sings." Her smile broadened like this was some sort of adorable creativity on my part.

"It's Sondheim. It's from *Into the Woods*."

"Ah." She nodded like she understood, though I knew she didn't. We had established in the first half of the session that Alyssa was woefully uneducated in classic musical theatre.

"I want to make sure I'm hearing what you want me to hear. Is your narrator saying what happened on Memorial Day was your fault?"

"It must be my fault or it wouldn't have happened."

She didn't nod. She didn't *mmm*. She just waited, and something about that silence removed the lid from my voice and let my words come burbling out.

"I know you're going to say 'It's not your fault, Jess,' but you're wrong. When I said no, he stopped, like, immediately. If I'd said it sooner..."

She nodded slowly. "Two weeks ago, I shared with you a little bit about trauma. I remember that you're not sure whether that word describes your experience. I just want to share another piece of information in case it's helpful. In a moment that someone experiences as traumatic, there are some common responses. Have you heard of fight or flight?"

I nodded.

"So, those aren't things that people *choose* to do. It's like flinching if something came unexpectedly flying toward you. Does that make sense?"

"Yeah, but I didn't fight or run away or whatever."

"There's another one that is less famous, probably because it doesn't rhyme. When people experience a trauma, sometimes they freeze."

I almost flinched as the memory hit me—lying on the floor, my limbs like rocks, my voice stuck in my throat. I swallowed the feeling away and wriggled farther down under the blanket.

"Since it's not a choice, a person experiencing this can't just *unfreeze* and do something to stop the traumatic thing from happening."

"But if I didn't tell him, how was he supposed to know I wanted him to stop?"

"I can't remember." She spoke slowly, watching me. "Did you tell him you wanted him to kiss you or to touch you in that way?"

"I—" I closed my eyes. "No. But do people really ask permission before they kiss other people? That doesn't sound like a thing."

"People do often check in with one another before initiating physical intimacy of any kind, including kissing—especially when they aren't in a romantic relationship together and haven't discussed boundaries before—just to make sure they are on the same page. And from your description, it sounds like he did more than kiss you without getting consent."

"Yeah, but—but once he did . . . that . . . then he could feel how my body was— So he must have thought I wanted it." I buried my face in my hands, as though if I blocked out the glow of the lamp, I could somehow unfeel the past.

The heating system clicked off again, leaving a sudden emptiness in the air around me. The cushion of Alyssa's armchair scrunched quietly as she shifted, waiting. I counted my breaths as they slowed.

Finally, she spoke. "Can you stop yourself from sneezing?"

"Umm . . . what?"

"If I threw some pepper at your nose, could you stop yourself from sneezing?"

A startled giggle escaped me. "Why would you throw pepper at my nose?"

"I don't know. I just meant—"

"You are so weird."

Her lips tugged up at the corners. "I'll own that. Okay, what if the wind blew pollen up your nose. Could you stop yourself from sneezing?"

"Definitely not. My allergies are the worst."

"So, that's an involuntary physical reaction to something that happens to you. The same kind of physical reactions can happen with sexual contact—even unwanted sexual contact. A physical reaction isn't proof of wanting or not wanting sex or any kind of intimate touch. And it's definitely not the same as consent."

"But that makes it sound like it's his fault," I whispered.

"What if we didn't have to decide on it being someone's fault today? What if we could just let the question of blame and responsibility go and think about your experience and the emotions that went along with it? If it didn't have to be his fault, would the trauma reaction—that *freezing*—sound more like your experience?"

I thought about her question. Then I tried to think about *it*. I couldn't. It was like the sun. The minute I turned my face toward it, I instinctively closed my eyes.

"What are you feeling right now?" Alyssa asked gently.

I had squeezed my eyelids tight as if I could block out reality like dust particles. "Humiliated. That's how I always feel when I think about . . . it. Or when I see him."

"Can you tell me more about that?"

"Whenever he brings it up, or when I remember, I just feel so embarrassed. And, like, horrified. That he saw me like that. That I was like that. It was like I lost control of myself, and I just felt so . . ."

She waited for me to continue, but I couldn't find the word.

"Would it be fair to say you felt vulnerable?" she asked.

"Yeah, maybe that's it." I was sweating and my muscles were taut.

"Thank you for sharing that."

She didn't say anything else. Neither of us did for the last ten minutes of the session. As I extricated myself from the weighted blanket and steeled myself to meet my mom in the lobby, Alyssa said, "We can talk more next week about your play, if you want, and whether we can come up with a plan for how you can feel safe if you decide to go to the show. But this week, remember: if your narrator is telling you that you aren't allowed to take care of yourself, she's telling you lies."

🔒 PRIVATE
Feb 3

REASON #54:
I lied to my (current) best friend.

Winter is a glorious season when Cam doesn't have practice every single day, meaning we can sometimes study calculus on weekdays as well as weekends. (I guess that's actually not too glorious . . . But hanging out with Cam is glorious in its own right.)

"I have conditioning tomorrow," he said, stretching out on the blanket under the stairs and ignoring his Calc book. "But we can study again on Thursday if you want."

I silently cursed Cam's sportsb—*base*ball—coach for giving him a Thursday off. I'd made it like a month without having to come up with a lie about what I did on Thursday afternoons. Because I definitely couldn't tell Cam *Hey, guess what? I'm seeing a shrink to have my crazy brain fixed!*

ALYSSA

(offstage)

Are you sure that's not your unreliable narrator talking?

I scooched myself into the farthest back corner of the homework cave, as far from Cam's languid form as possible, and braced my bare feet on the carpet.

"I see a therapist on Thursdays."

Cam sat up. I fixed my eyes on the knees of his Puma Purple sweatpants because I wasn't sure I wanted to see his reaction, but he just said, "That's great! Is it helping you deal with the bullying?"

"Kind of." I hesitated. "It's about what happened last year. With Noah. I—I kind of might have PTSD?" I didn't have to look at his face to know he was staring at me. My cheeks started to burn.

"Are you serious? But you told me . . . But really he— Did he—?"

"I, um, experienced it as a trauma?" I said, stealing Alyssa's words. The other words still didn't seem right.

"Oh my God. Oh my God." Cam tried to stand and smacked his head on the bottom of the stairs. He cursed, rubbing his head. "Are you okay? I guess you're not okay. Why didn't you tell me?"

"I'm sorry."

"Don't be sorry. You don't have to be sorry. Jesus." He scrubbed his fingers across his forehead like he was trying to erase the lines of his frown. "When exactly . . . ?"

"Memorial Day."

"You called me. You called me like ten times."

"It's okay," I whispered.

"No, it isn't okay, Jess." He remembered to crawl out of the cave this time before he stood and started pacing. "You called me ten times, and I didn't call you back."

I'd forgotten I'd done that. It had been in my initial panic after the event. By the next morning, I was pretty thoroughly enveloped in a guilt-fog. "You were busy."

"Yeah, eating hot dogs with my cousins. Playing at the beach. I should have picked up the phone. I should have made my parents drive me back."

"I'm not trying to make you feel bad."

He stopped pacing and crawled back into the cave. "No, I know. I just— God, Jess, I feel so awful. I wish there was something that I could do, and it turns out there's something I could have done, but I didn't."

"It's not your fault."

Cam scooched next to me, leaning his broad shoulders against the wall. He touched my hand, and when I didn't pull away, laced his fingers with mine. The warmth from his palm melted some of the jagged edges in my brain.

"It's not your fault, either," he said. "You know that, right?"

I brushed my thumb experimentally over the back of his hand. He squeezed mine tight, and little happy-flutters evaporated more of the guilt-fog away. "I'm trying."

"Do you want to talk about it now?"

"Not really."

"Okay."

We probably should have talked, at least about the ambiguous hand-holding and all. It didn't feel sexy, exactly. Just close. Happy. Warm. And that close-happy-warmness reminded me of another evening with Cam in the homework cave, him tipsy, me not, our lips meeting, the faint taste of cheap beer—and then the bit I'd forgotten: his pulling away and asking, *Is this okay?*

"Huh," I said.

"What?"

"Nothing. I just remembered you're a good person."

"Is it that forgettable?"

"Apparently."

He shoved my shoulder playfully but didn't let go of my hand. I leaned against him, and we both sat in silence for a while. There was another conversation we'd need to have—someday. But not today.

PRIVATE
Feb 17

REASON #55:
I'm going to Broadway, bitches!

Not really.

But I got accepted at Tisch!!!!! (Normally I do not condone the use of multiple exclamation marks, but in this instance it was essential to convey the true !!!!! of the moment.)

Starting in August, I will be a first year at the Rita and Burton Goldberg Department of Dramatic Writing. My mom had the day off from work and was on her phone when the notification email came. And instead of calling me like a normal mom, she drove to the school and pulled me out of Government to share the news. Slightly embarrassing but mostly thrilling.

I had my phone in my pocket, so I texted Julia and got back about a million exclamation marks and celebratory emojis. Then I texted Emily, and I was about to text Cam when I realized he'd probably prefer to hear the news in person. It wasn't until my mom asked, "What did your father say?" that I realized it hadn't even occurred to me to tell him. I'd send him an email when I got a chance.

I returned to Government, but it was impossible to focus on the nuances of executive privilege. Really all I could think about were the people I wanted to tell. Cam, Carly and Dee, Ms. Otashi, Mr. Barton—Creative Writing was next period; I could tell the whole lit mag staff at once!

Chloe.

She'd hear somehow.

I wondered if she got into Caltech.

When I walked into the Pubs Lab, the place was full of balloons and cupcakes and beaming word nerds.

"How did you even get all this stuff?"

Mr. Barton tapped the side of his nose, a thing literally no other human on earth does. "Emily tipped me off, and I had planning last period," he said. "But seriously, everyone, crumbs away from the computers or the yearbook assassins will come for me." He held his cupcake in the air. "To Jess!"

The class echoed his toast. I almost hugged him. If the whole class hadn't been there, I would have. I settled instead for snatching a chocolate cupcake. As the other word nerds engaged one another in bubbly chatter, I hung close to Mr. Barton. "Did— Did Chloe get into Caltech?"

"She decided to apply to UVA. She should hear soon."

My universe rippled for a confusing moment. "But . . . she's always wanted to go to Caltech."

"Since she decided she wanted to major in music, it really wasn't an option anymore."

Major in music? Chloe's plan was medical robotics. It was *always* medical robotics. Did she have a mid-senior-year crisis? Was majoring in music her version of my dad's new convertible?

"I'm sorry, Jess. I didn't mean—" Mr. Barton wiped some anxiety sweat off his forehead with a napkin. "I forgot you wouldn't have known."

"It's okay." I swallowed my feeling of disconnect along with a few stray cupcake crumbs. "What I really wanted to say . . . Well, I've been seeing a counselor."

"I'm so glad to hear that, Jess," he said, but he was nodding with such a clear lack of surprise that I knew my mother had already told him.

Freaking mothers.

"Yeah, so, you know in the fall you asked if Chloe was safe? You know, with Noah?"

His hands stilled on his cupcake wrapper.

"I said she was, but I'm not totally sure anymore. Like, she might be," I said quickly, somewhat alarmed by the way his body had gone all rigid. "And I'm not even sure if they're still together because he kind of yelled at me before break because she was mad at him or something?"

"They're still together." Mr. Barton's voice was as rigid as his body.

"Oh. Well, in that case, yeah. He just maybe isn't totally clear on the concept of . . . *consent*." I whispered the last word like it was a secret code or the most forbidden of curse words. I don't know why it was painful to say something so vague and clinical aloud. Maybe because I'd only recently realized that *I* hadn't been totally clear on the concept of consent, at least when it applied to me while rehearsing a scene with a theatre-mate/best-friend's boyfriend.

Mr. Barton nodded slowly, his whole body still tense. "Thank you, Jess. Thank you very much. I know it took a lot for you to . . . Listen, you've passed it off now, and Dr. B and I will take care of her. You don't need to engage with this anymore, okay? You take care of you."

My heart twinged at that. I don't know if it was relief at having passed it off or guilt for not being there for Chloe or a latent disappointment that things weren't the way they used to be—that I apparently didn't even know her or her life plans anymore. But the feeling softened as class wore on, with Emily's fierce hugs and everyone's millions of questions about details I didn't know yet. I was almost able to ignore Mr. Barton frowning into his phone in the corner and focus on the bubbles of joy still careening their way through my body.

NYU isn't 100 percent for sure, of course, because it costs

more than a Long Island wedding and I haven't heard about financial aid yet. But I will find a way.

I will take out student loans.

I will sell my pubic hair to black-market pervs.

I will break into Hannah's house and steal her mother's inexplicable collection of creepy porcelain shepherd children.

Broadway, here I come!

 PRIVATE
Feb 17

REASON #56:
I am crushing my life goals.

I waited by Cam's minivan for about ten minutes before I remembered he had baseball. I wasn't sure if I was allowed to watch the practice, but no one stopped me as I clanked my way up the sportsfield-riser-things.

Cameron is gorgeous. I know I say that a lot, and I used to think that meant I couldn't be asexual. But I have learned from my new, regularly scheduled video chat with Julia that the way I appreciate gorgeous men is actually pretty similar to the way people on a-/graysexual message boards describe their experience. (Yes, Julia googled it. I'm accepting bets on how long before the Russian hackers get in touch.)

For example, I thoroughly appreciated Cam's physique in those weird, tight baseball-capris and the short-sleeve shirt that was just loose enough to cling to his shoulders when he drew his arm back to throw the ball, but I did not actually want to have sex with him. It was more like, *Yes, these shoulders and man thighs have Jessica Lanza's seal of approval, but let's keep them at a distance, shall we?*

Cam noticed me at some point during the practice and glanced over periodically. It wasn't until his coach shouted for them all to "hit the showers" (he actually said that—unironically, I assume) that he trotted over to me. He was tomato red, and sweat plastered his hair to his face. When he pulled off his baseball hat—cap? Cap, right?—baseball *cap*, it left a wet depression in a circle around his hair where sweat had soaked into the band.

And if I'm being honest, he reeked.

"You are much hotter from a distance," I told him.

"What are you doing here?"

"I came to watch you practice."

"Really?" Even though he was obviously exhausted and panting, his lips pulled back in a grin.

"Yeah, and if it's okay with you, I'll come more often. It was pretty fun."

He tilted his head to one side like he was trying to figure out whether I was lying. "And what's the other reason you came?"

I flushed.

"It's cool. I'm not offended. But there must be another reason."

"I got into Tisch."

He whooped so loudly that his coach looked over to be

sure he wasn't being murdered, then caught me in a bear hug and swung me around.

"Put me down."

"Never." He whooped again.

"Lewis," the coach barked. "Pack it in. I'm not waiting around to close up the locker room just so you and your girl can do whatever that is."

My ears flamed as Cam finally set me down. "Wait for me? I'll drive you home and you can tell me everything."

I managed to say "Sure" without my voice croaking from embarrassment. I sat on the sportsfield-risers while Cam jogged to the locker room, and I deeply regretted that there were no showers available for me to hit. In the course of the hug, a considerable amount of his sweat had been sponged off on my cardigan.

And sitting there in the February chill, stinking of man, my fingers plinking a joyful rhythm as they fluttered against the metal seat, I realized: I am crushing the Senior Year Plan. I got into college. I will be getting the hell out of Stone Bridge. And—miracle of miracles—I'm actually having fun. Between rehearsals for *Restraint* and hanging out with Cam and Emily and my newfound appreciation for baseball (or at least the clothing in which it is played), senior year isn't turning out too terrible after all. My happiness is now a solid B. Maybe even an A–.

And as for that one goal I'm missing . . . Well, I'm starting to wonder if that's not for the best, too.

PRIVATE
Feb 25

REASON #57:
I have a security detail, apparently.

As expected, Emily had agreed to direct *Restraint* in the Spring Spectacle. It probably helped that I asked her when we were having a movie night at her house with Nic, whose immediate response was "Yes, yes, yes, you *must*! Can I help with costumes?" But I think another part of it is that little bubble of confidence I've seen growing in her all year. Last week, in the Pubs Lab, she actually spoke up and debated me on what was the best piece of student art for the lit mag cover. She won. I was impressed.

Dee had called dibs on Josephine (the bird), and Carly would be playing Amy (the toad). They'd also rounded up a handful of underclassmen to play the Vices, and Ben Ken would be up in the lighting booth. I'd agreed to help Emily with sound during rehearsals, but I found myself getting distracted and watching the action.

Or, more often than not, inaction.

"Nic, I'm breathing in feathers here." Dee pushed the headband of orange craft feathers higher on their forehead.

"Duh! You're a bird."

"Emily!"

"We'll work with the costume, Dee. Can we just practice with the ladder, please?"

"I can't climb down a ladder I can't see!"

"Nic!"

While the actors took ten for costuming adjustments, I paged through the script. It really was incredible, my words coming to life onstage. It made my skin ripple with goose bumps.

It also made me realize that my script wasn't quite right. I'd made a few minor changes to some of the lines, but the main issue was the ending. When Josephine climbed down the ladder, it never quite felt over, but I couldn't figure out exactly what was missing.

I was thwacking my pen against the last page of the script, running through possibilities in my head, when I heard my name. I looked at the stage, and my heart stuttered.

"Is she back there?" Noah asked, squinting into the dark house. He wasn't smiling. I couldn't tell if he was sad or angry, his brows low, his mouth drawn down and trembling. It was the first time I'd ever seen him onstage without a performance face on. "Hey, Jess!"

When evolution was handing out trauma responses, it

left me with none of the fight and a whole lot of freeze. Alyssa assures me that it's the same for many allistic people, not an autistic thing, but I couldn't help wishing I were more like Julia. She'd have been throwing punches already. I was an oak tree, rooted deep in my chair, grasping the soundboard and waiting for the axe that would fell me.

"Don't be a dick, Noah. We're having a rehearsal." Carly flounced her brown toad-cape at him.

"I need to talk to her."

"Is it about this production?" Emily hiked up the stage-left stairs. Her voice was soft but firm, and with her clipboard in hand and her teal hair wrapped up into a bun, she looked every bit as officious as Ms. Otashi. "No? Then get off my stage. Please."

Noah tried to brush past her, but Emily put a hand on his chest. "My sound tech is occupied. We'll be through here at six. Until then, please leave."

Perhaps realizing that there was something more going on than Noah being melodramatic, Dee and Carly had moved downstage, too. They flanked Emily at the steps, facing Noah with as much gravitas as one can when dressed as a bird or an amphibian. Nic bobbed from foot to foot in the wings, her arms full of deconstructed orange boas.

Noah's jaw quivered. "Look, I've got my girlfriend's parents lecturing me about consent all of a sudden, and I want to know what *your sound tech* has been saying to them."

Everyone's heads twisted to look at me. The underclassmen openly gaped. Panic thrummed through me, shuddering in my limbs.

Only Emily remained calm. "I'm sorry you're having trouble in your personal life, Noah, but that really has nothing to do with this production—or Jess."

"It does have to do with Jess, if she's been telling people— I mean, if she thinks—" His face scrunched up, and I wondered if he was trying not to scream or cry. "That's not what happened. I wouldn't do that. I'm not . . ." He tried again to push past, but my wonderful, heroic friends were an impenetrable wall. Dee actually grabbed his shoulder and shoved him back a few steps.

"I'd like to continue my rehearsal now, if that's not an inconvenience to you, Noah." Emily brandished her clipboard.

Outnumbered by my personal army and outmassed by the stage and the towering curtains behind him, Noah looked suddenly small. "I'm going to talk to you, Jess." His perfect stage projection and diction drove the words all the way to my seat in the back, but there was a quiver in his voice. Maybe he wasn't sad or angry, but afraid—afraid the guilt he was feeling was justified. Needing me to reassure him that it wasn't. "I'll be in the lobby."

He exited stage left. I needed to collapse or rock or scream or all of the above, but I couldn't. I couldn't let myself. Maybe I could have if it had just been Emily. But

Carly and Dee were there, and Nic, and all those underclassmen, and I could hear Ben Ken clomping down from the lighting booth—

"It's okay if you need to go home," Emily whispered. I hadn't even noticed her coming down the aisle toward me. Carly and Dee had followed, along with Nic, a trail of orange feathers drifting in her wake. "Whatever you need to do to take care of your mental health."

A jolt of electricity rushed through me like it was a live wire on my shoulder instead of Emily's gentle hand. I hadn't told Emily what happened with Noah yet.

And only just then did it occur to me that she'd guessed. Maybe right from the start, Emily had known. I always forget that some humans are actually incredible at reading other people's minds. *Emily Fernandez as . . . Captain Emotion!*

I forced my chattering teeth apart to say *No, I'm fine*, but what came out instead was "Yeah, I should go."

"I'll drive you," Dee offered, doffing their feathered headband and jacket.

"Oh." I hadn't even thought about how I would get home. "No, you need to rehearse."

"No, I don't." They grinned. "I'm already perfect."

There was a chorus of boos, and someone threw a balled-up sock at Dee's head. Dee ignored them all, bowing to me and offering their arm. "Milady?"

But I turned to Emily because something had just occurred to me. "Were you the other reader?" My voice popped and frizzed, punctuated by tooth-chatters. "Of my blog?"

"You have a blog?" Dee piped up. "What's the— *Rude!*" (That last was probably directed at Ben Ken, who'd just swatted them with his newsie cap.)

Emily half shrugged, her voice back to its typical mumble. "You're a good writer."

I wanted to say thank you, not just for standing between me and Noah today but for everything else—a whole year's worth of thank-yous—but my teeth were completely out of control, and it was reverberating down to my knees, so I just nodded. Then I grabbed on to Dee's proffered arm and let them escort me out the back door to the parking lot.

🔒 PRIVATE
Mar 1

REASON #58:
*In seventeen years of life,
I'd never really talked to my mom.*

A peace has settled over the apartm—town house. Admittedly, part of it is the fact that Julia is away at college again and our new weekly video chats aren't long enough for us to annoy each other too much, but my mom and I are fighting less, too. I've even voluntarily gone to church with her a couple of times, which wasn't as terrible as I expected. Mostly because (a) the ritual is still kind of comforting to my jittery autistic self, and (b) Nic is apparently Episcopalian and spends the whole service not-so-subtly waving at me and mouthing entire conversations across the congregation from her perch with the choir.

We went to the early service on the morning of my Big Party. The Big Party was Mom's idea to celebrate me getting into Tisch. I'm not sure she and I have the same definition of "big," and part of me was curious about who she intended to invite (her coworkers? my aunts? the cyberbullies?), but in the end, I convinced her to just have a celebratory dinner with Cam and his folks. Realistically, neither she nor I have the social skills for a larger gathering.

After we got home from church, she flooded the house with purple and white balloons. (Would you believe that NYU's school color is also purple? Once a Puma, always a Puma, as they say.) We started cutting out little movie clapboards and writing the names of the guests on them as place cards (her idea).

Maybe it was the relative peace in which we'd been living or some sort of divine prompting from my morning daydreaming in a church pew that inspired me to ask, "Why didn't you tell me about Dad's affairs?" She stopped writing in the middle of Cam's dad's name.

"I wanted you to have a good relationship with your father," she said without looking up.

"It's not a good relationship if it's based on a lie."

She sighed and finished writing. "Anger isn't healthy."

"It can be. That's what my therapist says."

She put down her pen and raised her chin to look me in the eye. I tried not to squirm. "I never lied to you. And I'm not sorry for keeping things from you. I was protecting you, and I was protecting myself. Can you understand having something you don't want to talk about?"

"Unfortunately," I muttered. "But you *weren't* protecting

yourself, because I thought it was your fault, so I was—" I took a shuddering breath. There was no avoiding this moment. "I'm really sorry. For treating you like dirt."

She pulled me into a hug that crumpled the little clapboard I was still holding. "You don't need to apologize for anything. Honestly, I thought it was my fault, too. For a long time."

Unfortunately, I could understand that, as well.

"It's almost a reflex I have, to apologize for everything, even things that have nothing to do with me. I've done it my whole life." She took the clapboard from me and smoothed its wrinkles on the NYU-purple paper tablecloth. "Your father has the opposite problem. He never believes anything is his fault no matter what he does. You know, he once went off the road in a snowdrift because he had decided to go meet one of his—um—friends in the middle of a blizzard, and when he got home, he yelled at me for an hour because apparently if I had remembered to put a bag of kitty litter in the trunk of the car, he would have been able to get himself out of the ditch on his own and wouldn't have had to wait for a tow truck." She smiled like it was a moment of fond nostalgia instead of the most screwed-up thing I'd ever heard.

"And you think *anger* isn't healthy?"

"It was years ago."

"All of it?"

"At this point? Yes." She was still staring at the blindingly purple tablecloth, and she looked kind of sad, maybe even a little lost. A prickling suspicion crept up the back of my neck.

"You wouldn't . . ." I ran my tongue over my incisors. "I mean, if he asked you to take him back, you wouldn't, right?"

She took a slow breath. "No." She looked up, and I was relieved that however deeply her frown lines were etched in her forehead, her mouth was set in determination. "I made a mistake, staying with him that long. I knew it deep down for a long time, but seeing you this year . . ." She shook her head. "My first priority is you girls, and I see now what damage his example has done to you and Julia—"

"And to you."

"And to me," she conceded. "So, no. I will never take your father back."

"Good," I said. It was weird talking to my mom about relationships. I mean, I'd never had a romantic relationship, so I didn't have a lot to go on, but I think I was on pretty solid ground in believing that when a man lies to you and cheats on you and blames you for all his mistakes, you should maybe think about breaking up with him.

"But just because I'm no longer in contact with your father doesn't mean you can't be."

Hah. "I don't really—"

"I'm not saying you have to." My mom reached out and squeezed my arm. "Just that if you wanted to, it would be okay. Whatever relationship you want with him—or no relationship at all—it's okay."

Maybe someday, in like a million years, if he decided to become a different person, I would hang out with him again. But right now? With everything else I'm dealing with? I don't have the energy to sort through any more lies.

"And you . . ." She hesitated. "You're not still seeing the boy who . . ."

I winced. "I have never dated anyone. The—the thing that happened—was not with someone I was dating or have any desire to date."

"Oh, Jessie." She reached out for me again, but this time, I dodged.

"Remember how like five seconds ago we were talking about things we definitely *don't* want to talk about? This is one of those things."

She opened her mouth, probably to say something else super awkward.

"And you still haven't said you forgive me for treating you like dirt about Dad."

She stepped closer and put an arm around my shoulders. "Of course, I forgive you." I let her hold me for a long moment, but when she kissed the top of my head, I wriggled away.

"You know, you used to like to snuggle," she said. "Julia never did. She was up and running as soon as her legs would support her. But you just liked to be held. If I'd let you, you'd probably have kept nursing until—"

"Oh my God, *please* do not tell that story when Cam gets here."

"All out of my system." She held up her hands in surrender.

"Good."

"I'm really proud of you, Jess," she said. "I'll miss you, but I'm really proud."

"Thanks." And then, since the conversation was already hopelessly far down the sappy and ridiculous path, I added, "I'm proud of you, too. I know I suck at showing it. But it's really awesome what you do for those kids at the hospital. And I appreciate all the stuff you do for me."

"Oh my gosh, *please* do not say that when Brittany and Christopher are here!" she wailed. I threw a balloon at her head. She threw it back. And when Brittany and Christopher (and Cam) knocked on the door, the table wasn't set, and the kielbasa and cabbage wasn't ready, but the balloon war was raging.

I'm sure I need not mention that Cameron "Magnificent Shoulders" Lewis and I emerged victorious.

PRIVATE
Mar 14

REASON #59:
Even people who hate me are impressed by my genius.

My first opening night in almost a year.

Technically it wasn't really an *opening* night so much as the *only* night—the Spring Spectacle draws such a pathetic audience, it's best not to spread it out—but my nerves were jangling like it was the biggest show of the decade. I was grateful for the black weighted poncho Nic had designed for me. Not only did the pressure help keep my anxiety from spiraling, it turned pacing the hallways of the nearly abandoned school into a distractingly rigorous workout. By the time I returned to the lobby, my T-shirt was damp with sweat.

I didn't go into the auditorium right away. As one of the student directors, Emily had some clout in determining performance order and had convinced Ms. Otashi to put Noah's skit first so that I'd be able to skip it. I lurked in the corner of the lobby as the audience filed in. Drama kids, some still not speaking to me. Parents of drama kids, who had no idea who

I was but whom I avoided on principle. Mutinous younger siblings who were unlikely to abide by the no-talking-during-the-performance rules that had been laid down in the car ride over.

I don't know why I was bothering to people-watch. My theatre friends (and Nic) were already backstage getting ready, and my mom had insisted on arriving an hour early and was already sitting in the front row. That was the extent of my people. Julia couldn't come home from college because of midterms, and Cam had an Away Game (which I have learned means An Excuse for Missing Several Hours of School So You Can Drive Far Away to Play the Same Sport That You Could Just As Easily Have Played with One of the Other High Schools in Your Own City). He offered to fake an injury, but that seemed excessive when I was 100 percent positive my mom would film the show on her phone and broadcast it to the entire universe later. Besides, he'd just found out about his baseball scholarship to UNC like two days earlier, and I didn't want to be responsible for his skills deteriorating.

I checked my phone for the time (five minutes to curtain), then checked my phone again to be triple-extra sure that I'd put it on silent.

"Jess!" Mr. Barton's voice boomed across the lobby.

I froze like an about-to-be-roadkill deer. Mr. Barton was striding toward my lurking corner.

Chloe was not. She hovered between the front entrance

and the doors to the auditorium, caught between opposing forces—one dragging her toward the theater and her boyfriend's skit, the other toward her father, to rescue him from being tainted by her slut-of-an-ex-best-friend. Hannah, Brooklyn, and Alexis were standing next to her.

"I am so excited to see your play on the big stage!" Mr. Barton beamed.

I was still looking past him to Chloe and the cyberbullies. My anxiety spiked. I started rocking up and down on the balls of my feet.

Hannah's stage whisper assaulted my ears. "Oh my God, she is such a freak. I can't believe they let someone that sick go to a normal school."

I saw the force that overcame Chloe's inertia.

It started at the base of her spine, straightening her, forming the words that came blasting from her lips: "Being autistic isn't an illness. It's a form of neurodiversity."

I flinched as her voice rang off the tiles. Mr. Barton spun around.

"Well, obviously, *you're* not—" Hannah began.

"Don't insult me by minimizing my disability. *You accept all of me, or I don't accept you.*" Chloe sang her last sentence on a non-melodic, Sondheim-esque riff that sparkled with ferocity. Her ballet flats smacked the tiles as she marched to the auditorium doors.

"I'm sorry. I have to . . ." Mr. Barton jogged past the frozen cyberbullies and into the theater.

"Ugh." Hannah rolled her eyes at the doors as they clicked shut. "I guess she thinks accepting *all of her* should include the angry bitch part."

Brooklyn gasped, and Alexis reeled as though Hannah had clobbered her. "Please tell me you did not just call a Black woman an angry bitch."

My chest clenched, my anxiety rising with the tension in the lobby, and there was only one thing to do. I fled—not out of the building but down the hallway that leads to the Fine Arts Wing. Just as I passed the double doors near the front of the auditorium, applause erupted. I flinched from the noise. My legs stopped supporting me, and I crumpled against the wall, knees tucked to my chest, rocking. I retreated into my mind, letting everything else fade.

I don't know how long the shutdown lasted, but when I started to come back to myself, my first thought was of Chloe.

I wondered how my twin tornado was doing on the other side of the wall. I'd been called a lot of things in my life (weird, creepy, a computer, sick, crazy, even the R-word), but no one's ever accused me of being an angry bitch. At least not that I know of. Maybe in speaking her truth, she'd thrown off the suffocating weight of her mask. But I wondered whether she'd also exposed herself to something worse: a trifecta of racism, sexism, and ableism.

My head thunked back against the tile wall. I'd been reading all of the internet's blog posts by autistic people of color, but I couldn't go back in time and be more supportive of Chloe. I wasn't even sure how to turn any of what I'd learned into action to support autistic people of color right now. I wasn't even sure how to take action to help *myself*. Maybe Dr. Barton would have some ideas. The storms inside ourselves are bad enough without facing storms from the outside, too.

My body finally felt regulated enough to stop rocking. There was another smattering of applause from inside the auditorium—the end of a skit, maybe Noah's. Maybe not, depending on how long I was shut down. The stage-left door was like five yards and a few stairs away from where I was sitting. When it squeaked open, I said a silent prayer to Lin-Manuel Miranda that Noah had exited stage right.

Lin-Manuel answered my prayers this time. It was one of the new Drama Freshmen, standing at the top of the stairs, bracing the door with her back and easing a giant papier-mâché rabbit head through the opening.

I staggered to my feet, dragging my poncho up with me. "Let me help."

I held the door while she hauled the rabbit head through. The papier-mâché caught on the doorstop with an ominous crunch.

"*Merde,*" she whispered. "Well, I guess we don't really need it anymore." She kicked the rabbit head down the stairs. It landed in a deflated heap on the tiles below.

As the freshman followed her mangled costume-piece

down the stairs, the stage lights came up on the next skit. I started to ease the door closed, but then—before I could think better of it—I slipped inside.

Nostalgia hit me like a cannonball to the chest. It was the smell, mostly: sawdust from set pieces and the slight tang of teenage sweat. Techies flitted in the dark, the only light coming from the oozing glow of the stage lights that reached past the black side curtains and from a book light clipped to the director's podium stage right.

Devi Sharma was at the podium on a headset, whispering cues to Ben Ken up in the booth and whoever they had on soundboard tonight. She must have been the director of the gaggle of performers out on the stage dressed as rag dolls (or scarecrows—hard to tell). Behind Devi, a heap of humans wriggled on the Stage-Right Orgy Couch. I didn't want to know what *they* were doing.

I settled down against the wall to watch the rag doll/scarecrow skit. Most cast and crew used the stage-right door that led to and from the parking lot since stage right was significantly larger, but I was happy to be among the smattering of anonymous techies on stage left. I felt simultaneously like an outsider and like I was finally returning home after a yearlong sea voyage, still wobbly on land.

A handful of sophomores were performing a scene from *Death of a Salesman* (Ms. Otashi's favorite play, so I guessed they were failing her class—they were certainly failing onstage) when the door squeaked open.

"They should oil that thing," Carly breathed, settling beside me on the floor.

I nodded. During a real show, no one would have come in or out in the middle of a scene, because of both the noise and the spill of light from the hallway. But Spectacles were more lax. In fact, they were famously casual.

So, why was my body thrumming with a buzzing anxiety that even my most furious hand-fluttering and tongue-scrubbing wouldn't quell? Was it because my play was premiering? Was it the possibility of running into Noah? Was it Chloe and the cyberbullies in the audience? I remembered the plan Alyssa and I had agreed on. *Deep breaths. Do what you need to self-regulate. Repeat the mantras: I have a right to be here. I have a right to exist. I matter.*

The audience dutifully applauded the Murder of a Salesman as the stage lights came down. Techies carried out Dee's stool and the cardboard tree, matching them with the little squares of glow tape that spiked their positions.

"Here we go," Carly said, rising and pulling her cape over her shoulders.

The play went just as we'd rehearsed. Emily stood at the podium whispering lighting cues into her headset, while Dee and Carly hit every one of their lines, and the actors playing the Vices took all their movements very seriously.

Especially Nic. She'd been delighted to step in at the last minute when I finally figured out what was wrong with the ending. We'd raided Julia's closet for her costume since they're the same size. When it was her turn to lower her cage bar, she spun, hiding the word pinned to the back of Julia's cocktail dress (SLUTTY) and revealing the sash we'd pinned to the front: HUMAN.

Dee descended the ladder from their stool and went to stand behind Carly. As they removed Carly's blindfold, Ben hit them both with a follow spot and brought down the stage lights. It was pitch-dark except for that single beam as Dee unhooked Carly's cloak and hung it on the tree so that the whole audience could see the words painted on the back: SENSITIVE, VAIN, SHREWISH, BOSSY, SLUTTY.

I wondered how many of those words would be painted on Chloe's cloak, along with ANGRY BITCH. LOUD, according to the mall's Angry Perfume Lady. I wondered how many more words were painted there, words that hadn't occurred to me yet.

Finally free from the weight of the cloak, Carly rolled her shoulders and rose, accepting Dee's hand as they led her downstage where the freshmen and Nic were waiting: COMPASSIONATE, BEAUTIFUL, CONFIDENT, INTELLIGENT, and HUMAN. They took Carly's arms and lowered her off the stage to the floor of the house. The spotlight followed her as long as it could as she walked up the center aisle toward the auditorium doors. Then the spot went dark.

There was a long pause—too long—and my rib cage squeezed tight against my straining lungs and heart.

Then the applause exploded.

I say exploded, but it wasn't anywhere near the standing-O level of applause we got for *Romeo and Juliet* last fall. Then again, there were like a quarter of the number of people in this audience. As whistles and whoops assaulted my ears, Ben brought the house lights up. I edged forward on hands and knees between two of the black curtains that helped hide the wings from sight, ignoring my internal narrator's screams of *If you can see the audience, they can see you!*

Mr. Barton was the first person I saw. He was standing (because of course he was) and he was also the one giving the piercing whistles, two fingers tugging down the corners of his mouth. Next to him, Chloe was sitting, not clapping, but her lips were slightly parted as she stared at the seat in front of her. I knew that face. Her thinking face. Her something-really-interesting-just-happened-and-I'm-not-sure-what-to-think-about-it-but-I'll-enjoy-figuring-it-out face. She sat back in her chair, and she didn't seem weighed down at all. Maybe Hannah's words didn't bother her as much as they bothered me. Or maybe she was used to shaking them off.

I lay on my belly and slithered out a little bit farther. Alexis and Brooklyn. Both clapping. Alexis's mouth was open in a kind of awed almost-smile. Brooklyn leaned over to whisper something. Alexis nodded.

Hannah wasn't there.

As the applause died back, I returned to the safety of the wings. I closed my eyes and took a few deep breaths, filling myself with the sawdust and sweat of the stage. *No matter what they say, I matter. I belong.* A final whistle from Mr. Barton reached me. My mom was out there somewhere, too. I'd have to go find her. She was my ride. And I also kind of wanted to know what she'd thought of the play.

I took another breath and rolled my shoulders, cracking out the stiffness from hunching on the floor. I let the poncho slip off my back, and the weight of the evening fell away, too.

It was time to greet my adoring public.

PRIVATE
Mar 19

REASON #60:
I hear voices.

Specifically, Alyssa's voice. Like, all the time.

SCENE: CHLOE passes JESS in the hall. A slight drawing-together of her eyebrows suggests that she is feeling something more poignant than mere animosity—something more like sadness or regret.

          ALYSSA
          (offstage)

You are not responsible for Chloe's happiness or unhappiness, Jess. She is her own person and can make her own choices. You're allowed to set boundaries to protect your mental health.

SCENE: When JESS comes out of her apartment, CAM is scrubbing at the side of his van with a dirty baseball shirt. The words that had been drawn on with window markers are partially erased, but the letters "l," "u," and "t" remain suggestive of the message's original contents.

> ALYSSA
> (offstage)

You do not have to feel guilty for being friends with Cameron. He has chosen to be friends with you and to care about you. Respect his choices. Wouldn't you gladly shoulder the same inconveniences for him?

Without a word, JESS removes her cardigan and helps CAM scrub the van.

SCENE: JESS is on the bus when she pulls out her phone and sees a text from EMILY. She jumps and immediately calls EMILY back. After several rings, she leaves a voicemail.

                    JESS
Hey Emily, it's Jess. I'm so, so sorry.
I forgot we were supposed to meet after
school, and I'm already on the bus. If
my mom's home, I can get her to drive me
back, but if you have a ride, you might
just want to leave because that will be a
while. I'm so, so sorry.

She hangs up, then bangs her head repeatedly
against the phone.

                    ALYSSA
                  (offstage)
Do you expect your friends to be perfect?
Do you care about them less when they make
mistakes? Then do you think it's possible
that Emily can—and does—forgive you?

SCENE: HANNAH comes up behind JESS in
               the cafeteria and "accidentally"
               jostles her elbow. JESS's soda
               cup tips, drenching her lunch
               and dripping onto her orthopedic
               shoes.

                    ALYSSA

                  (offstage)
You have not "driven them" to bully you.
They are responsible for their actions.
Even if you thought someone made a mis-
take, would it be okay for you to treat
them unkindly?

                    JESS
No.

She turns and faces HANNAH.

                 JESS(CONT'D)
Please stop.

   Beneath her thick layer of bronzer, Hannah's cheeks reddened. She glanced over her shoulder for reinforcements, but Alexis and Brooklyn weren't there. My own reinforcement materialized at my elbow. Emily righted the now empty cup and piled a stack of napkins in the pool on my tray. Hannah was the color of cherry Kool-Aid before she managed to sputter, "It was an accident."

   "Stop bullying me," I said, not loudly but firmly. Alyssa's voice in my head and Emily's defiantly fuchsia hair in my peripheral vision gave me the confidence I needed. "Your behavior is unacceptable."

I squelched away, leaving behind a trail of sticky footprints.

I didn't expect it would do any good. In fact, it might just prompt her to bully me more. But it *felt* good. Emily and I shared her slice of pizza and watched an extended interview with Renée Elise Goldsberry on her phone.

"Thanks for forgiving me," I said. "For standing you up yesterday."

Emily tilted her head to one side. "It was really no big deal."

"As long as you realize that my forgetfulness was not due to a lack of appreciation of our friendship."

She giggled. "Nerdier words were never spoken."

"Sorry to break it to you, but I am a nerd. I totally understand if you don't want to hang out with me now that you've had this revelation."

"I'm still kind of amazed that you're willing to hang out with *me*."

A laugh burst out of me before I could stop it. "What? You're always so cool, and I'm such a socially deficient mess."

Emily squinted. "No, you're not. You're so . . . invested in everything and so good at the stuff I want to be good at, and willing to help people get better at theatre and writing and stuff. And I'm just a sophomore. Most of the time I feel like an extra on a movie set. I'm still shocked that you'd even want to talk to me."

Huh. "Well, if I were making a movie of Stone Bridge High School, you'd definitely have a speaking role, because you're awesome. In fact, I'd make you a lead. And I'm glad we're still friends even when I stand you up."

Emily's ears turned copper. "It's totally fine. You didn't even do it on purpose."

Through the cafeteria windows, I watched Chloe's Robotics class steer one of their mechanical critters around the patio.

ALYSSA
(offstage)

```
A true friend listens and forgives. Did
you ever consider that you might have some
reasons to feel angry, too?
```

🔒 PRIVATE
Apr 1

REASON #61:
My promposal was sweeter than yours.

"Do you want to go to prom?"

It was April Fool's Day, and Virginia was blooming. As we pulled out of the parking lot, a cherry blossom tree bowed a pink farewell in the morning breeze. The asphalt was dusted gold with pollen.

I sneezed.

"Cameron, what in the name of Lin-Manuel Miranda and all that is holy makes you think that I would ever—*ever!*—want to go to prom? I didn't go last year, and that was before I was Stone Bridge High's most infamous boyfriend-stealing slutbag."

He tore his eyes from the road to glare at me.

"Joking. I know I'm not a slutbag, it wasn't my fault, blah blah, et cetera."

"Those jokes aren't funny."

"They kind of are."

"No."

There was an awkward pause of the sort that I am often talented enough to inspire. Then Cam said, "To be clear, I wasn't asking *whether* you were going to prom. I was asking you *to* go to prom. With me."

I gawked at him. I'm sure he asked on the drive to school because he knew I couldn't escape. I briefly considered hurling myself from the minivan and into the drainage ditch. "You mean . . . as friends? Or as a date?"

"How about a friend-date?"

"That is even more confusing." I squinted at him, like that might help me read his mind. He looked totally relaxed, hands loose on the wheel. He glanced over his shoulder before changing lanes.

Finally, I said quietly, "I don't want your pity."

He snapped his head toward me, then swung the van into the parking lot of the 7-Eleven. I cracked my head on the plastic of the door frame.

"*Jesus.* You should have your license revoked."

"Sorry." He twisted in the seat and took me by the shoulders. Then (probably noticing my abject terror), he let me go. "Sorry. I'm not hitting on you. I just— Look at me, or focus on me, okay? I want you to know I'm being serious when I say this. I've thought about it a lot, and there is no one else that I would rather spend prom with. Friends, dates, I don't care what you want to call it. I just think I will have more fun at prom with you than with anyone else."

"Hmm. But could you have as much fun *after* prom with me than anyone else . . . ?"

"I'm being serious."

"I know. Sorry." Across the parking lot, two guys I recognized from my time lurking at baseball practices were climbing into a pickup truck. One of them called back to a sundress-clad girl on the sidewalk. She gave him the finger, laughing. "I feel it only fair to warn you that I won't be up for any shenanigans. By which I don't mean to suggest that you are not sufficiently hot to inspire—"

"I am not expecting shenanigans," he said gravely. "I'm not even sure what a shenanigan is."

"I meant—"

"I got you. Listen, here is all I am expecting: I am expecting that we will laugh and stuff our faces and probably spend at least half the time talking about movies or whatever you're reading in AP Lit. If things are too loud and chaotic for you, we can hang out outside. I do not expect anything romantic to occur. We don't even have to dance if you don't want. We can just sit on the side and throw Doritos at the cyberbullies."

I considered before saying, "Counterproposal: we stay home and make nachos and binge football movies."

"Counter-counterproposal: we go to prom for at least one hour. And after that, whenever you want to leave, we go to IHOP and see who can eat the most waffles."

"Tempting." I ran my tongue over my teeth. "I'm going to ask you a serious question. Will you give me a serious answer?"

"If it's a real serious question and you're not just saying that ironically."

"It is serious." I searched for the right words, something that wouldn't lead to a whole conversation about sexuality that I wasn't ready to have quite yet. "Isn't making out or . . . whatever . . . with a hot field-hockey player more fun for you than eating waffles?"

I'll give Cam the credit he deserves by admitting that he considered before answering. "In some ways, definitely. But it's a different kind of fun. And despite the stereotypes, guys can think about more than one thing."

"But for *prom*—"

"I know prom is supposed to be this special night, and I know the typical 'special' thing you're supposed to do is get laid," he conceded. "But we're graduating, you know? And you're going north, and I'm going south. It just seems more 'special' to spend time with you than to make out or—um, whatever—with a girl I don't really know. I mean, Kate Heston's nice and all, but I'm not going to miss her next year."

"Well, good, because I definitely saw her making out with Grayson in the North Stairwell on Friday."

He watched me for a long while. When I didn't say

anything more, he got out of the car and started into the 7-Eleven.

I found him near the Slurpee machine. "Okay, then."

"Okay, what? Prom dates?"

"Unromantic, waffle-eating prom dates," I reminded him.

He smiled. "Deal."

🔒 PRIVATE
Apr 18

REASON #62:
My smug moral superiority can be deflated by snack food.

We got ready for prom at my house. I discovered that "getting ready" mostly involves a girl pricking her finger while she tries to pin a tiny flower to a buttonhole on a guy's (deliciously tight-fitting) tux, followed by a guy shoving a bracelet made of ribbon and flowers onto the girl's wrist, the girl immediately going into sensory overload because flowers are apparently incredibly itchy and an all-around weird thing to have attached to your arm, and then her mom figuring out a creative way to attach said flowers to her braid, which is not itchy and by all accounts quite beautiful, although the girl can't see it because it's behind her head. Also, there were lots of photos.

We opted for dinner at the upscale burger place on Maple because it seemed wrong to have a pre-prom meal at Five Guys. (And because my mom's suggestion for the perfect pre-prom feast had been stuffed cabbage. I may understand her better these days, but that doesn't mean I have to tolerate her strange fascination with waterlogged rabbit food.)

Cam kept glancing over at me on the drive to the restaurant. I was kind of proud of the flowy black jumpsuit-dress I'd found at the hospital thrift store. I say *I* found it, but Emily was the one who'd spotted it first. That was unsurprising, given how I had been mostly standing in a corner overwhelmed by the racks and racks of color, and Nic and my mom had been talking religion. Again. They are very boring people when they are in the same room.

The jumpsuit was gorgeous—sleeveless with a high bateau neck and floor-length, voluminous legs that had swirled around when I'd spun in the dressing room. I never imagined myself wearing a prom dress, but this thing was just perfect.

Cam glanced over at me again. "You look—" He swallowed and gripped the steering wheel tighter, focusing on the road. "Sorry. Not being romantic."

"Right. Don't forget that," I warned. But something warm bloomed in my chest.

Prom was loud. I had to put on my noise-canceling headphones as soon as we entered the hotel ballroom, and it immediately became apparent that they weren't going to be enough. After one song proved torturous, Cam took me by the elbow and guided me toward the patio where twin glass doors muffled the speakers. Jeff Watkins and his boyfriend waved as we squeezed past, and I waved back before following Cam outside.

Even though the sound was more bearable out there, I decided to keep the headphones on. I was mostly not-embarrassed by them—but only because Cam didn't seem embarrassed by them, and anyway, who was going to be looking at me when hot-shoulders-baseball-god was next to me wearing a tux?

"I'm going to go get us some drinks and food," he said when the first slow song started. "Be right back."

"I'm sorry we have to be out here."

"You don't need to be sorry."

"Yeah, well, I just keep thinking you could have taken out a normal human and had a normal prom."

He frowned. "No human is *normal*, and there's no human I'd rather hang out with than you."

I swallowed, trying not to let the warm bloom in my chest spread up to my cheeks.

"And in case your therapist hasn't told you this yet, you don't have to apologize for being you."

"Ugh. Stop lecturing me, and go get me snacks." I appreciated his broad be-tuxed back as he retreated into the ballroom, then sat on a wrought-iron bench next to a concrete planter of sickly pansies. My cheeks were definitely too warm. Hopefully my blush would subside by the time Cam got back. Cam, my friend who would rather hang out with me than any other human.

The warmth in my cheeks flared. Okay, this was definitely a crush. So did that mean that I was allosexual but found tongues repulsive? Or I was somewhere in the middle of the graysexual spectrum? Or I was 100 percent asexual but not aromantic? How many possible combinations were there, and how would I figure out which one I was? Thinking about it, my happiness began to frizz, transforming to a knot of anxiety.

ALYSSA

(offstage)

```
You don't have to figure this out today,
or even tomorrow. You are who you are,
whether you have a label for it or not.
Don't pressure yourself.
```

No pressure. I took a deep breath.

The music swelled again as the door opened. I stood, then plunked back down when I realized it wasn't my friend-date-crush.

It was Alexis.

"Hey." Her shimmery, bright-coral gown swept the ground when she walked toward me. She stopped about six feet away. So much for relaxing. I forced myself to deepen my breaths, willed my heartbeat to slow, as I focused on the glittery combs sticking out of her sleek, piled-high curls.

"My dad always says, you gotta own your mistakes and make them right." Her voice sounded strange through my headphones. "So this is me, owning it." She drew a long breath. "I knew about Hannah's blog. I never told her to stop. And I never reported it to the administration or anything. And none of that was okay, and I know it. I'm not going to ask you to forgive me, because you shouldn't have to. I needed you to know that *I* know what I did was wrong, and I regret it, and I'm going to talk to Vice Principal Yarmouth on Monday to let him know what's been going on."

I shook my head to clear it, then shook it again. "Please don't."

Her teeth found her lower lip, scraping off a bit of her pink-orange lipstick. "Are you sure?"

"Yeah. I don't want this to be a thing. Or more of a thing."

"Are you worried she'll—?"

"I'm not worried. I'm not scared of her. I'm just—" I closed my eyes to concentrate on finding the right words. "I'm here at prom with my friend. My *best* friend. I'm having fun. I'm going to an awesome college next year. That other stuff . . ." I shook my head and opened my eyes. "I just don't care about Hannah Brewer. My friends don't care about Hannah Brewer or anything she has to say about me. I'm ready to move on."

She frowned, gnawing on her lip. "Okay. I guess if you're sure . . ."

"Yes. And . . . I'm sorry for the unkind things I said about you on my blog, too. It was wrong. That's why I took it down."

She waved a hand. "Forgiven."

"Thanks."

She nodded once and said something more, too soft for me to make out through the headphones. Then, she turned and walked back inside. Cam passed her in the doorway, balancing two cups and an overly full plate of cheese puffs in his arms. He hurried toward me, some of the syrupy liquid in the cups sloshing over his hands.

"That was Alexis Jones. Are you okay?"

"Fine. She was just saying sorry. Apparently Hannah was the only one writing the blog; Alexis just knew about it."

"And she didn't do anything about it? That's awful."

"It's actually less awful than I thought she was." A breeze rippled the hair on my arms, and I hugged my elbows.

Cam shook his head. "I really thought she was nice."

"Maybe she is. I mean, everyone makes mistakes, right? I never made much of an effort to get to know her." Punch dripped from Cam's fist. I took one of the cups from him and licked the orange liquid from the side. It fizzed on my tongue.

"Happy prom," I said.

"Happy prom." We tapped our paper cups and took a drink.

I peered through the glass doors at the pulsing, gyrating horde within. "Which one is the Alexis who's dating your lineback?"

"Quarterback." Cam stepped up to the doors, shading his eyes against the glass. "Umm, there, by the buffet, with the really tall blond hair and the blue dress."

Her hair was indeed very tall. The blue of the dress was harsh, as was her facial expression and the jabbing of her finger into her date's chest as she berated him about something, perhaps related to the orange punch that was now dripping from his earlobes and the end of his nose.

"I can see how you would have thought she was a bully," I said. "I mean, *I* don't think that because I no longer judge people, but I can see how *you—*"

I gurgled and choked as Cam used his baseball prowess to toss a cheese puff directly into my mouth.

🔒 PRIVATE
Apr 24

REASON #63:
I gave up on my (former) best friend.

The best part of a half day is that Cam can drive me home. Unfortunately, he wasn't the one waiting for me by the grayish-white minivan in the overflow lot.

It was Chloe.

"Hey," she said. The skirt of her yellow sundress fluttered its own hello as the wind whipped around us.

"I didn't know you parked in this lot." It was a kind of passive-aggressive thing to say, since I'd seen her Volt in the Senior Lot when I was walking past. After almost a year, I was still in the habit of looking for it.

"I just came up to talk to you."

I said nothing. The air was warm, and the wind tugged at my ponytail. My eyes watered from the pollen, but I didn't dare dry them. God forbid Chloe should think I was misty-eyed over her.

"We should go inside and sit in the lobby," she said.

"Why?"

"Your allergies will be better inside. They're always bad on windy days."

"That's not what I meant."

"Oh." She ran her thumb over the bracelet on her wrist. "I'm sorry about your notebook. I know you'll never forgive me, but I had to tell you I'm sorry."

"I forgive you."

Her forehead crinkled. "You do?"

"Yes."

Neither of us said anything for a while. I don't know if she was waiting for me to say something else. Maybe *It was no big deal*—but it was. Maybe *I'm sorry for seducing your boyfriend*—but I hadn't. Maybe just a blanket *I'm sorry*—but I'd said that a thousand times since last June, and I couldn't believe that the thousand and first would make a difference.

I glanced over my shoulder. Cam was hesitating by the flagpole in front of the school, his shoulders hunched like an indecisive yeti. I waved—a gesture I hoped he would take as a "please save me" but that Chloe would misinterpret as a friendly hello.

"Here comes Cam," I said. "I'm sure you have places to be, so . . ."

She glanced at her phone. "I have a Robotics meeting soon, but first, I need— I want to say—" She chewed her lip for a minute before she forced out the words. "I also want to apologize for the other things I said. And did."

A bubble of something that wasn't quite hope inflated in my lungs. "Really?"

"Yes. Noah told me you were acting out a scene when you kissed him. I was so angry at first, it didn't even occur to me that you might have meant it as acting, but . . . My dad has been giving me a lot of lectures about dating and consent lately, and I realized that you might not have even thought about it. I mean, you didn't have any experience with dating, so you didn't realize what you were doing."

"Doing what?" I wished my voice had been less shaky, but my whole body was trembling at this point.

Chloe shrank, tucking her chin as she spoke. "Just, you know, putting that pressure on him to . . . kiss you back, and . . . I am trying to say that there was no excuse for me bullying you over it. I'm very sorry."

I clamped my jaw. The thing inflating in my chest was definitely anxiety. Or maybe a scream.

Someone touched my shoulder, and I jumped. "Everything okay?" Cam asked.

He was asking me, but it was Chloe who said "Yes."

"Jess?" Cam persisted.

I nodded. "Yeah, I'm fine. Thanks, Chloe, for . . . yeah."

Her shoulders relaxed. "Great. It has been so hard not being friends. I've missed you, and my dad said you're going to New York—and congratulations, I know how much that means to you—but now we only have a few more months to make things . . . right. Between us."

I nodded. My lungs tightened. I rocked up and down on the balls of my feet, pushed my tongue hard against my teeth.

"Maybe we can hang out this weekend. Noah and I were thinking of getting tickets for *Pirates of Penzance* at the community center. We could all go. You too, Cam."

I shook my head, then kept shaking it.

"Have you seen it already?" she asked, her hands tensing. "We can do something else."

"I can't—" I swallowed. "I can't be friends with you right now, Chloe."

"But you said you forgive me." Her shoulders clenched, her jaw working in an expression I knew too well.

"I did. I do. I'm not mad at you, I just . . ." Cam's hand moved from my shoulder to my arm. He pulled me into a gentle side hug, supporting me. I have never been more grateful for another human being. "I'm just working through some stuff right now, and I can't deal with this." It was hard enough dodging Noah in the halls. I couldn't hang out with him on weekends.

"I get it," Chloe said, her hands now flapping by her ears. "You don't."

Cam squeezed my arm and tugged me toward the van.

"I do. You can't forgive me for being mad at you and for making new friends, even though I can forgive you for seducing my boyfriend—"

Cam abandoned his subtle attempts to pull me away and threw me over his shoulder.

"—and making my parents harass me and Noah about our love life."

"You don't know what you're talking about, Chloe," Cam bellowed as he set me gently in the passenger seat.

"Just leave it, Cam." My hands were shaking too much to buckle the seat belt.

"I will, but only because she's not worth it." As he crossed to his own door, he shouted, "You leave her alone, or I swear to God . . . !" He left it at that.

I put my head between my knees as we drove away and didn't take it out again until Cam set me down outside my apartment door and I needed to dig out my keys.

He laid me on my bed and brought me a can of orange soda and a box of Cheez-Its and an apple, fussing over me like he was his mother until I snapped at him to get out.

It was only after he left that the tears came. They broke in waves, drenching my pillow, then subsiding while I caught my breath, only to return again with the force of a typhoon. Cam must not have gone far because at some point, a box of tissues appeared at my elbow.

Then, at 8:13 p.m., when my salt tears had shriveled my eyes like slugs and I had too much of a headache to think straight, I chugged the orange soda, copied every single one of these posts into an email, and hit send. She won't read it. Why would she when she has Noah's side of things?

It will just be something else for her to tear to shreds.

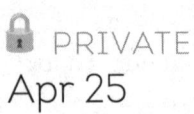
PRIVATE
Apr 25

REASON #64:
As much as I rag on Andrew Lloyd Webber, when it comes right down to it, I'm a sucker for melodrama.

I managed to avoid Mom this morning by pretending I had my period. I lay in bed eating chocolate and watching film adaptations of *Hamlet* with a heating pad on my stomach. Cam visited for an hour or so, but I was on the Zeffirelli adaption (the one with Mel Gibson), so he didn't stay long.

"Why do you bother watching this crap?"

"Helena Bonham Carter is never crap. Also Glenn Close. And Sir Ian Holm. There's a lot to like if you can get over, you know, everything else about it."

"But why do you *start* with this one?"

"Reverse alphabetically by director's last name."

"Why not regular alphabetically? Then you could start with Branagh."

"Bennett. The 1980 BBC adaptation," I corrected. "But then I'd have to *end* with this one. And this one's total crap."

That was when he left.

When I heard the knock at the door this evening, I assumed it was Cam again. Mom was working the night shift, and I'd taken advantage of her absence to venture downstairs in search of more chocolate. I was still in my pajamas, and the only chocolate I could find was a half-full canister of unsweetened cocoa powder in the pantry. I debated making brownies, but that seemed like too much work, so I was just stirring the powder—and like four times as much sugar—into some boiling water to see if it would turn into cocoa when the knock came.

I wiped the chocolate off my hands onto my pajama pants and answered the door.

It was Chloe.

"I thought you were Cam," I said. It sounded stupid but less confrontational than the other things I was thinking.

What are you doing here?

You are the last person I want to see right now.

Please, for the love of Lin-Manuel Miranda and all that is holy, go away.

She stood on the doorstep in her favorite blue sundress, shifting from one foot to the other. "Can I come in?"

"Why?"

"I read your email," she said.

I stepped back to let her past.

After I had closed the door to keep the pollen out, I followed Chloe to the living room. She was still standing, but her body was slumped. She was exhausted. Either she'd stayed up all night reading my blog or she'd been crying. Maybe both.

"I'm sorry that I didn't respond to your texts last summer," she said.

Then she lost it.

I left her sobbing in a heap behind the couch and went to find some tissues. We'd gone through a lot of them in our apartment/town house lately, and in the end, I had to settle for a roll of paper towels.

Chloe's tornado lasted over an hour. It was loud and whirling, sucking out her tears and her sobs, leaving her crunched into the carpet, gasping. But my winds remained calm. Maybe I didn't have any tears left after last night. Maybe my brain was already so thoroughly melted that there was nothing for a tornado to take hold of. Maybe she and I were so distant that the same storm could no longer rock us both.

When her meltdown subsided, she lifted her head, taking a moment to reorient herself to my living room, then another moment to notice the paper towels. She nodded her thanks, still waiting to regain her voice.

I closed my eyes, reciting *Hamlet* soliloquies in my mind until she said, "Thank you."

I opened my eyes. She yanked off her foggy glasses and wiped them on the front of her dress—three quick wipes—and it was like a knife to my heart. We'd been apart for so long, and yet every movement she made was so familiar. Like no time had passed. Like we were still best friends.

But we weren't.

"Why are you here?"

Chloe blew her nose into a paper towel, rubbing it raw, before saying, "I broke up with him."

"Okay."

Reading my mind, she added, "How I treated you is my fault, though, not his." She squeezed her eyes shut, a few more tears oozing down her cheeks. "I didn't even talk to you—or listen to you—and I blamed you."

A few of my own leftover tears leaked out in solidarity. "Yeah, that sucked."

She choked on a laugh-sob. "Yeah."

Then, in response to a guilt-fireball expanding in my chest, I scooted beside her. "Even without Memorial Day, you had other reasons to hate me, or at least be frustrated with me. I mean, I was kind of a steamroller."

"You weren't."

"I was. I just rolled all over you all the time and dominated your life—"

"I made my own choices," she said. And then, in her best Dr. Barton imitation, "Don't take away my agency."

I laughed. "Still."

A silence settled over us. I picked at the fibers of the

carpet, shredding them with my fingernails. Chloe's hands were stuffed under her knees, a gesture I recognized only too well. "You can flap in front of me." She kind of jolted, so I added quickly, "You don't have to. Just if you're comfortable. I mean, I want you to know I won't judge you for self-regulating."

She tugged her hands out and let her fingers flutter. "I know. I got so used to . . ."

I swallowed, my face heating in advance of the awkward I was about to voice. "I also just need to admit . . . I know I was never really sensitive to the racist BS you have to deal with. That's something I'm working on. Maybe your mom mentioned. She's been . . . she's given me some stuff to look at. I want to be better." Then, since that sounded too tentative, "I will do better."

She nodded once, her thumb moving fast over her wrist. "I wanted to tell you, too, that if you're . . . In a couple posts you implied you might be asexual or gray-ace or . . . so I wanted to tell you it's okay to be who you are and . . . yeah, all that."

It was my turn to awkward-nod. Obligatory allyship statements, check. I wondered if Chloe felt the same emotion soup I was feeling—a little swell of happiness from being seen and not judged, a little swell of anxiety that she might push the conversation into territory I didn't want to traverse with her, and a great big swell of discomfort because knowing the correct thing to say and actually understanding what someone's going through are two very different things. Especially if the person saying it isn't particularly close to you anymore.

I ran my tongue over my teeth. "You and Alexis and Brooklyn don't sit with Hannah at lunch anymore."

"Yeah. We needed . . . a break, I guess."

"Are they good friends to you? Alexis and Brooklyn, I mean."

Her fluttering slowed. "They are."

"Good. I'm—I'm glad. And your dad said you're going to UVA to be a music major now?"

She blew a frustrated breath. "He keeps telling people that. I'm going to UVA because they have majors in both biomedical engineering and music. I might want to double major."

"Ah. That makes more sense. Very on-brand of you, taking on two of the most difficult and complicated degree programs at the same time."

"I can do it," she said, her volume nearly doubled.

"I know," I said quickly. "I meant you're *good* at doing hard things in school."

"Oh. Thanks."

This conversation was having a detrimental effect on my respiratory system. I took a few subtle deep breaths to loosen my clenching lungs. In the twilight outside the living room window, the wind agitated the trees. The branches clacked against one another, adding an erratic beat to the ceaseless rustle of the leaves and occasional bark of a squirrel.

"Are you and Cam dating now?"

I tore my focus away from the outside world. "Not really. Not in the mood to date anyone, actually."

She nodded and swallowed. "Your email woke me up to a lot of things that were wrong about me and Noah."

"Did he—?" Acid reflux clawed up my throat. "With you, he never—?"

"No," she said. "He never, um, pushed me to do anything I didn't want to do. He just . . . Memorial Day isn't the only thing he's . . . I don't think 'lied' is the right word. I think he believes the things he says. It's almost like he has to . . . like, if he believed anything were ever his fault, he'd fall apart."

"Maybe a little falling apart would do him good," I said. I thought of him that day in the auditorium, practically begging me to reassure him that I had, in fact, consented, and he had not, in fact, done anything wrong. If I was honest, I still felt a little guilty for not reassuring him, even though Alyssa said it was the right choice.

"He seemed resigned when I told him we had to break up," Chloe said. "I think he knew it was coming."

"He probably did."

I hadn't seen it coming, though. I'd kind of accepted the status quo—Noah and Chloe together, me and Chloe apart. The sudden change quaked the ground beneath me. For the first time in nearly a year, she was in front of me, listening to things I had to say. I had a lot of things I wanted—needed—to say. But I couldn't get them out. Because if I started speaking my mind, would I be able to stop?

```
SETTING:      Jess's living room.

AT RISE:      CHLOE and JESS sit across from
              one another. Between them, a
              mountain of crumpled, snot-soaked
              paper towels provides a physical
              and metaphorical barrier.

                      CHLOE
You have some things you want to say to
me. Please. Get them off your chest.

                      JESS
Well, since you're asking . . . I com-
pletely understand that you were angry.
I'd been the one who kept it secret, so
Noah probably seemed more trustworthy. In
retrospect, I should have called you the
instant it happened and told you myself
and made sure he'd never done it to you.

A beat.
```

JESS (CONT'D)
But I tried to talk to you a hundred times
last summer. After all the years we'd been
friends—after everything we'd been through
together—you couldn't even listen to my
side? If you were too angry in the summer,
you couldn't have listened to me in the
school year? Even when you came to me to
suggest we try to mend our relationship,
you didn't want to give me a chance to
explain. And the bullying . . . I want to
forgive, but the words "I'm sorry" don't
make the memories go away.

"You have some things you want to say to me," she said.

"Someone should burn you at the stake." She jerked back, so I hastily added, "I mean, as a witch—because you keep reading my mind. It was supposed to be a joke."

"Oh."

Well, *this* sucked. Definitely not BFFs anymore. Our friendship had survived horror movies and jewelry heists, parents' divorces and fracturing life paths, accidental insults and intentional slights, but now we were a broken Christmas ornament, held together by Elmer's glue. If one of us breathed wrong, we'd shatter.

"Things aren't going to go magically back to the way they were," I said.

Her chest caved, and her head sagged. "I know. But I don't want to graduate and go our separate ways without even having the chance to try to . . . improve things between us. If you never want to see me again, I understand. But if you would be willing to try talking, or hanging out once in a while, once a week, or even once a month, so that I'd have a chance to listen to the things you need to say . . ."

I was nodding before she'd even finished her sentence.

🔒 **PRIVATE**
May 25

REASON #65:
I'm staging a new story, and it's already a hit.

The sun had set, the bugs were out, and I had never laughed so hard at a Shakespearean tragedy.

(To be fair, *Richard III* is technically categorized as a history, but the full title of the originally published version is *The Tragedy of Richard the third, Containing, His treacherous Plots against his brother Clarence: the pittiefull murther of his innocent nephewes: his tyrannicall vsurpation: with the whole course of his detested life, and most deserved death.* So.)

The backdrop was a sheet slung between two oaks in the downtown park. LED lanterns strung between the trees illuminated the patch of stage and all of us onlookers sprawled on our picnic blankets around the field. Richard swirled his cape, asking us, "Was ever woman in this humor wooed? Was ever woman in this humor won?!" He raised his arms, beckoning for applause, and we obliged with whoops and cheers.

Cam leaned so close, his breath tickled my ear. "I have

never thought of this play as a comedy, but it totally is. Richard is hilarious!"

"I know!" I whispered back.

Alexis leaned across from her blanket beside us to say, "Just wait."

The shift came suddenly in the final act. One minute we were all laughing away with the underdog king and his clever schemes, and then he was snapping at his right-hand man—straight-up rage-yelling—and we realized the toady was about to die.

"Oh, shit," Cam murmured.

"Yup," said Alexis.

"He's totally been murdering people."

"Yup."

"And I was laughing about it."

I shushed them both and leaned forward, glad that the semidarkness was hiding my gleeful grin. Alexis had been right. This production was awesome.

When the show ended, I exploded to my feet, clapping. On the next blanket over, Emily and Nic had done the same.

"That was so, so, so good!" Nic squealed. "He made me feel like such a terrible person! It was awesome!"

Emily belly-laughed. The lantern light reflected off her blindingly yellow hair.

While Alexis ran backstage (or back-sheet?) to congratulate her brother (the treacherously murthered Duke of Clarence), Cam and I shook off the blanket and folded it into my backpack. Chloe marched back from the lighted tree where she'd been reading a music history textbook for her first semester at UVA.

"Wasn't Richard amazing?" I gushed. "He was so funny!"

"He wasn't funny. He was killing people."

"Well, I know, and you realize that toward the end, which is the brilliance of—"

"You realize it at the beginning. When he kills someone."

I shook my head. Chloe was not the person with whom to discuss Shakespearean antiheroes.

When Alexis returned, we joined the small mob of theatre-goers making their way back to the parking garage. I swatted a mosquito on my arm. "It seems criminal to be this close to the gelato place and not actually get gelato."

"Gelato!" Nic cheered, like a battle cry, and veered toward the outdoor mall.

"I'm not running," Emily called after her, though she picked up the pace of her walk.

"Well, I totally am," Alexis said. "C'mon, Chlo, you know you want gelato." She grabbed Chloe's hand and skipped off after Nic.

"Are we running?" Cam asked me.

"I think you know the answer to that."

We ambled across the field. The path was poorly lit, but I had faith that the gargantuan football/baseball star standing next to me could take out any tyrannical usurpers that came our way. I could barely make out Alexis and Chloe ahead of us, just their shapes bobbing across the lawn and the occasional squeals of laughter that the wind flung our way. It made me feel something. Some kind of happiness, maybe. Or contentment. Like they had a life, and I had a life, and if those lives sometimes collided, that might be okay.

"Tonight seemed to go okay," Cam said.

"Yeah." Though Chloe and I had eaten lunch together a couple of times in the cafeteria and exchanged a few emails, this was our first real attempt at doing something together. I'd been surprised when Alexis had invited me, but I couldn't really say no—not when she had prefaced it with *because you're the only other person in this school who knows how to appreciate Shakespeare.*

"Richard was epic," Cam said. "He totally had me the whole time."

"And even without panzer tanks!"

Cam gave my shoulder a gentle shove. "Maybe you should add that one to the blog. Reason number one hundred: I give my friends a hard time for enjoying Jazz Age Shakespeare movies just because the bad guys happen to be Nazis."

"Nah. That's more of a reason to love me."

Cam blew air out of his lips like a derisive horse.

Cam's the only one besides me who has access to this blog. I gave him the password because I wanted to try being more honest with people I trust. (And because he held my Five Guys fries like five feet above my head until I did.)

The blog dedicated to my sluttiness, on the other hand, has vanished. I don't know why, but I suspect it might be that, despite honoring my request not to tell the administration about the bullying, Alexis took some action or other. I wonder what she has on Hannah Brewer. I'm a little jealous.

"You haven't posted in a while," Cam said as we walked through the narrow alley between the toy store and the pizza place, our shoes scuffing along the uneven brick walk. "Does that mean you've run out of reasons to hate you?"

"Oh, no." I squashed another mosquito on my arm, wiping the tiny carcass and a generous film of sweat off on my jeans. "Those are endless. Although the blog is pretty comprehensive at this point."

"Maybe you should start a new one. Reasons to hate Richard the Third."

"Reasons to hate Andrew Lloyd Webber musicals."

"Reasons to hate AP Calculus."

"Reasons to hate small blood-sucking insects and whatever deity thought it was a good idea to create them."

"Reasons to love Cameron Lewis's awesomely hot shoulders."

My face flamed so intensely, I knew it was only a matter of seconds before I combusted. "That's it. I'm changing the password."

"I'm only teasing."

"Nope. You are never seeing that blog ever again."

"Well, then I guess I'll have to get my daily dose of Jess humor somewhere else."

"Umm, like by actually hanging out with me?"

"Yeah. Like that. In fact . . . I think we should spend a lot of time together this summer. If you want."

He was looking straight ahead, and his cheeks had gone a little pink. I tried to keep my voice as casual as he'd tried to keep his, but I figured I failed as badly as he had. "Yeah?"

"Yeah. I know you're not ready to figure out . . . like, sexuality or . . . umm, textures or whatever. But we could still spend time together. No pressure, no shenanigans, but lots of waffles and Shakespearean panzer tanks?"

"That sounds . . ." I paused and checked in with my body. Slightly faster heartbeat, happy flutters in my hands, a warm, melty feeling in my brain. "That sounds really good."

Emily was accepting her gelato cup from the guy behind the window when Cam and I walked up.

"Jess!" Nic squealed. "They have *Nutella!*"

"Yes, please."

Once Cam and I had our scoops of creamy goodness, we joined Nic, Emily, Chloe, and Alexis on the benches around one of the islands of landscaping in the center of the mall. We made a lot of toasts with our gelato cups.

To summer!

To graduation!

To NYU and UVA and Chapel Hill and Columbia!

To the incoming vice president of the SBHS Drama Club and her gorgeous and talented girlfriend!

Cam gave an exaggerated sigh around a mouthful of frozen strawberries and cream. "Reasons why gelato is proof of a benevolent God."

"Mmm. Thank you, Lin-Manuel Miranda."

Chloe choked on a laugh. My lips twitched up at the corners, all on their own. I ran my tongue over my teeth, sucking up every last smudge of chocolate.

When our brains were sufficiently frozen and our gelato cups insufficiently full, we began the slow march back to the parking garage. It was after eleven o'clock, and the sugar high made us all giggly—and me clumsy. After my third stumble, Cam caught my arm.

"Do you need me to carry you? I'm sure my shoulders could handle it."

"Don't make me beat you up."

He chortled.

We filed into the alley one by one, leaving just enough room for the stranger coming in the opposite direction to pass us by. It was a man in a black leather jacket, a glowing cigarette between his lips. I took courage from Cam's warmth directly behind me, just in case it was one of those aforementioned tyrannical usurpers.

The stranger didn't make any menacing moves, but as

he passed Alexis, she spun around, mouth wide in horror. As he passed Chloe, she spun, too, her hand shooting up to her ears. Then he passed me, and I suddenly understood.

It actually was King Richard.

I gasped as I spun, staring after his leather-clad back. Nic was last in line, and as the actor passed, she squeaked, "Oh my God—it's him! It's Richard the Third!"

"Shhhh!" we admonished in unison. Then our laughter detonated.

"Y'all!" Alexis shouted between laugh-bursts. "When you pass Richard the Third in a dark alley, you *do not* call attention to yourself!"

We laughed harder.

I wonder what the actor thought, walking away in the dark while a bunch of hysterical teenagers shrieked behind him. But then again, I guess it doesn't matter. We had a right to be there, collapsing on the dirty sidewalk with stitches in our sides from laughing too hard after eating too much frozen cream. Anyway, do we care what a treacherous murtherer thinks?

I tilted my head back and took a deep breath of summer sky. Maybe I will start a new blog.

Reasons to always turn on your phone light in dark alleys.

Reasons to celebrate Memorial Day with Shakespeare productions in the park.

Cam wrapped one of his magnificent arms around me

and helped me back to my feet. Nic laced her fingers with Emily's, leaning her head onto her shoulder. Chloe whispered something to Alexis and a laugh ricocheted through the alley.

Reasons to never judge a play by its first act.

Acknowledgments

When I told my then seven-year-old daughter that this book would be published, she said, "Mom! Your dream!" It was a magical moment. But this dream come true is thanks to an unquantifiable amount of work and support from many wonderful people who are not me, and my gratitude is fierce and sincere.

Thanks to fellow author and much-better-than-Jess actress Rachel Renner, my first reader and the most insightful, kind, and enthusiastic critique partner and cheerleader an author could ask for. Thanks also to my SCBWI critique groupies: Jennifer Bohnhoff, Michele Hathaway, Diane Mittler, and Chris Ottaviano Shestak. You keep the process fun, the memes weird, and the journey far from lonely.

Thanks to my dream agent, Susan Hawk, who got my sense of humor from page one and whose excitement about Jess's story was instrumental in finding it a publishing home. Thanks also to my thoroughly delightful editor, Andrea Tompa, who not only gave this book its publishing home but saw immediately what I was trying to achieve with this story and helped it become the best it could be. (And who also didn't give up with me when, in our initial conversation, I somehow [inevitably] ended up on a tangent about *Star Trek*.)

Thanks to Juan Botero at Candlewick for his astute contributions to the book's revisions. Also hearty thanks to the designer, Pam Consolazio; copyeditors Susan VanHecke and Julia Gaviria; proofreaders Tracey Engel and Martha Dwyer; Terry Borzumato-Greenberg, Emma Long, Michelle Montague, Stephanie Pando, Sawako Shirota, Karen Walsh, and the whole marketing team; and all of the other staff at Candlewick who do the parts of the job that—as Jess might say—are not areas in which I excel. This book would not be out in the world without you!

A special thank-you to the readers who helped me make each character's experiences as authentic and accurate as I could, whether or not I shared their lived experiences: Baylee Thurman, Lydia K. Valentine, and Basil Wright. Any errors or shortcomings are my own responsibility.

I also must acknowledge my senior year of high school Destination Imagination comrades, Margot, Sid, Alorah, Julie, Ingrid, and Bonnie, for the chemistry jokes Chloe puts into *The Maltese Electron*, all of which appeared in our fabulously nerdy chemistry-themed play *An Electron Affair*, winner of the Jefferson Region DI competition (2005–2006). It was awesome, and I understood roughly half of it.

Finally and most gratefully, to my family. My parents, Cathie and Sam Metallo, encouraged me to read widely and without restriction and passed on their belief in the value, impact, and joy of the arts. I am in this career because of their love and support.

And to my husband, Stephen, and children, Clara and Catherine. This job sometimes means odd hours and emotional upheaval, not to mention many years of hard work with few or no returns. You have given me your unwavering logistical and emotional support through it all, never doubting that I'd sell a book even when I doubted it myself. Stubborn as I am, I probably would have given up without you. I owe this book to you, and I love you.